FIRESTORM

Also by Taylor Moore

Down Range

FIRESTORM

A NOVEL

TAYLOR MOORE

WILLIAM MORROW

An Imprint of HarperCollinsPublishers

HarperCollins books may be purchased for educational, business, or sales promotional use. For information, please email the Special Markets Department at SPsales@harpercollins.com.

FIRST EDITION

Designed by Kyle O'Brien

Title page photo © SMP.adobe.com

Library of Congress Cataloging-in-Publication Data

Names: Moore, Taylor, author.
Title: Firestorm: a novel / Taylor Moore.
Description: First Edition. | New York: William Morrow, [2022] | Series: Garrett Kohl series; vol 2 | Summary: "DEA Special Agent Garrett Kohl must rescue a CIA officer after she has been kidnapped in Texas by a brutal band of mercenaries in this pulse-pounding thriller for fans of C. J. Box"— Provided by publisher.
Identifiers: LCCN 2021060829 (print) | LCCN 2021060830 (ebook) | ISBN 9780063066557 (hardcover) | ISBN 9780063066564 (trade paperback) | ISBN 9780063111561 | ISBN 9780063242005 | ISBN 9780063066588 (ebook)
Subjects: GSAFD: Suspense fiction.
Classification: LCC PS3613.O5685 F57 2022 (print) | LCC PS3613.O5685 (ebook) | DDC 813/.6—dc23
LC record available at https://lccn.loc.gov/2021060829
LC ebook record available at https://lccn.loc.gov/2021060830

ISBN 978-0-06-306655-7

22 23 24 25 26 LSC 10 9 8 7 6 5 4 3 2 1

Cowboy is a way of life that transcends race, creed, color, and gender. It's the wildest of spirits, the purest of hearts, and the gentlest of souls. Cowboy is dogged determination, a job done right, and a fight won against all odds. Cowboy is what the world needs a little bit more of these days. It is to those rare few that I dedicate this novel.

FIRESTORM

PART ONE

My God sent his angel, and he
shut the mouths of lions.

—Daniel 6:22

1

Garrett Kohl had spent the better part of his DEA and special operations career taking a series of calculated risks, but he'd never done anything quite as stupid as this. Blasting across the lake through the foggy darkness in a Super Air Nautique G25 Paragon, he pondered everything that could go wrong, which was a hell of lot to consider in a place run by the Garza Cartel.

With the sudden thought of slamming into a limestone jetty at thirty-five knots, Garrett yanked the throttle, killed the motor, and let the wake boat drift to a lazy stop. With no wind, the stagnant fishy air hung heavy like a soggy sponge. It was a smell that normally put this avid angler in the best of moods, but tonight there was simply way too much at stake.

As a seasoned combat veteran from the U.S. Army's 10th Special Forces Group, Garrett was no stranger to being behind enemy lines, but this rendition assignment with his task force partners in the Texas Rangers and CIA had jacked the pucker factor up to eleven. Breaking more international laws than he cared to count, Garrett shoved those thoughts to the back of his mind and focused on something he could control—finding the drug lord they were supposed to meet.

Garrett raised out of his seat and glanced up at the moon and stars, which had pierced the clouds and bathed the shoreline of thick carrizo cane in a soft amber glow. Lifting the 4X night vision binoculars to his eyes, he panned the reed-covered beach in the green glow of his optics, spotting a dry creek bed about fifty yards out. But for a prowling bobcat and an overturned jon boat there was really nothing to see. No pier. No fishing village. And no murderous cartel boss with a duffel bag full of cash.

Looking down at his map, Garrett clicked on a penlight and aimed the beam at the upper-right corner. According to his GPS, they were right where they were supposed to be, an isolated cove near an old rural community called Rancho Culebra. The plan was for him and his mission accomplice, Texas Ranger Cade Malek, to meet up with their confidential informant (CI) Ray Smitty and a drug kingpin named Emilio Garza.

Had he not been in dangerous country on assignment, Garrett would've longed to explore the area around Lake Amistad. The sixty-five-thousand-acre body of water on the Rio Grande was a desert oasis, with rugged terrain not unlike the arid ranchland where he grew up on the Texas High Plains. It was tabletop flat in places and scarred by deep ravines and jagged cliffs in others—wild, remote, and lonesome—just the kind of land he loved.

Garrett eased back into the driver's seat and looked around. More fisher than skier, he wouldn't have traded his own Skeeter bass boat for the Nautique, but it was perfect cover for two ne'er-do-well ranchers out looking to make a deal with the devil. According to their fabricated backstory, Garrett and his brother, played by Malek, had a penchant for whiskey, wild women, and worldly possessions.

Despite having a hangar full of vintage muscle cars and a fleet of helicopters they used for hunting feral hogs, their entertainment cup was sadly only half full. They'd burned through a chunk of their daddy's oil fortune, and as a result, the old man had put his foot down. Despite giving them an allowance fit for a Saudi sheik, they wanted more. And they wanted it however they could get it.

Garrett only hoped Garza didn't notice that he and Malek looked nothing alike. The ranger was tall and lanky, a short-shorn towhead, while Garrett was just below six feet, with long dark hair, a bronzed complexion, and athletic build. But whatever similarities they lacked in looks they made up for in banter. The ball-breaking between the two came off as natural, as if they'd been tormenting each other since the playpen.

Malek, wearing a burnt palm cowboy hat and coyote-colored hunting shirt, was sitting up on the bow, keeping a close watch on the dark horizon. "Helluva good night for fishing, ain't it."

"Good as it gets." Garrett gave a nod. "Quiet too." But for the occasional small wave lapping against the hull, it was dead silent. "Probably got a few minutes until showtime if you wanna throw in a line."

Malek gave a slow shake of his head as he scanned the shoreline. "Don't think I'd enjoy it too much given what we got on our plate."

The ranger sounded a bit anxious, and Garrett knew why. Aside from the obvious danger, the operation to capture a Mexican drug lord was an opportunity of a lifetime. It could make or break their careers. Of course, that was assuming they weren't killed in the process.

"This thing will be done before you know it." Garrett let out an easy chuckle. "Hell, I lay you odds we'll all be having margaritas over in Del Rio before noon."

Malek swiveled around. "Think so, huh?"

Damn sure hope so. As a former Green Beret, Garrett never took odds on high-risk operations. Too many variables. Also, it was bad luck. He'd cussed more than his share of soldiers for doing just that.

But Garrett needed Malek calm and collected so he doubled down on the lie. "Oh yeah, I can taste the huevos rancheros, pinto beans, and corn tortillas right now."

Malek shot a glare. "*Corn*, did you say?" Disgusted, he turned back and raised his binoculars. "Knew something was off about you, Kohl."

Feeling as though he was living out the lyrics of a Lyle Lovett song, Garrett had to laugh. Apparently, Malek was a *flour* tortilla man. For some Texans, that was a personal conviction of the highest sort. Garrett was about to connect his partner's dislike of sweet tea to latent communist leanings when the ranger perked up.

Malek lowered his voice. "See some lights up there." He pointed to a spot about a hundred yards west where there was a break in the fog. "Think that's the village?"

Garrett turned the key in the ignition and the six-hundred-horsepower motor rumbled to life. He clicked the throttle forward and the motor grumbled into a grind. As they eased through the mist, he followed the halogen lights to a rusted gas pump where a couple of turquoise rowboats were tied to the rickety pier. Behind the dock were five cinderblock shacks. The ragged curtains danced in the windows, making the place look more haunted than abandoned.

Knowing it'd be a great setup for a cartel ambush, Garrett reached back to secure the Nighthawk Double Agent pistol tucked into the back of his belt. He'd swapped his DEA-issued Glock 17 for the 1911 before the cross-border trip. Deep cover officers are all about the details and carrying his service weapon just wouldn't do. It was the same reason he'd altered his appearance from rodeo rogue to well-to-do land baron.

The shift in disguise had required a barber visit and a slight trim to his thick beard, taking him from ruffian to rancher in a matter of minutes. But Garrett didn't hide the sleeve tattoos of death skulls, tomahawks, and screaming Comanche warriors atop galloping mustangs. With his faded Wranglers, Twisted X moccasins, and untucked Howler Brothers pearl snap, his look fell somewhere between cowboy and frat boy.

Garrett turned his black Lone Star Dry Goods trucker hat backward, raised up in his seat, and took in the village. Other than the wafting stench of fish guts from the pier and some freshly burnt trash, there were no signs of human activity. He nosed the Nautique up to the dock, yanked back on the throttle, and drifted up to the far end beneath a halo of yellow lamplight.

Malek reached for the gnarled wood piling that jutted up from the planks and brought the wake boat to a halt. After tethering it to the dock, he turned back. "Right on time and exactly where we're supposed to be." The ranger's voice still held a nervous edge. "But something doesn't feel right."

Garrett felt the same but wasn't going to give in to any bad juju. At least not until he had a good reason. "Remember, man, we're holding a good hand of cards here. Garza wouldn't take the risk to meet us in person otherwise. So, just play it easy. And play it loose. Like a couple of drunk bubbas about to spend ten million dollars on trashy women, Caribbean fishing trips, and big-game hunts in Alaska. Got it?"

Malek, a confirmed bachelor and avid outdoorsman, seemed to drink in the idea. "Already there, man." The toothpick in the corner of his mouth raised with his wide grin.

Although Garrett hated to admit it, he was a little nervy too. For the first time in a long time, he had a lot to lose. And most of it had to do with an orphan from Afghanistan he'd brought home to the ranch on a protective custody assignment. Garrett thought of the boy as his own son and wanted to adopt him, but all those plans were hinged on repaying a debt to the CIA.

In exchange for covering up past transgressions, Garrett was conscripted as an off-the-books black-bag operator. And his first assignment began with the cross-border *snatch and grab* involving Garza, who had become public enemy number one after torturing and murdering a Texas Ranger and sending a hit team after Garrett's own family.

Tempted to get riled at the thought of it, he kept calm by going over his cover story—poking any holes yet to be poked. And the biggest hole out there was their CI Smitty, a two-time loser in the Texas prison system and a low-level crook who had started running drugs for Garza. Smitty could either rat out the drug lord or spend the rest of his life in prison.

Despite his shortcomings, which were many, the former convict had a brilliant scheme. His idea was to lure Garza into a meeting with two brothers, Garrett and Malek, who owned a large ranch contiguous to Mexico. But the land itself wasn't the real draw, it was the gas pipeline crossing the border that got the drug lord's attention. Smitty had devised a plan to use what was known in the energy industry as a "pig," a maintenance device that travels the length of pipelines for cleaning and inspection. Retrofitted, they'd been used in the past to transport drugs and cash. If there was a better way to smuggle contraband across the border, Garrett had yet to see it.

At the sound of an inbound motor, Garrett turned, just as he heard the *uh-oh* from Malek. Through a break in the mist, he saw two sets of lights, which meant Garza had broken the deal and brought his thugs along for the meeting. Garrett and his partner might be holding a good hand, but the drug lord had stacked the deck. And worst of all, the whole damn operation hinged on Smitty, who wasn't even a joker. He was the Uno card that had somehow slipped into the box.

2

Ray Smitty surveyed the lake's dark shoreline, careful to avoid the drug lord's suspicious glare. Emilio Garza wasn't just known for killing those who crossed him, he was known for sending a distinct and unsettling message—usually written in blood. As their five-hundred-fifty-horsepower Pavati wake boat moved through a dewy fog, Smitty cursed himself for agreeing to an operation in this borderland graveyard just south of the Rio Grande.

Agreeing to it, hell! It'd been his stupid idea!

Knowing what he knew now, prison would've been a much smarter choice. The problem was that Smitty didn't make smart choices. He made foolish choices. Drunk choices. Choices based on fear. And the greatest fear of them all, right up there with being skinned alive by Garza, was what would happen to his daughter if he messed up again. His *darlin' girl* had made many a prison visit to the Wynne Unit over in Huntsville, but she was just a tot back then.

Savanah was just shy of middle school now, a young woman in her formative years. These were ones she'd remember—the ones he couldn't miss.

Between inheriting her mother's good looks and his bird-dog sense for finding mischief, Smitty knew she'd be a magnet for the wrong sort—the sort like him. If he was going to keep her from falling into that trap, then he had to stay clean. He had to be home. In other words, he had to be a father.

Smitty had been out of trouble for a while now. But the trouble with trouble was that it was damn near everywhere. The deal he was making with Garza was his do-over, a chance to make things right after all his misdeeds. Of course, prison was a better alternative than what would happen if things went wrong. And they were about to go wrong. That was for certain. Smitty turned to Garza, and gave an easy smile.

Wearing a white guayabera and tan linen chinos, the cartel head looked nothing like the short and pudgy Pablo Escobar or Joaquin "El Chapo" Guzman. Garza was tall and slender, with sharp features and a handsome face. He could've passed for any run-of-the-mill successful Latin American businessman were it not for his sullen eyes—permanently fixed in a psychotic glare.

Smitty knew better than to judge anyone by their looks. His whole damn life he'd been accused of looking like a weasel. Of course, favoring a musky rodent might've had nothing to do with a gosh darn thing. His mother-in-law looked like a slutty Martha Stewart but couldn't cook a Pop-Tart. *Sometimes crap just looks like stuff.*

Finishing up whatever he was texting, Garza brushed the dark hair from his eyes and slipped the phone into his shirt pocket. "Good news for you, Ray. Your friends are here."

The report told Smitty one very important and frightening thing. Garza's spies were out there watching.

"Told you to trust me, didn't I?" Smitty faked a laugh that came out nervous, blowing any effort he'd made to cover his fear. "Knew they'd be right on time. No doubt."

Garza pulled his Cabot Diablo 1911 from the glove box and tucked it in the front of his belt. Made of Damascus steel and forged with pieces of an old meteorite, the silver and black pistol looked more like a work of art than a functioning firearm. But Smitty had seen the drug lord use the .45 semi-automatic before at close range. It was as deadly as it was beautiful.

Garza's brazen display of the weapon was his way of letting their new business partners know this was no ordinary kind of deal. Of course, that should've been evident by the machine-gun-toting body-guards in the Supra SA550 wake boat trailing not far behind.

Having lost trust in his Mexican *sicarios*, Garza had contracted a new team of mercenaries made up of members of Guatemala's elite special operations forces known as Kaibiles. What they lacked in resources, they made up for in an inventiveness born of poverty and jungle hardship. These cutthroat killers were short and stocky, strong as oxen, built like their indigenous ancestors. They operated on raw instinct and an animalistic will to survive.

Smitty scanned the beach ahead through breaks in the low-level clouds settling atop the lake, searching for help, which he'd been assured by Garrett and Malek was out there. He fought to keep from squirming, knowing that the drug lord was studying his every move. A bad vibe from Garza was as good as a bullet to the head.

The Pavati's motor dulled to a rumble as they drew near to the dilapidated wooden pier in front of the village. As the boat drifted beneath a ring of lamplight, Malek took the rope from the Kaibile gunman who'd moved from the driver's seat to the front. The ranger tied it to the cleat of the Nautique and brought both boats side by side.

Smitty couldn't help but admire Garrett's coolness under pres-sure. Despite the mercenaries, he didn't make a fuss. He just dug around in his cooler, pulled out a Tecate, and tossed the can to the bodyguard, who nearly lost his balance trying to catch it. The Kaibile was confused but content—cold cerveza in hand and a smile on his face. *A brilliant move by the undercover agent.*

Garrett bellowed out a greeting like a drunken college kid, *"¡Una chela muy fria, amigo!"*

Smitty rose from his seat, following the drug lord's lead, and trailed him the few feet to the bow. Garza waved off the confused guard who stepped back to the boat's controls, still wearing a baffled grin, wondering what the hell he was supposed to do with his beer.

Not missing a beat, Garrett tossed another Tecate to Garza, who fortunately seemed amused by the antics. No doubt, the cartel boss was more accustomed to cowering than bravado. But Garrett had made sure Smitty built these traits into their profiles. The drug lord knew to expect two drunk buffoons, arrogant and clueless as they were greedy.

Not to be outdone in coolness under pressure, Garza cracked his Tecate, blew off the suds and took a sip. He raised it and smiled. *"¡Salud!"*

Smitty didn't know much Spanish, but he knew the toast could mean to health, wealth, or security. He prayed for all three but knew it was for naught. Neither Garrett nor Malek would call off the mission, even when targeted by a boatful of mercenaries.

Garrett polished off what was left of his own beer, crushed the can, and tossed it onto the pier with a clank. He opened a fresh one, popped up, and took a couple of faux stumbling steps to join Malek at the front of the boat.

Garrett reached to Garza to help him aboard. "Welcome, my friend! Step on in!" He thumbed over his shoulder where the maps were laid out on the table. "Got everything set up already. Overlay of the pipeline. Schematics for the pigging device. All you need for making lots and lots of money."

Garza left Garrett's arm hanging, took another sip, and looked around just as Garrett had done. "Why don't you join me first?"

Garrett looked over both shoulders and shot Garza a skeptical glare. "Bit risky, ain't it?" He let out a drunk-sounding chuckle. "Thinking them *federales* you got down here would love to get their hands on a couple of gringos."

Garza shook off the notion. "You're in *my* world now." He tilted his head toward a bottle of Herradura Selección Suprema on the table. "To celebrate our partnership."

Garrett looked a little antsy and Smitty didn't blame him. The drug lord had already broken the deal by bringing his entourage of Guatemalan commandos.

Before Garrett could make another argument, Garza added, "I insist." He draped his arm around Smitty's neck and pulled him close. "I like to get to know the people I'm doing business with first."

Although the gesture was meant to look like a warm embrace, Smitty knew it was a warning. And Garrett was aware of that too. The drug lord's offer was not to be refused.

"That's the good stuff, man." Malek looked to Garrett like a kid brother begging for permission. "Can't turn down Suprema, can we?"

An awkward moment passed as Garza stared Garrett down. The tension in the air hung as thick as the humidity, and Smitty suddenly became very aware of the gunmen in the boat thirty yards off their stern. They were out of the light, but he could see the rifles in their silhouettes.

Garrett turned his death glare on Malek. "Guess not." He held out his hand to be helped to the other side.

Garza clasped Garrett's hand and pulled him over into the Pavati. As he moved wobbly to the back of the boat, the Texas Ranger leapt over next. Once secured, Malek moved to the stern where Garrett was already sitting with his back to the open water. He had downed his second Tecate in preparation for the *good stuff* and helped himself to a sloshing shot of the Herradura. It was a ballsy move but right in character.

Looking as though Garza might've bought into the lawmen's ruse, Smitty let out a sigh of relief, hopefully not too loud. He'd just begun to feel like things might be okay when the cartel boss drew the pistol from his waistband and aimed it at Garrett.

3

Terrence "Trip" Davis, of the Texas Ranger Reconnaissance Team, scanned the five little cinderblock shacks of the fishing village through the green glow of his night vision goggles. Since Garza had already welshed on the deal by toting along a boatload full of heavily armed bodyguards, Trip expected it wouldn't be the drug lord's only surprise.

The good news was that the mist had lifted, giving him a better view. The bad news was that he still couldn't see much. His view of Garrett was blocked by the henchmen's Supra, which was floating behind Garza's boat. Blind to what was going down on the other side, Trip shifted focus to the perimeter, now bathed in light from the full moon and stars.

The petite blonde beside him turned and asked again, "See anything?" She had her own night vision binoculars, but they were of lesser quality than the Steiner scope fixed to Trip's Daniel Defense M4V7 rifle.

He took another hard look but came up empty. "Sorry. No dice."

"What's the range?" she pressed.

Same as the last time. Trip pretended to recalculate then let loose his answer in a Texas drawl, smooth and easy as his temperament.

"'Bout . . . two hundred yards." He turned to Kim, who had taken a knee beside him, her binoculars trained on the boats across the cove.

As a combat veteran from 5th Special Forces Group, Trip had seen a few strange things, but nothing compared to this. The hush-hush mission into Mexico was out of the ordinary, but the attractive blonde beside him with the suppressed H&K MP7 submachine gun took the cake. Kim Manning couldn't have weighed more than a sack of sugar, but she was a heavyweight in authority. He didn't know exactly who this was, but she had CIA written all over her.

This wasn't the first shadow war that Trip had been roped into by Garrett. Back in Afghanistan, his old buddy had recruited him into a mountain warfare unit that hunted terrorists on horseback. As the only snuff-dipping, pickup-driving Black cowboy in the bunch he was a bit of a rarity, but so was his skillset. He was a superb rider and a helluva good shot.

After the Army, Trip became a state trooper and was selected to be a Texas Ranger. He joined the SWAT team, completed the Precision Rifle Program, then later moved on to Ranger Recon, conducting intelligence gathering and drug interdiction on the Mexican border. He'd worked a couple of task force operations with the feds but nothing this high-level.

For this mission, he'd ditched his badge, ID, and normal attire, which typically fell somewhere between cowboy and commando—Stetson, blue jeans, and an Under Armour polo. But for their weaponry, which they could dump if need be, anyone they encountered would suspect them as a couple of lost campers who'd gotten themselves in a whole lot of trouble.

Trip moved from prone to a knee, slid a couple feet right, and repositioned against a stack of red Spanish tile inside of an old adobe structure that looked like the Alamo. He snatched a brittle blade of dry grass from a crack in the floor, let it loose, and watched it drift in the breeze.

"Wind's kicking up out of the west." Trip raised his rifle and rested the crosshairs on the head of a Garza gunman. "Turn that boat a smidge and maybe we can see Garrett."

Kim nodded. "Okay, well at least that's good news."

"Yeah . . . but there's something else." Trip debated whether to mention the bad news.

Kim turned looking anxious. "Now what?"

He pointed to the wave of mist floating over the village. "Fog's rolling back in."

"*Dammit.*" Kim raised her binoculars for another scan of the area.

Trip kept his scope trained on the boat flanking Garrett. There were four stocky gunmen on board, all carrying Tavor X95s, a strange but deadly choice of weapon for cartel henchmen. Assuming the bullpup rifles were select-fire and not commercial-grade variants, each shooter could unload a thirty-round mag in ten seconds. Garrett and Malek would be dead in about two.

"What do you think?" Kim looked to Trip. "Got a shot?"

Trip didn't mind pulling the trigger on some cartel dirtbags, but he was a law enforcement officer, not an assassin. He'd not be afforded the same immunities as Kim. Aside from that, there were friendlies behind the target. His stray round was no better than one from Garza.

Given Kim's casualness with taking preemptive lethal measures, it assured his suspicions that she was CIA. Only the Agency operated under a *kill first, sort it out later* mentality. Trip needed to slow this thing down before it got out of hand. "I got four good shots. But soon as I pull the trigger, so will they. And Garza won't hang around. He'll haul ass once the bullets start flying."

Kim didn't miss a beat. "Take him out first then."

Ah hell. This thing was going down right here and now. Trip kept the crosshairs on the gunman furthest to the left, the only one who had his Tavor shouldered and pointed at the Pavati. With the center of his reticle on the henchman's spine, Trip did his best to get a read on their body language, trying to determine if they were in a standoff. Then suddenly a solid gust spun the gunmen's boat just enough to reveal that Garza was pointing his pistol at Garrett.

Trip rested the pad of his finger on the trigger, sat the crosshairs on the drug lord's chest, and held his breath. He was just about to fire when the fog dropped like a curtain, settled over the boat, and his target was lost in the dewy haze.

4

arrett wasn't all that surprised to see the gun. He'd looked down the barrel of more than a few, but they'd always belonged to a young hothead just trying to get in his bluff. Garza, however, was no dope-slinging rookie or someone who wasted time with theatrics. The mission wasn't just compromised, they were about to be executed on the spot.

With his pulse racing, heart pounding, the words of Garrett's old mentor from the DEA came to mind. Joe Bob Dawson likened the rapid adrenaline-fueled thump of the heart to a *war drum*—a signal that your primal instincts were kicking in to help you survive.

It was no doubt a psychological trick, a way to keep calm in life-and-death situations, but for Garrett it was just what he needed—right when he needed it. His muscles twitched, vision grew sharper, and hearing became keener, so keen that the crackle of gunfire from across the cove immediately registered that Trip and Kim had been found.

Garza donned a victorious smile. "I would ask who you work for, but I suspect it will take a while to get to the truth."

"You're right about that." Garrett allowed himself to sink in his seat, trying to get his head below the gunwale in case Trip had a shot. "But I'm up for the challenge if you are."

Garrett's swagger was purely for show, knowing that the interrogation and tortures would be a fate worse than death. But he needed some time to think.

Garza gave a nod to his guard in the driver's seat then turned back to Garrett and smiled. "Challenge accepted."

A turn of a key and the Pavati's powerful motor rumbled to life and idled in a low growl. Without even a shred of an escape plan, Garrett glanced at Malek and Smitty, both of whom had lost any pretense of an easy disposition. In a matter of minutes they'd be deep in the heart of cartel country without any hope of rescue.

DESPITE THE *SNAP* OF SUPERSONIC rounds strafing overhead from whoever was attacking from behind, Trip kept his eye on the target, or at least where he suspected it to be behind the drifting haze. He had just cursed the *damn ass fog* when another gust of wind parted the mist and gave him a clear line of sight. Setting his crosshairs on a gunmen, he notified Kim that he'd *acquired a target*, to which she responded with the two-word command. *Send it.*

No sooner had the words left her mouth than Trip squeezed the trigger, his suppressed rifle coughed, and a 5.56 round *whapped* the gunman in his sights with such force that he went headfirst into the lake. With the water still rippling, Trip eased his crosshairs a sliver to the one on the right turning to fire. But before the guard could get off a single round, Trip found him dead center of his reticle and sunk two bullets in his chest.

Trip lined up on a third, who had good enough sense to try and duck for cover, took three rapid shots, and hoped for the best. His last round clipped the top of the gunman's scalp, which popped up a spray of dark crimson. It wasn't by any stretch a good hit, but he'd take *good enough* so long as it knocked the guy out of action.

Trip ducked when a bullet *zipped* past his ear and slammed the adobe wall he was using for cover. He had just wiped the debris from his eyes and risen to search for Garrett when he lost visibility in the drifting mist. With Kim now at the back of the room in a full-on gun battle, Trip ducked low, moved next to her behind a crumbling adobe wall and joined the fight.

She was leaning around the left edge, letting rip with her H&K, emptying one magazine after the next. Trip thought she was wasting ammo until he eased around the corner and saw the half-dozen muzzle flashes, bursting from the brush cover of the mesquite only thirty yards out.

GARRETT RUSHED THE DRIVER BEHIND the boat's controls, but hit the deck with a thud, as the slack in the line caught with a sudden jerk. Scrabbling to a knee, Garrett turned to the Supra, finding only one of the four guards were left. Even under fire, Trip had done some damn good shooting.

The barrel of the last guard's Tavor was hanging over the starboard side, gliding from right to left hungry for a target. As the machine gun rattled to life, Garrett hit the deck and the gunwale above him was shredded to kindling. The boat driver took three rounds in the back and slumped forward, his deadweight on the throttle forcing the motor into a furious growl.

Looking to the bow, Garrett saw that Garza, who was straddling Malek, had clamped down on the ranger's throat. Punching and kicking fruitlessly to free himself from the drug lord's grip, his veins bulged and his face grew redder with each missed breath.

Garrett lunged for the ignition, killed the motor, and scurried to

Malek, crawling beneath a hail of bullets that ripped the boat's interior. Chin so low it scraped the deck, he clambered to the cartel boss, grabbed his pants legs, and yanked like hell.

Malek broke loose, landed a solid right hook to Garza's jaw, and leaned against the inner hull, gasping for air. The punch-drunk cartel head turned a bit wobbly and set his unfocused gaze on Garrett, seemingly in shock at the sudden turn of the tables.

Garrett yanked his Nighthawk and aimed at Garza. "Don't move!" He looked to Malek, who was struggling to breathe. "Sit tight, pardner. We got one still out there."

Lying flat as a pancake to avoid the next barrage, Garrett turned in every direction to locate Smitty, but the only other person aboard was the dead driver. With their CI missing in action, Garrett turned again to Malek. "Where's our friend?"

"Overboard," Malek barked out.

Damn! Garrett's heart sank. "Hit?"

Malek shrugged, still huffing. "Don't know."

Garrett eyed Garza, still dazed and woozy, then turned back to Malek. "Got your pistol?"

The ranger reached back and pulled his FN 509 from his jeans and aimed it at Garza. With the cartel boss covered, Garrett turned his thoughts on the last gunman. If Smitty was overboard he had to go in and get him. He hated to think the poor guy was bleeding out in the water.

Garrett was contemplating his next move when he heard the *crack-crack* of a pistol, the full-auto discharge of a Tavor, then a sudden splash. Easing up over the side, Garrett searched for the last gunman, but found no one left. The guards' boat was unmanned and drifting away.

Scrambling to his feet, Garrett moved to each side of the boat in search of Smitty but found nothing but the blackness of the empty water. With the rest of his life to play the "what if" game on Smitty, Garrett raced to the bow to unfurl the line from the cleat. Garrett turned to Malek and threw him a zip tie that had been stuffed in his back pocket.

The ranger labored to his feet and delivered a solid kick to Garza's chin, knocking him on his back and out like a light. Malek flipped the cartel boss over and shackled his wrists. He looked across the cove to where the gun battle was raging. "We need to get over there."

"I'll worry about them." Garrett leapt back into his Nautique, dashed to the controls and threw himself into the driver's seat. "Get him back to our side before his reinforcements arrive. We'll be right behind you."

Expecting an argument out of Malek, Garrett cranked the motor, turned the wheel, and jammed his palm on the throttle. Although he could no longer hear the gunshots over the boat's snarl, he could still see muzzle flashes on the shoreline. His friends were in a fight for their lives.

5

Trip drew back inside the doorframe and threw his back against the wall. Dropping a spent mag that banged on the concrete, he yanked the last one from his chest rig and jammed it into his rifle. A quick pop of the bolt release put him back in action. He had just swung around to fire when a spray of rounds clipped the edge and sent him reeling for cover.

A moment to regroup and Trip hung his rifle around the corner, finding more than a dozen muzzle flashes in the darkness. He braced his rifle barrel against the doorframe, rolled onto his offset red dot, and rested it on the forehead of a gunman crouched behind a pile of bricks. Trip pulled the trigger, sunk the target, and slid left, locking onto the next.

Downing the gunman, Trip scanned right, spying three fighters maneuvering through the thick mesquite brush around the side of the structure. He snapped his rifle onto the first in line and fired, then moved to the next, who had just collapsed with a double tap from Kim. Another popped up from behind a rock wall and swung his Tavor in their direction, but Trip's red dot was already hovering over the gunman's right eye. A squeeze of the trigger, a jar of the head, and the fighter's body sank behind the barrier.

With another flurry of rounds that sent him scurrying for cover,

Trip took a quick glance back at the lake to find Garrett's Nautique zooming up. He nudged Kim, who was still firing through the window and got a reaction that was somewhere between pissed and desperate. But before he could suggest retreat, the blonde spy was already tearing a path toward the boat.

With rounds cracking overhead and chipping the adobe walls all around him, Trip hung his rifle around the ledge to provide cover fire, landing another round on a charging gunman. But where one went down, two took their place. He and Kim were about to be overrun.

WITHIN THIRTY YARDS OF THE beach, Garrett jerked back on the throttle, but he was way too late. The Nautique slammed into the limestone with an ugly crunch beneath the hull. Sucking in a breath, he found his footing and sprinted to the front. From the muzzle flashes coming from in and around the building, the fighters were closing in fast.

Garrett had just raised his Nighthawk and banged out three rounds when a volley of lead *zipped* and *buzzed* overhead. He ducked behind the bow and shot into the darkness, where the enemy were fanning into an arc—returning fire from covered positions behind the thick brush.

As Kim made a running leap into the front of the boat with Trip on her heels, Garrett jumped into the driver's seat, jerked the lever in reverse, and heard the flustered whine of the revving motor. A flurry of rounds cracked above, then *clack-clack-clacked* into the boat's hardtop roof, churning the plastic into brittle shards that rained down on Garrett's head.

Trip scrambled to his feet, raced to the bow, and leapt over the side to free the boat from the bank. With a few sudden jolts, the Nautique rocked back and forth until the sickly drone of the motor morphed to a low steady rumble, scraping across the limestone back into the lake.

Garrett yelled to his friend over the echoing gunfire, "We're good, Trip!" When he got no reply, he called again, "We're good! Let's git!" Kim's eyes met Garrett's with a mutual recognition that his friend might be down. Garrett shouted again, surprised by hearing the uncertainty in his own voice. "Come on, man! Now or never!"

Before Garrett could move, Kim had already dropped her MP7, dashed to the front and hopped overboard. With the supersonic *snap* of strafing rounds, he ducked and raced to the front as bullets ripped through the console and shattered the controls.

Garrett leaned over, reached out to Kim who was struggling to keep Trip's head above water but couldn't meet her outstretched hand. He leaned further and had just clasped her hand as bullets raked the port side, devouring the fiberglass from bow to stern.

Palming the gunwale, Garrett threw his legs over the side, hurled himself into waist-deep water and moved behind the hull, which had drifted parallel to the beach. He and Kim hauled an unconscious Trip back behind the boat, taking shelter from rounds that churned the black water. Thumbing the catch release button, Garrett dropped a spent mag into the lake, yanked a fresh one from his belt and jammed it into the Nighthawk.

Looking back at the lights of the fishing village two hundred yards across the cove, Garrett hit the slide release to chamber a round and turned to Kim. "You gotta swim for it. Get out of here, while you still can."

She looked out at the dark expanse, then back to Garrett. "There's no way. I can barely keep him afloat standing here. We'd drown."

"Not him. Just you."

"I'm not leaving him." Kim's eyes went fiery. "Or you! Forget it!"

"It's the only way." Garrett grabbed hold of Trip's lifeless body from Kim and pulled him close. "Maybe you can get us some help."

The notion was almost laughable. Most Mexican law enforcement officers were bought and paid for by the cartel. They'd be no use. But there were still a few good Samaritans out there—the kind who remember what life was like before their home was run by cartel outlaws.

Kim eyed the fish camp. "You see anyone over there?"

Garrett shook his head. "There's a dirt road coming in from behind the village. Leads to a little town about seven miles south. Find somebody you trust that will get you back to the border."

"Somebody I trust?" Kim's skeptical glare revealed what Garrett believed to be true. Trusting anyone in cartel country would be a risk. But it was a helluva lot better than staying behind. She pointed at the boat. "Help me back in. We've got Trip's gun and my own. We can—"

"How much ammo?" Garrett interrupted, unsure why he bothered to ask. The boat was zeroed in. Any attempt to retrieve the guns would be met with a hail of lead.

Before she could answer, a rifle barrel swung around the hull. The guard had just opened fire when Garrett leveled his pistol and cracked off a round, clipping the gunman's shoulder and ripping out a hunk of flesh. His second shot landed center mass, which sent their attacker sprawling. The splash gave way to a lull in the gunfire and an eerie unsettling silence.

6

Smitty was still clutching the drug lord's Cabot Diablo pistol when he eased into the driver's seat of the Supra. Now presumed dead, there was strong temptation to skedaddle into the night and disappear forever. But that was the *old* Ray Smitty. The new one had made a commitment to his wife, a promise to be the husband and father he should've been from day one.

With the knock of gunfire echoing across the water, Smitty yanked the night vision binoculars from the guard he'd just shot and panned the dark shoreline on the other side of the cove. In the green glow of his optics, he saw Garrett, Kim, and Trip huddled behind the Nautique, with a dozen or so men from the hit squad swarming in around them.

Smitty had fulfilled his obligation to bring in Garza to the meeting, which met his terms of the deal. Nobody would've blamed him for escaping. The problem was that he'd come to think of Garrett as a friend, even if the feeling wasn't mutual. But it didn't take much pondering to know what the DEA agent would do if the shoe was on the other foot.

Slipping into the seat, Smitty flipped the ignition, and the Supra's five-hundred-seventy-five-horsepower motor roared to life. With a boat full of dead Kaibiles, he stuffed the Cabot pistol into the back of his blue jeans, turned the wheel, and aimed toward the fight.

With the throttle jammed forward, it took only a few seconds to cross the cove, but it felt like a lifetime as he watched Garza's gunmen surround the Nautique. Roaring in from behind, Smitty tried to keep Garrett's boat between him and the swarming hit squad. But almost immediately their bullets were *thwacking* his hull.

SPENDING THE LAST OF HIS last rounds providing security for Kim as she climbed in Smitty's boat, Garrett holstered his Nighthawk and waded up to the swim platform of the Supra. With bullets popping and chopping the black water all around them, Garrett groaned as he heaved Trip's soaking wet body onto the deck. Once secured, he clambered up himself and collapsed atop Trip, shielding his friend from the lead barrage.

Nearly slipping off the back when Smitty hit the throttle, Garrett felt his shirt catch as Kim grabbed his sleeve. He took her handoff of the Tavor rifle, racked the slide, and ripped away full auto at the gunmen in their wake. It was less of a defensive move and more of a middle finger to the enemy. But burning through a thirty-round magazine had never felt so good.

7

Asadi Saleem brushed the dust from his jeans as he approached a colt that Garrett had come to call Grizz, short for Grizzly, because of the thick winter coat that made him look like a bear. The animal had shed the hair by early summer, but the nickname stuck. Despite his relatively sweet personality, and having been under a saddle for ninety days, the sorrel had woken up a bit humpy that morning and gotten the best of Asadi with an unexpected buck.

A little dazed and disoriented from the fall, Asadi searched the top rail of the round pen to where Butch sat coaching. The old man lifted the straw Resistol from his head, wiped his brow, and ran an open palm over his thick white hair. He always did that when solving a problem.

Asadi wasn't hurt from the fall, nor was he afraid of the horse, although he didn't favor the idea of taking another tumble. His only worry was letting Butch down. Disappointing him or Garrett was always the first thing on his mind.

Butch called to him in his gravelly voice. "Ease up, sonny. Slow but steady. Let him see your determination."

Asadi turned from Butch to the horse then back again, clearly at a loss given the unfamiliar five-syllable word.

Butch clarified. "Let him know you ain't putting up with no crap."

That Asadi understood. He gave a quick nod, making a mental note—*determination* means *no crap*. With middle school approaching at the end of August, he had to get his vocabulary up to speed. And he had to do it fast.

Asadi approached Grizz cautiously enough not to spook him but briskly enough to convince Butch, not the colt, he was unafraid. Among the many things to be learned since his arrival in Texas was the cowboy code. The rules weren't written or spoken but rather lived out during everyday life. It wasn't wrong to be afraid, only to be ruled by fear. But conquering it was easier said than done.

"Hey, Outlaw!" Butch beckoned with a big wave. "Come visit a minute."

Thankful for the reprieve, Asadi walked over to where the old man was perched atop the fence. Behind him, and their little white farmhouse, an orange fireball of sun filled the sky, burning a blurry mirage on the horizon of the flat dusty plains.

Butch noticed it too. "Beautiful now, but it's gonna be a scorcher."

Asadi agreed with a nod and practiced his English with a topic of conversation that seemed to dominate all others between Garrett and his father. "No rain?"

Butch shook his head. "Afraid not." He patted the top rail with a leather-gloved hand. "Come have a seat."

Asadi scaled the fence, sat beside Butch, and stared back at Grizz since he knew that would be a topic of conversation. He was desperately worried he was failing at his job.

Butch rested his hand on Asadi's skinny shoulder and gave it a squeeze. "A horse can talk, you know?"

With his English lacking at times, Asadi wondered if he'd heard correctly. He looked to Butch curiously to confirm. "You say . . . horse talk?"

"Better believe it, sonny." Butch turned to Asadi to make sure he could see his smile. He spoke a little slower, as he often did when he wanted to drive home a point. "Not like you and me. And not like they talk to each other." He took a moment to study Grizz. "But they speak with their bodies. Their eyes. And their ears."

"Ears?" Asadi repeated with suspicion.

"Just look." Butch pointed at the colt. "Where are they pointed?"

Asadi jabbed a thumbed into his chest. "At me?"

"*Exactly.*" Butch's voice went from gravel to gravy when he talked to or about horses. "He's looking right at you. And do you know why?"

Asadi shook his head. "Maybe he angry."

Butch coughed out a laugh. "No way. Not at all. No, he's looking at you because he doesn't want you to give up on him and he's worried you might quit."

Asadi looked to Butch, certain the old man was joking. "How you know?"

"By doing exactly what we're doing right now time and time again for one. But even more importantly, I have a God-given gift to understand animals in a way most folks don't."

Asadi's face screwed together. "You be serious?"

"Better believe it." Butch smiled. "You see, in the Bible it says God gave animals to us, but I think it's the other way round. I think God gave us to them." He scanned the length of the top of the caprock cliffs behind the corral. "People forget that we were all partners once, back before the apple and everything got all messed up. Since then, it's been a battle of wills between man and beast."

Asadi turned to Butch. "Like war?"

"Yeah, one only to be rivaled by the one between husband and wife." Butch winked at Asadi. "But that's a lesson for another day."

Asadi was confused and his face must have showed it. "You say . . . Grizz own me?"

"In a way, I suppose." Butch shrugged. "You see, my point is that for him to be at his best in this world, he needs a partner. And so do you."

Thinking he understood, Asadi gave a timid response, "He want—be my *partner*?"

"*Exactly*. Like two best friends, who work together for a purpose. For something they love. Something bigger than themselves." Butch thumbed back at the hayfield. "Like taking care of this ranch here."

Asadi looked from Grizz to Butch. "Like you and me."

Butch mussed Asadi's hair. "You know, if my own kids had been bright as you, I'd have had a lot more." He pointed to Grizz. "What can you tell about his eyes?"

After careful study, Asadi found them different than he expected. They weren't fierce or blazing. They were nervous. "He a feared?"

Butch gave a slow nod. "Yep. Might be a little afraid." He turned back to Asadi. "And I think the reason is that he doesn't want to let you down."

Finding that hard to believe, Asadi shot Butch a skeptical glare. Still though, he could relate. The last thing he wanted to do was disappoint Butch. "*Me?*"

Asadi looked to Grizz, whose body spoke volumes. With that in mind, he relaxed, climbed down from the fence, and eased to the colt with the confidence of a friend coming to help. After a gentle stroke across Grizz's neck, Asadi took hold of the reins near the bit and slid the toe of his boot into the stirrup.

And with this new understanding, the language gap between horse and rider started to fade. Asadi and his colt partners. And they were both on their way to being their very best in this world.

8

Garrett fought heavy eyelids destined to clamp shut. His sleepless night, coupled with the effects of a second margarita, was a recipe for some solid sack time. But there were toasts to be made, and was no better place for he and Kim to make them than Memo's Restaurant in Del Rio. Most notable of their triumphs was the fact that Trip suffered only a concussion. The tough-as-nails bull rider had taken a back full of lead while pushing them off the shore.

Fortunately, the body armor saved his life, but it had done nothing to cushion the blow when he'd banged his head against the boat hull. Had it been anyone else, the injury would've warranted a lifetime of teasing. But Trip was the guy with the biggest smile and an encouraging word—the one you could count on through thick and thin. Garrett would carry their secret to the grave.

While Garza's extradition hadn't gone down exactly as planned, a win was still a win. They'd all be celebrating this one for a very long time. Of course, all the accolades would fall to the Texas Rangers, and more specifically their intrepid, albeit sketchy CI. Garrett couldn't help but shake his head and laugh at the debt of gratitude he owed a redneck yokel like Ray Smitty, who'd turned out to be their guardian angel.

Kim raised her glass in a toast. "To bringing a murderer to justice." Her voice was low enough that no one around them could hear.
Memo's patrons more a bit more accustomed to small-town locals
than narco hunters. So, it was probably best to keep a low profile.

Garrett couldn't help but think that Kim looked a bit girlish and
innocent right then and there. It was a rare look for the no-nonsense
CIA operations officer he'd met in Afghanistan. Whether decked out
in 5.11 Tactical garb or her Hermès business suits, Kim was a helluva smokeshow. But there was something about that white Mexican
dress, with the embroidered flowers and off-the-shoulder neckline,
that took her beauty to the next level.

A quick sip of her margarita and Kim asked, "Bother you at all
that the rangers will get the press on this one?"

"Got to be honest. It's going to hurt a little seeing Garza do the
perp walk with no DEA around. But I'm just glad it's done." Garrett
gulped some ice water, still thirsty from the night's adventures. "How
about you? You're the one who really got the wheels in motion."

"Whenever CIA makes the news it's rarely a good thing." Kim
chuckled. "And at the end of the day, the people who matter will
know. I'll get the credit where it counts."

Garrett had learned over time not to ask questions about *the people* to whom she was referring. He assumed they were her higher-ups
at the Agency, maybe even a few at the National Security Council,
someone with direct access to the president.

It was wishful thinking, but Garrett had to ask, "So, I'm off the
hook after this, right?"

Kim smiled. "Not by a long shot, cowboy."

"Then what's next on this list? I'm ready to even up the ledger."

"Doesn't work that way." Kim seemed to enjoy watching him
squirm. "But you already knew that, didn't you?"

In fact, he *did* know that. But Garrett was growing tired of the uncertainty, particularly when it came to the Afghan boy he wanted to adopt. "When do we make this Asadi thing permanent?"

Kim's joy seemed to fade. "Still working on that one."

"What's there to work on? With the Taliban back at the helm there's no way in hell we could ever send him back. Should be a done deal."

Ceding the country to the enemy had been a bitter pill for Garrett to swallow. But nothing could be done about it now. The past was the past, and the focus of his future was giving Asadi a permanent home with a family who loves him. There was no looking back.

Kim put her margarita on the table and stared at it. "I'm afraid there's a complication."

"*Complication?*" Garrett swirled his finger in the air as if waving a magic wand. "Just do that presto-change-o CIA thing you do and make it happen."

Kim looked up slowly. "Turns out Asadi has family over there."

"So what?" It was a kneejerk reaction, but Garrett felt it to his core. "Afghanistan isn't even remotely safe. Especially for him. You know that better than I do."

"No, not in Afghanistan. Across the border from his village."

"*Pakistan?*" This revelation shocked Garrett even more. "*Where* in Pakistan?"

Kim paused again, clearly reluctant to deliver the news. "Waziristan."

Garrett's blood boiled. "You kidding me? That's in the heart of Taliban country." Working to control his temper, he lowered his voice. "Just as bad as sending him home. Maybe worse."

"Not anymore," Kim argued. "Taliban has moved back across the border. Waziristan would be safe for him now."

"But we'd be sending him to the people who sheltered our enemies. Gave them food. Clothing. *Weapons.* They're just as bad as any terrorist in my book."

"They weren't helping our enemies, Garrett. They were helping other Pashtuns. Other Muslims. Historical allies."

"Same thing, Kim. No matter how you want to spin it. Those people have blood on their hands. My blood. My friends' blood. The Taliban and Al Qaeda may have moved out of there, but nothing's really changed. They hate us. And they'll hate Asadi too."

Kim sighed. "Look, the situation is complex."

"Not to me," Garrett shot back. "After testifying against the Taliban butchers who razed his village, you can't tell me there won't be people looking for Asadi to get revenge. People who probably came from the *exact* part of that country. Sending him back would be a death sentence."

"He'd be protected," Kim argued.

"How can you be sure of that?"

Kim let out a huff. "His uncle is very powerful. A man of influence."

"*Uncle?* What uncle?" Garrett's distrust of the CIA was in overdrive. Work with them long enough and you start to get a feel for when you're not getting the whole story, which was most of the time. "Everyone in his village was murdered. And Asadi never mentioned any other family."

"Well, he's a *distant* uncle. Asadi doesn't know him. Or his aunt and cousins. But they're there. I promise you. I checked them out personally."

"*And?*"

Now Kim looked exasperated. "And what?"

"What makes his uncle uniquely qualified to keep Asadi safe?"

Kim looked around the way intelligence officers do before dishing out the goods. "His uncle is a tribal chief."

"You mean a *warlord*," Garrett corrected.

"Whatever you want to call him, he's highly respected. No one crosses Omar Zadran. Not the Taliban. Not Al Qaeda. Not even Pakistani intelligence. He's very well connected. Nobody goes against him. *Ever.*"

"How can you be so sure? You've seen how these guys horse-trade. How do you know this *Zadran* won't make a deal with the Taliban? Swap Asadi for someone he really wants."

"Because we know, Garrett."

"*How* do you know?"

"Because we've known him for a long time. We're working on a deal."

And there it is. Asadi's uncle was a CIA asset, or at least someone willing to cooperate. But it didn't mean he was kind or moral, or that he would be decent to Asadi. It meant he was getting something from the U.S. in return. Usually that was weapons or money. Sometimes both.

"Okay, Kim, what do you have cooking over in Waziristan that is so important you would ruin the life of an innocent eleven-year-old boy?"

Kim shook her head. "I can't get into that."

Garrett bristled. "Well, you better give me something. Because I ain't letting him go if he's going to be a pawn in some kind of damn CIA shadow war."

Kim looked around again, clearly uncomfortable with the conversation. "Look, you know as well as I do, we need to know what's happening in Afghanistan. Through Zadran and his extensive contacts, we have a window into that world. A window we desperately need. Now that the Pakistani government has thrown their support to the Taliban, we have less support in the region than ever. Zadran even has ties to ISI. He's our eyes and ears now."

The Inter-Services Intelligence, or ISI, is Pakistan's primary intelligence agency, known to play both sides of the war on terror. After the U.S. pulled out of Afghanistan, Islamabad's fig leaf didn't just drift away, it was blown with the force of a hurricane. Of course, what could you expect from the country that was hiding Osama bin Laden?

Garrett could tell she was holding back. "You've got something up your sleeve, I can tell."

Kim lowered her voice. "You've heard about 'over-the-horizon' operations, right?"

OTH, among other things, was the concept of using surrogates in places that the U.S. military and intelligence community were denied access. Garrett was doubtful it would work effectively in Afghanistan, which mostly had to do with the failure to detect the attacks planned for September 11, 2001. As an undercover operative, he was a big believer in boots on the ground.

Garrett shook his head. "Don't tell me you've bought into all that crap."

"I don't make policy. I just do my job to the best of my ability."

"And this is your job now?" Garrett guffawed. "Armchair intelligence gathering."

"Zadran is the poster boy for OTH. And it's my job to make sure it works."

Garrett knew it wasn't easy for Kim to reveal that information and he understood why the deal with Zadran was so important. But it did nothing to assure him of the boy's safety. "Okay, I appreciate your honesty and I trust your judgment. I know you care for Asadi and would never suggest a solution that would put him in harm's way. But he's never even met these people. They're strangers."

"I know, Garrett. But you always knew this day could come. You said it yourself. You'd support him going back if he has family there."

Garrett had said those very words and meant them. But that was months ago. That was before he realized he could never let the boy go. "Maybe they don't even want him. I mean, if they knew Asadi had a good home. That he was happy here. Maybe Zadran would—"

Kim shook her head. "Not how they think over there. All goes back to Pashtunwali. It's their code of loyalty. Zadran believes he has a duty to tend to his family's orphaned child and there is no changing that. It's been their way of life for millennia."

Garrett raised his hands, palms up beside him. "Doesn't Asadi get a say in this?"

Kim looked genuinely pained. "He's a child and his family wants him back."

Garrett started to speak then stopped himself.

Kim sat staring at him, clearly not ready to let it go. "Got something to say? Then say it."

"If you leave us no choice, then maybe Asadi and I will go another way."

"There *is* no other way."

Garrett shrugged. "We'll see."

Kim leaned forward and looked around to make sure no one was listening, then asked with gritted teeth, "You mean you'd kidnap him?"

"It's not kidnapping if it's your own damn son."

"Yes, it *is* still kidnapping. And he's not your son."

Garrett shook his head, frustrated over the fact that *legally* she was right. "He's not my boy, officially. Not yet. But I'm all he's got now."

Kim let out a long sigh as her eyes went from fierce to forgiving. "I know it hurts. But we always knew—"

"This was a possibility," Garrett finished. "Yeah, I remember. All I'm saying is that if what you're suggesting is how it plays out, then maybe there's another option."

"Taking off with Asadi is *not* an option." Kim's words had a tone of both frustration and pain. "This is coming straight from the CIA director, who is talking with the deputy director of national security. They see Zadran as a foothold in an area of extreme importance to the safety of our country. And they're not going to let that go over a kid."

Garrett wondered if he should just shut up and do what was necessary if the time comes. "Okay, maybe you're right. We'll just wait and see then."

It was clear by the look on Kim's face that she wasn't buying his sudden change of heart. "We *will* find you, Garrett. We will track you down no matter where you go. You know that."

"I've got no doubt you can find almost anyone in the world if you've got a mind to, but the day I go off the grid will be the last time you ever see me again. Or him."

Garrett's boast was no bluster. In Army Special Forces he'd been trained by some of the best in the world to evade and survive in the harshest conditions known to man. And given his role as a deep cover narcotics officer, he'd learned how to operate beneath the radar, develop new identities and live undetected. If it came to that, he and Asadi would be ghosts.

"Even if that is true, then what, Garrett?"

"Then we make a new life."

Kim was clearly anguished. "And what kind of life would Asadi have as a fugitive? No home. No school. No stability. You'd be looking over your shoulders every moment for the rest of your lives." Before Garrett could respond she pressed on. "Look, just don't do anything rash. Let me work things from my end. And then if it's time for drastic measures, we'll talk."

Kim's reasoned and rational argument had bested his emotional half-cocked plan. It was all true. Life on the run is no life at all, which meant the CIA operative had to find an alternative. She might be a magician, but she wasn't a miracle worker. Even Kim had her limits.

9

Garrett yawned and rubbed weary eyes, nearing the end of his twelve-hour drive home with Trip from the border. They made a pit stop at Perini Ranch Steakhouse in Buffalo Gap, the meal on Garrett of course, then swung through Abilene. Slipping past Sweetwater, home of the world-famous Rattlesnake Roundup, the duo shot through Post, named for C.W. Post, the breakfast cereal manufacturer, who founded the town in 1906 to create his own Utopian society.

From there they'd continued to Lubbock and then north to Amarillo, playing a soundtrack made up of regional music legends like Buddy Holly, Bob Wills, and Waylon Jennings. The stretch of highway that'd taken them from the Rio Grande to the Canadian River ranged from desert to prairie, ramming against the Caprock Escarpment, a two-hundred-mile stretch of caliche mesas running from New Mexico through West Texas to the Oklahoma borderline.

Garrett was glad to have Trip along for the ride, even though his inquiries could get downright intrusive at times, and even worse, bordering on sincere. But his friend had a big heart and tended to ask meaningful questions. It had always been his worst quality.

Trip leaned the passenger seat back, let out an exhausted sigh and closed his eyes. "Thinking maybe that CIA gal got a thing for you, Quanah."

Trip had taken to calling Garrett by a nickname given to him by his childhood best friend. Nobody found Garrett's Native American heritage more interesting than Tony Sanchez, an avid Texas history buff and expert on regional indigenous cultures. *Quanah* was in reference to Quanah Parker, son of Comanche chief Peta Nocona and Cynthia Ann Parker, a settler's daughter, who was kidnapped at an early age but assimilated into the tribe.

Both Sanchez and Trip, who were descendants of a Texas Ranger and a Buffalo Soldier respectively, liked to point out that it was in *their blood* to go after Comanches. It'd been their primary excuse when the ball-breaking got a bit rough on their elk hunting trips in New Mexico.

Garrett pointed out that it was in *his blood* to take the scalps of his enemies while they peacefully slept. Although his friends laughed it off, he noticed that the trash talk suddenly declined, possibly due to the bowie knife that he always kept nearby.

Garrett shot Trip an incredulous glare. "What are you talking about?" It took him a moment to realize that by *a thing*, Trip was referring to something romantic. "Think that bump on the head gave you brain damage."

"You know *exactly* what I'm talking about." Trip cocked an eye open. "Way ya'll were looking at each other. Batting eyes and all that mess."

"I never batted a damn eye a day in my life."

Trip chuckled. "I'm just saying, man. If I was you, I'd—"

"You'd what? Make a move? Go on ahead, Trip. Ya'll were the ones all cozied up on the beach under the stars."

"Cozied up!" Trip shook his head, clearly riled by having the tables turned so quickly. "Almost got me killed by them bushwhacking pygmy assassins. Cozied up? You *must* be crazy."

It was Garrett's turn to chuckle, having gotten the better of his friend. "I'm spoken for with Lacey. You know that. Finally got the girl of my dreams and I'm not screwing it up."

Trip looked as if he was fantasizing, likely at the thought of Lacey. "Yeah, you got the girl of *everybody's* dreams. We'll just see for how long."

Growing up, Lacey Capshaw was the high school crush of every teenage boy in six counties. It had only taken Garrett a couple of decades to get her attention. He didn't mind that Trip was jealous. Who wouldn't be? But the *how long* comment was a shot across the bow.

Garrett looked at his friend askance. "What's that supposed to mean?"

"Means you don't have a history of staying in one place too long. Kind of live like that Kwai Chang Caine dude from *Kung Fu*. Just drifting from place to place your whole damn life."

"Yeah, you're one to talk, rodeo star. Girl in every town." Garrett cut eyes at Trip. "Haven't seen you shopping for wedding rings. Putting down any roots."

"My rodeo days were a long time ago. And I'm not talking about *my* love life, Quanah. My girl and me, we got an understanding. I'm talking about *yours*, son. I'm talking about Lacey."

Garrett couldn't believe how quickly Trip had spun the conversation focus back on him. "Times change and so do people. Got a boy to look after now. Never had that before."

"And a hot lady, to boot?"

Garrett conceded with a smile. "And a hot lady to boot." He turned to Trip, whose eyes were clamped shut again. "You convinced now?"

"Convinced you're committed to that boy. Maybe Lacey too. Still not sure about your CIA boss, though. I don't know much, but I do know *the look*. And she's got it for you."

Garrett shook his head. "So, we're back on her again?"

"Just saying. I know what I know."

"Well, I know what I know too. And know that after what happened down in Mexico, all I want is for things to get back to normal and slow the hell down. That's it."

Trip smiled. "Same here. Ready for a few cold Carta Blancas. Some of Mama's home cooking. And a little *me time* out on Lake Meredith."

Garrett perked up at mention of Mrs. Davis's home cooking. "And I can be expecting an invite . . . when?"

"You've got a standing invitation with my mom. You know that."

Garrett's mouth was already watering. "And she knows what I want, right?"

"The four Cs?" Trip chuckled. "Catfish. Coleslaw. Cornbread and cobbler."

Garrett had to laugh. Even Trip knew it by heart. "Just making sure." He turned to his friend for the next request. "When you want to head out to the lake?"

"Nah, don't believe so, man." Trip took a moment, scowled, then shook off the suggestion like it was the worst idea he'd ever heard. "Thinking maybe that's a one-man job."

Garrett turned back surprised. "You're joking?"

"*Hell nah*, I ain't joking. Last time we went to Ute, you drank all my damn beer." Trip cocked an eye, looking deadly serious. "And my most recent memory of you on a lake ends with me almost getting killed. Nope. Uh-uh. Hard pass, buddy."

Done arguing, Garrett just shook his head and laughed. Letting his friend catch a little much-needed rest, he shut up and watched the road. Unfortunately, his mind drifted to the Asadi situation. While Garrett's visceral reaction to Kim's bad news was heartfelt, he wondered if he was thinking of the boy's well-being and not just his own. If Asadi wanted to be with blood relatives, then he would have to let him leave. But the thought of it alone was almost too hard to bear.

10

Garrett dropped Trip off in Pampa, a gritty little oil field and agriculture town, once the stomping grounds of folk singer legend Woody Guthrie and Dog the Bounty Hunter, who not everyone claimed as a native son. The former residents of note captured the community in both look and spirit. Whether it was the rusted pumpjacks to the south or the windswept ranches and farmland to the north, it was a place with a deep soul and tough-as-leather exterior.

Pampa was put on the map by a businessman named Timothy Dwight Hobart who'd ventured from Vermont to Texas after the late 1800s. He'd at one time managed over a million acres of land in the Texas Panhandle and went on to run the nearby JA Ranch, founded by Scots-Irish businessman John George Adair, his wife Cornelia, and an illustrious cattleman, trailblazer, and Texas Ranger named Charles Goodnight.

Garrett took Hobart Street past the hospital and slowed north of town at a state trooper speed trap before shooting up Perryton highway to the ranch. With the broad plains on either side and the Caprock on the horizon, he finally felt at peace. But it wasn't until he hit the bumpy caliche road to their farmhouse that the world felt right, and he could let his guard down.

His change in disposition was partially due to the summer

sunset—a thousand shades of yellow, orange, and red. And some of it was kindled by the smell of fresh cut alfalfa, lying in concentric circles beneath the half-mile-long center pivot irrigation system. But it was mostly the sight of Asadi driving that John Deere tractor. Whether on the back of a horse or working the soil, the orphan from Afghanistan wore a permanent grin. Farm life suited him, there was no doubt about it.

Garrett was about to turn into the field to say hello when he noticed the white Ford F-150 pickup parked in front of the house. He pulled his black GMC three-quarter-ton Sierra beside the empty fleet vehicle and saw the *Talon Corporation* sign on the door. Beneath it was a bird of prey with outstretched wings and claws, like the iconic emblem on the Pontiac Trans Am. Odds were the truck belonged to the oil company taking over for Mescalero Exploration, the energy firm owned by the wealthy Kaiser family, who'd reigned over the Panhandle for decades.

With the patriarch only recently dead and buried, Garrett assumed all drilling would come to a halt. And that suited him fine since the Kohls owned the land but none of the oil beneath. As J. Paul Getty once said, *the meek shall inherit the earth, but not its mineral rights.*

Curious to find out who was poking around on the place, Garrett put his truck in park and opened the door. Immediately the oven-like August heat smacked him hard. He was moving toward the porch when he saw the Talon employee sauntering around the corner.

Garrett spoke first in a direct tone, "Can I help you with something?"

The guy looked startled by the question. "Oh, hi there! Didn't see you pull up."

Garrett's first impression was this guy wasn't a local. He had slicked-back silver hair and wore a starched white dress shirt and navy sport coat. Too damn stifling for the one-hundred-two-degree heat. He *was* wearing cowboy boots, but the cuffs of his blue jeans were way too short, just above the ankle. No way in hell this guy was from Texas.

The stranger thumbed over his shoulder at the house. "Knocked on the door but nobody answered. Thought you might have been in the barn around back."

Garrett was tempted to rake this guy over the coals for venturing around the property without permission, but he was too tired from the long drive. All he wanted was a hot shower, a cold Shiner Bock, and to prop his feet up on the couch.

Instead, Garrett was fielding a brand-new aggravation. "You the new landman?"

"Don't care for that term." The stranger shook his head in disgust. "Bad connotation."

A "landman" was the guy or gal working for an oil and gas company whose job it was to secure mineral leases, procure easements onto the property, and settle surface issues with the landowner. There were good ones and bad ones, but he'd never thought of it as a dirty word.

Maybe Garrett had enough energy to give this guy a little hell after all. "And what connotation would that be?"

The guy ran his fingers through his hair for no real reason as he stammered through his answer. "Well, you know. Someone out to take advantage of you."

Garrett crossed his arms. "What makes you think someone could take advantage of me?"

"I mean . . . not *you* in particular," the man stammered. "But I'm sure you've heard the stories about the ones out to steal your minerals. Pollute your beautiful land. That kind of thing." He smiled with the finish of his answer, clearly happy with the delivery.

Garrett didn't budge. "I'll have to tell my brother that. Seeing as how he's done a good bit of land work himself."

The man looked confused. "Bridger's the one who sent me out here."

Garrett was about to inquire further when his dad and Asadi pulled up in the white Ford flatbed dually pickup. Both doors flew open at the same time, but it was the boy who broke forth like a race-horse from the gates. He slammed into Garrett, wrapping him in his arms, and didn't let go until getting his fill. Their three weeks apart had felt like an eternity.

Garrett returned the embrace, yanked off Asadi's cowboy hat, and mussed his thick black hair. "Looking pretty good on that John Deere, Outlaw. You're gonna put me out of a job."

Butch ambled up in no particular hurry. "*Gonna?*" Loaded for bear, the old man launched in with a trademark dig on Garrett's work ethic. "Told you the day you brung him here. Kid's half beaver, half plow horse. Outworks you and your brother on the best days you ever had." He cocked an eyebrow. "Which were few and far between, I might add."

Used to his dad's not-so-subtle barbs, Garrett ignored the insult. Of course, shirking hard work had been Bridger's favorite pastime. It was possible Butch was lumping the two siblings into one, as parents tend to do.

Before Garrett could state the obvious fact that they had a visitor, the old man piped up, "See you met Mr. Holloway."

Garrett offered his hand in the obligatory salutation since Texas custom dictated it, even when meeting a sorry son of a bitch like this one. "Garrett Kohl."

"Tom Holloway." Looking a little less nervous, the man shook Garrett's hand and glanced at his truck with the big screaming bird on the side. "Talon Corporation as you can see."

Since it turned out Holloway wasn't a trespasser, Garrett felt a little guilty. "Sorry I was a bit curt. Didn't know you'd been here."

"Oh, I haven't. First time. No, I met your father over in Canadian." Holloway added with a smile and nod, "When we had our meeting."

"*Meeting?*" Garrett turned to his dad. "What meeting? When?"

"Couple days ago." Butch seemed a bit sheepish, which was rare. "At Bridger's office."

Garrett's dad was a less chipper version of Clint Eastwood's character in *Gran Torino*. There was nary an occasion that he didn't go from crank to crazy in the blink of an eye. Garrett was tempted to give him the *why in the hell wasn't I informed* routine when he remembered he'd given strict instructions not to be bothered unless it was an emergency.

Garrett turned back to Holloway. "Guess you better fill me in."

Holloway seemed to relax as he gave his spiel. "Not surprising to you or anyone else, I'm sure that following the untimely death of Preston Kaiser, the fate of Mescalero Exploration has been on everyone's minds. With over half a million acres under lease, the energy company's holdings are quite a prize."

Garrett shook his head and laughed. "We've had a nice little vacation with Mescalero shut down. But all good things must come to an end, I guess. When do you start drilling?"

"Oh, we're not looking to drill, Mr. Kohl. We're looking to dig." When Garrett didn't respond Holloway continued. "Rare earth minerals are the future. Not hydrocarbons."

"Rare earth minerals?" Garrett knew very little about them other than what he'd read in a few articles. They'd made a huge find down around El Paso, and there were discoveries just north in Colorado and Nebraska. But he'd never heard mention of it in the Texas Panhandle. "What makes you think you'll have any luck with that here?"

"Because we know where they are." Holloway flashed a used car salesman's smile. "According to Mescalero's geological records, your property is rife with them."

Garrett didn't know what to think. On the one hand, he hated the idea of another *boom* of any kind. It meant construction, traffic, and lots of outsiders swarming their community. On the other, it meant good paying jobs for those in desperate need. Aside from that, mineral leases came with big money. While material wealth had never particularly been on the forefront of his mind, he had responsibilities now. And a college fund for Asadi was at the top of the list.

Moreover, Kohl Ranch was falling into disrepair and their herd was dwindling. A cash infusion could turn his thirty-year plan for the family business into a three-year plan. It was something to consider. Still though, Garrett had learned over the years that the devil is in the details when dealing with energy companies. And he'd be damned sure to press his attorney brother on every single line of the contract.

Garrett turned back to his dad. "What did Bridger say? Guess he's seen the terms."

Butch looked deflated. "Afraid the terms are the same as they were under the Mescalero lease. Not good. We get some fees for surface damages and new roads but nothing more."

"But this isn't an oil and gas play," Garrett argued. "It's a whole new deal."

"Afraid not," Holloway interjected. "Not according to your lease. When the Kaisers bought the minerals, it included everything subsurface, to include what we're mining for now."

Garrett was primed to argue but didn't doubt Holloway was correct. Garrett's grandfather, among many other farmers and ranchers in the area, had signed the deals back in the drought of the 1950s. Desperate to keep what they had afloat they essentially signed over the rights to everything beneath the surface with no way of knowing what that would mean for generations to come.

In Texas, minerals were the dominant estate, meaning the surface owner has less rights than the ones who owned the resources beneath. Even in court, their objections would fall on deaf ears. They could even be forcibly removed by law enforcement if they tried to stop it.

Butch piped up. "Had a good discussion with Bridger on all this and he tells me we're not without some recourse. Said we'll have a say on how this looks in terms of road construction, and keeping trucks and heavy machinery away from our house and the horses."

Holloway perked up with Butch's mention of this small silver lining. "That's right, Mr. Kohl. You'll have *some* say."

Butch perked up too, but not in a good way. "You come on here digging up my ranch and I'll have a *big* say on what happens."

"Within reason," Holloway clarified. "Some things can't be changed." He scanned the entirety of the ranch and swung his arm across the horizon. "Like where we dig, for example. The minerals are where they are. Nothing can be done about that."

Garrett knew that Talon's lawyers had already thought that through. He'd talk to Bridger, regroup, and see what they could do, if anything, to keep their pristine ranch from being destroyed.

"Now hold on a minute." Butch marched up to Holloway. "You never said this thing was going to be right in my backyard."

"You'll be compensated for any inconvenience, Mr. Kohl."

"It's not a damn *inconvenience*," Butch shot back. "It's the destruction of the land I've devoted my life to protect. Now I couldn't stop Mescalero from drilling it full of holes and running trucks up and down the road all day, but I can stop you from digging a pit to Hell."

It was Holloway's turn to look sheepish. "Well, I was hoping it wouldn't come to this."

"Come to what?" Garrett asked.

"If you'll look at your Mescalero lease, you'll notice a clause that specifically gives our company the right to dig where we want. Take whatever operational steps necessary for extraction. Same reason an oil company is allowed to drill water wells for drilling and hydraulic fracturing. It's necessary for company operations. It's right there in your terms. Plain as day."

"You need water?" Garrett pressed.

Holloway gave a nod. "Big part of the mining operation. But you'll be compensated."

"I don't want to be compensated." Garrett pointed to the center pivot irrigation system in the hayfield by the house. "Water around here is scarce enough. I want a guarantee you won't suck this place dry."

Since Garrett returned home from Afghanistan nine months prior, he had added two more pivots to their original holdings. Between the new land he purchased and the investment in the irrigation system, he had taken on significant debt. Horses and cattle had kept Butch afloat, but for Garrett to return, and to have something to pass on to Asadi, they needed a moneymaking enterprise. Access to good water wasn't just nice to have, it would literally save the ranch.

"Can't promise we won't make a dent on the water table. Hard to predict." Holloway shrugged. "But I can tell you we'll only take what we need and no more."

Garrett couldn't believe it. This company was going to kill his hay operation. "Who's your boss? I gotta talk to someone about this."

"Our headquarters is in Chicago." Holloway reached into his

inside coat pocket and took out a business card. "I'll give you the number if you want to lodge a complaint."

Before Garrett could take it, Butch moved nearer to Holloway. "You never mentioned anything about water before."

Holloway looked as if he'd never really thought about it. "I mean, who really needs that much water out here, Mr. Kohl. You're in the middle of nowhere."

"No son, *you're* in the middle of nowhere." Butch jabbed his finger into Holloway's chest. "This is my home. It may be flyover country to you, but it's the heart of everything in the world that matters to me." He tilted his head at Garrett and Asadi. "And it's their future."

Holloway took a few steps backward and returned the business cards to his pocket. "I'm sorry, sir. But all that's irrelevant in the eyes of the law. You just have to accept that."

Butch advanced toward Holloway. "Like hell I will!"

Moving quick, Garrett caught his dad by the shoulder. "Whoa, whoa, not like this, Daddy. Won't do any good." He could feel Butch trembling with rage. "Got to handle this in a legal way. Bridger will know what to do."

Holloway made a beeline for his truck, opened the door. "I'll send the plans over to your son in Canadian." Before hopping in and closing the door, he added, "I'm really sorry, Mr. Kohl, but you can't stop progress."

Garrett couldn't help but chuckle. Butch had written the book on stopping progress. It was an angry dissertation built upon the actions and philosophies of ill-tempered curmudgeons through time immemorial. If the codger hadn't backed down to blizzards, wildfires, and tornadoes, he damn sure wouldn't kowtow to this landman who wasn't a landman. Whether Tom Holloway knew it or not, Talon had picked a helluva fight by setting foot on the Kohl Ranch.

11

Smitty had never returned home a hero before in his life. On parole for sure. Drunken stumblebum many a time. But never once with his sword held high. And the worst part of it was that he couldn't tell a soul that he had risked it all to save three others. Not only had he signed a plea deal with the feds, but he'd sworn an oath to that feisty little blonde named Kim who'd threatened him with tortures he couldn't even pronounce.

What hurt the most was that he couldn't tell his daughter. His wife probably figured him for a perennial disappointment but his *darlin' girl* still thought he hung the moon. Of course, bringing Garza to justice had bought him his freedom, and that was all that mattered. He just wanted some peace.

Smitty pulled into the run-down trash dump of an RV park on the outskirts of Canadian and read the paint-chipped sign at the entrance to Misty Mobile, which he'd redubbed *Misery Mobile*. His wife, Crystal, was out in front of their orange and white Shasta camper, spraying down their daughter, Savanah, with a garden hose. The fanbelt on his nineties model Chevy pickup had a distinctive shriek that caught their attention.

As usual, his wife's hair was windblown and bushy, the texture of frayed burlap. A fresh dowsing of peroxide left it shammy yellow, with a few odd patches the color of Styrofoam. She was wearing her Daisy Duke getup, a red skintight tank top and denim short shorts. It meant she was either getting off shift at the bar or getting ready to start one.

Upon seeing Smitty pull up behind her gold Pontiac Fiero, Crystal barely registered an expression. His daughter, in gym shorts and one of his old undershirts, was for some reason covered in mud. She lit up like a Christmas tree and made a break for his truck, but her mother yanked her back and kept scrubbing at her mousy ringlets.

Smitty parked on the brown patches of what was considered their lawn, shut off the truck, and stepped outside. "Well, what happened here?"

"Been on the river catching crawdads!" His daughter's reply was more of a boast, probably because she knew he'd be jealous. She slithered past Crystal and darted to Smitty for a wet hug.

With her arms tight around his waist, he reached inside the truck, and pulled out her south of the border souvenir. On the front of the T-shirt was a mustachioed, sombrero-wearing cartoon worm that was coiled into a shot glass. The Don Chucho Tequila slogan beneath it read DON'T BE AFRAID, which Smitty assumed meant don't be afraid to eat the worm. It wasn't appropriate for an eleven-year-old, but for a guy who was afraid of everything it struck a chord.

"Seriously?" Crystal wasn't happy, which was evident by the way she threw her hand on her hip. "Why don't you just get her a pack of Newports while you're at it?"

"I know, I know." Smitty pushed the air. "But hear me out first."

Crystal's face said everything. She wasn't interested in an explanation, but that didn't stop him from giving one. "You see now, it's just that it was the first time I'd ever been overseas, and I wanted her to have something . . . *exotic*."

Crystal still wasn't impressed. "She can't wear it to school, you know."

Smitty conceded with a shrug. "Just thought she could wear it when she's just hanging out with her buds. You know. Down at the arcade or whatever."

"Arcade!" Savanah burst into laughter. "This isn't *Stranger Things*, Dad! Arcades don't even exist anymore."

"They do so! Seen them down in Pampa awhile back."

Even Crystal laughed. "Those places were full of slot machines! And they shut those down a long time ago. Not a good hangout for your daughter and her *buds*."

She did the air quotes. He hated when she did air quotes.

"Well, when I was her age, kids hung out. Went places. Did things. Weren't sitting around on the couch playing Minesweeper all day."

"*Minecraft*, Dad!" Savanah laughed even harder. "Not whatever . . . you just said."

"You know, Ray, if you'd spent more time in school instead of *going places* and *doing things*"—Crystal made air quotes again—"maybe you'd have stayed out of trouble."

Smitty didn't bother to fight her. It was all true.

Possibly recognizing he wasn't in the mood for teasing, Crystal's eyes warmed, and her voice softened. "And speaking of trouble. How *are we* in that department?"

Smitty snatched the beach towel off the ground and handed it to Savanah. "Why don't you dry off inside and grab me a Pearl." He'd been dreaming of a cold beer the whole trip home. "I'll be there in a minute."

Always the dutiful daughter, she did as she was told. It was obvious Crystal wanted to talk. His wife waited until the screen door slammed behind Savanah to begin. "So, what happened? You do everything you were supposed to do?"

For a man who'd spent his entire life lying, sworn silence was a fitting punishment. Now that Smitty wanted to tell the truth, the whole truth, and nothing but the truth, he couldn't. She didn't know about Garrett, Malek, or Trip, and she sure as hell didn't know anything about the CIA. All he could do was confirm that the plan worked, they were safe, and their lives were their own. "Yep. It's done. We're in the clear."

Crystal moved close, took him into her arms, and buried her face in his chest. She sniffed a little and stifled a sob. "Now what?"

Ray drew her into him tight. "Now life goes back to normal. I get a regular job. Make some money and get us out of this dump."

Crystal pulled back and surveyed the dusty grounds of the RV park. As if on cue, a pack of mangy dogs darted from behind a dumpster to beneath an abandoned Airstream. "It ain't so bad, really. Get a nice breeze up here around evening."

"Breeze is God's doing. I want to build something on my own." Smitty turned to find Doris Gunderson, their nosy next-door neighbor at her window, eavesdropping again. "And I want a place with some *privacy*." Stressing the word sent Doris retreating behind the curtains. Smitty looked into Crystal's eyes. "What do you think? Land of our own in the country? Some horses?"

Crystal smiled. "Think if you want all that, I'll need a better job than what I got."

Smitty never liked her working at Crippled Crows anyhow. The bar was full of derelicts from every walk of life. Convict cowboys. Meth-head truckers. Oil-field roughnecks and roustabouts of the trashiest sort. The only thing he still liked about his old stomping grounds was the fact he'd met Crystal there. But they both needed a change.

"Got a buddy doing some dozer work over in Borger says something might be opening up. Reckon I'll head over tomorrow and see if there's anybody looking for a hand."

Like Smitty, the town of Borger had a checkered past. It had once been a wild and wooly Old West kind of oil boomtown in the 1920s, and a hub of organized crime that included bootlegging, gambling, and prostitution. Robbery and murder were so rampant that the governor ordered the Texas Rangers, under the command of legendary Captain Frank Hamer, who later killed Bonnie and Clyde, to move in and bring the town under control.

Crystal's hand flew to her chest. "Oh wait! You haven't even heard. There's a new company in town that's took over Mescalero. Talon Corp. Paying big money. Great benefits."

Smitty hadn't seen Crystal this excited since her nemesis at Crippled Crows got a wicked case of conjunctivitis and had to wear an eye patch. He didn't want to burst her bubble, but he didn't want to get her hopes up either. His criminal record was a hell of an albatross.

"Well, I ain't ever heard of Talon," Smitty confessed, "but that don't mean nothing. There's a million of them companies around."

She shook her head. "Not like this one. To hear folks tell it, they got deep pockets."

"Kaisers got deep pockets too."

"No. I mean *real* deep. Like this company's got big mining projects all over the country. Colorado. Nebraska. Wyoming."

"*Mining?*" Now Smitty's skepticism was on nitrous. Rumors around the Texas Panhandle spread like wildfire. At times he wondered which of the two did more damage. "You had me up to then." He shook off the suggestion. "Nah, I'll just stick to what I know."

Crystal's hand was back on her hip again. "And what's that?"

"Oil and gas."

"Well, I hope you got a time machine then, Ray. Because them oil boom days are long-gone. And they ain't coming back."

"There'll be something out there," he assured, not really knowing if there would be. But when she gave him those eyes, the ones that said *not even for me*, he relented. "Alright, alright, there's bound to be a main office somewhere. I'll talk to them tomorrow."

Crystal took him by the hand and led him inside the camper. There'd be plenty of time to find a job. For now, he just wanted to enjoy having his life back. That, and a cold one.

12

As Garrett stared across his kitchen table at Lacey Capshaw, he couldn't help but think on what he'd nearly lost. Of course, he couldn't tell her what happened on the Garza operation and really had no desire to. His beautiful high school crush with ice blue eyes, thick chestnut hair, and killer curves had pledged her heart to him. And in return, he'd given her his own.

She hadn't just been a girlfriend, she'd been a surrogate mother to Asadi, and had helped them turn their old farmhouse into a beautiful home. But it wasn't just the help she'd provided in picking out paint and new furniture, it was the warmth of her smile, and the melody of her laughter that brought their world to life. Even his dad admitted as much. He said Lacey was the daughter he'd never had. Of course, he actually did have one. They just hadn't spoken in months.

Grace lived down in Midland, but they'd had a big blow-up over something Garrett couldn't recall and each one was waiting for the other to concede defeat. Long bouts of brooding silence were a family tradition, like fireworks on Christmas Eve and soul-crippling insults. Butch was like the Bizarro-world version of Joel Osteen to anybody but Asadi, who he treated like a prince. There'd been a hole in the man's life that hadn't been filled until the kid joined the family.

Lacey got a pass too, even though she was always on Butch to eat healthier due to his high cholesterol. The man was in every way the opposite of a good patient, particularly when it came to dietary restrictions. Butch had once chucked his boot at his television for Rachel Ray having merely suggested you could substitute sour cream with Greek yogurt.

Lacey passed the plate of fried chicken first to Asadi, who was bouncing in his chair. "You really that hungry, young man?" She cut a stern look at Garrett that was meant to be playful. "Need to talk to someone around here about feeding you better."

With eyes like saucers, Asadi snatched a couple of drumsticks from the heaping platter. His nodding was the next level of enthusiastic. "*Tenk you.*"

Butch looked as eager. "If I could move like that without cracking my pelvis, I'd be just as jumpy." He shot her a smile. "Been out bailing hay all day and never took a lunch break."

Lacey sent a helping of mashed potatoes counterclockwise around the table. "Alfalfa looks beautiful." Adding with a pass of the cream gravy, "Smells like heaven too."

"Well, it couldn't have come at a better time. To keep the herd and remuda we got, we're damn sure gonna need every bale. Unless we get some rain soon."

"You're not the only one worried." Lacey restocked her plate. "The drought is all anyone can talk about at the café. Bad out there. Bet you're glad you got those center pivots now."

Garrett had purchased the land adjacent to their property from their longtime neighbor, Kate Shanessy, taking their property from nine thousand to seventeen thousand acres, a little over twenty-six square miles.

Garrett shook his head in disbelief. "Still can't believe Kate sold to us. Never thought she would, you know, with her girls and all. Thought there might be some hard feelings."

"Them girls don't give a rat's ass," Butch guffawed. "But the truth of the matter is Kate would've never sold to anyone but you."

"Don't know about that," Garrett countered.

Butch had a twinkle in his eye that accompanied his teasing. "Always had a crush on you."

"Daddy that's just sick. She's—"

"*Old?*" Butch's face morphed into a scowl. "Well, so am I. But that doesn't mean I can't appreciate something that catches my eye." He winked at Lacey. "And damn sure doesn't mean I don't have an *appetite*." Butch took a big bite of his chicken leg to drive home the point.

Garrett shook his head. "Again, Daddy. Just. Plain. Sick."

If Butch wanted a female companion, there were plenty of local widows nearby, Kate being one of them. There was no need to go scouring the earth. The week before Butch had yelled at some poor customer service rep from a "single ranchers" dating website over the fact that he couldn't download their networking app to his landline. It was proof positive that the old man was too out of touch to be carousing online.

With another pass of the fried chicken, Lacey asked with a timid smile, "So, this it for a while, Garrett? You don't have any more trips planned, do you?"

The quick switch of topic took Garrett off guard. He stumbled a little in answering because he could honestly say he didn't know. Kim Manning lived for the next mission. If he had to guess, she was already in the planning stages.

Garrett gave a shake of the head. "Nah, I'm here for a while." He added with the caveat, "Far as I know." Taking another drumstick, he handed it off the platter to Asadi, who was eagerly awaiting a third helping. "Supposed to head down to Amarillo this week and check in."

Since taking a bullet nine months earlier, Garrett had been on mandatory desk duty at the local DEA office. Given his recent performance, he knew he was fit enough for the field, but some bureaucrat back at headquarters in Virginia still thought otherwise.

"What then?" Lacey asked.

This mother of two understood the kind of work he did was dangerous, but it didn't mean she wasn't planning for the future. And if his future included an early death at the hands of deadly drug runners, she wasn't on board.

"Well, hopefully I'll get an assignment here." Garrett immediately regretted using the word *hopefully*, but it was the God's honest truth. And he didn't want to lie to someone he loved.

Lacey looked disgusted. "Sounds uncertain."

"You gotta understand, Lace, navigating the process at DEA is a bit tricky. Takes time to finesse something like that."

"How much time?" she shot back.

The moment was bordering on awkward, one of those unexpected *defining the relationship* conversations that happened to be playing out in front of his dad and the boy. But Asadi, who was too consumed with his drumstick, didn't even notice. Butch, on the other hand, who got the hint, eased his chair back and grabbed his plate as he stood.

"Just remembered I need to check on something out in the barn." The old man was no stranger to confrontation. He almost lived for it. But inquiries of the romantic sort were tantamount to the Spanish Inquisition. "Come on, Outlaw. Grab your plate. You can eat while we work."

Oblivious to the reasoning behind the sudden exodus, Asadi scooped up his meal, snatching two more drumsticks for the road. It wouldn't be the first meal they'd eaten on the job. Of course, a meal on the tractor or out working cattle usually consisted of saltines, summer sausage, and cheddar cheese, not Lacey's famous fried chicken. But the boy made no fuss, just followed Butch out the door still gnawing on a leg.

Garrett had expected Lacey to object, but when she didn't, he knew it was serious. Before he could ask, her eyes softened and her face fell. She was embarrassed.

"Garrett, I'm sorry. I didn't mean to run everyone off from supper. I feel awful."

Garrett shook his head and laughed. "Don't worry about those two. They're happiest with the horses." He tilted his head toward the barn. "Asadi would sleep out there if we'd let him."

Lacey looked genuinely relieved. "I don't just mean them. I mean you too."

Having just taken a bite of potatoes he waved her off. "Trust me, I'm good."

"Not about dinner. For putting you on the spot. Especially in front of your family."

"Don't sweat it. Nothing gives me more pleasure than to watch Daddy squirm."

Lacey chuckled again. "Can't say I've ever seen him move that quick. But seriously, I don't want to put pressure on you. A lot has happened since you've moved home. And it's all happening fast."

"Lacey, I'm glad it's happening fast. You're my future. I want you to know that."

"I believe that, Garrett. I really do. But you have to understand that my life isn't my own. I have two kids to consider. And their dad lives *here*. If you take some assignment somewhere else, I can't go. I won't leave my children under any circumstances. You know that, right?"

Garrett fully understood her predicament. Because of Asadi his life wasn't his own either. And he still hadn't ruled out making a run for it if they tried to take him away. But he'd made an open-ended deal with Kim that tethered him to the CIA. He couldn't make any promises to Lacey until his obligation was fulfilled.

"I hear what you're saying, and I'd never expect you to leave your kids behind. I'm working on my situation. With everything in me I'm working on it. I promise." Garrett hoped she believed him, but it was clear by the look on her face that his words weren't doing the trick this time. "What is it, Lacey? Something else is going on."

Lacey's hesitation was obvious. There was reluctance in her voice. "Well, it's Travis again."

Travis. Garrett hated that name. Lacey's ex-husband, a successful doctor who lived in Amarillo, had been a constant thorn in his side. In nine months of dating, they'd still never met, but Garrett had heard enough to form a good opinion. Travis Mansfield had cheated on Lacey, multiple times during their marriage, acts of infidelity he'd attributed to a prescription drug addiction coupled with alcohol abuse.

Doctor Travis had cleaned up enough to get joint custody of the kids, but Garrett didn't buy the *victim of the disease* excuse he'd sold to everyone else. In fact, he didn't buy the fact that Travis's sudden epiphany came from his sobriety. It was more a case of a man who once had everything, suddenly concluding that Lacey no longer wanted him. *His* woman had found true happiness with Garrett, and it just killed her ultra-competitive ex-husband to know there was something he couldn't have.

Garrett recognized the poor effort he made in hiding his contempt. "So, what did *Doctor Feelgood* do this time?"

Lacey ignored the jab like she always did. "Well, he made this big plea about how he wants us to do more as a family."

"A family!" Now Garrett's contempt wasn't masked at all. "But you aren't a family. You're divorced. He had his chance, and he blew it. Multiple times. In case you forgot?"

"No. I haven't forgot. And I told him that very clearly and in no uncertain terms. *But* he told me he's reading some book his therapist gave him about coparenting. About how just because you're not a *traditional* family unit, doesn't mean you're not still a family, blah blah blah."

"That sounds like the biggest load of bull—"

"I know, Garrett. I know. But it got me to thinking."

"What's there to think about? It's a load of crap."

Lacey was less contrite now and getting more worked up by the second. "Well, I was thinking about *family*, for one thing. It's not my children's fault that theirs isn't together."

"And it's not yours either," Garrett fired back. "Travis chose to party rather than be there for you and the kids. There are consequences for that and he's paying for it now."

"I know that too. But the kids are caught in the middle. In a place where they get screwed out of a normal childhood."

Normal childhood? No such thing. Garrett's mother died when he was a little older than Asadi. Butch had turned to the bottle in the early years, leaving Garrett, Bridger, and Grace to fend for themselves. But it was in that tragic memory, reliving what he'd gone through, that he started to think things over. Because he'd suffered doesn't mean Lacey's kids should too.

Garrett took a deep breath. "Alright, what does this new kind of family thing entail?"

"Just doing more together. Activities like going bowling. A Sod Poodles baseball game. Going for a hike at Palo Duro Canyon. Stuff like that."

Sounded like a *traditional* family to Garrett, but he didn't say any-thing. "Okay, you're a wonderful mom and I know you've always got your kids' best intentions at heart." He sighed, louder than intended. "If this is what you need to do for them, then we'll get through it."

Lacey smiled, clearly relieved to get that revelation off her chest. "Thank you for being so understanding about this."

Garrett nodded graciously, but all he could think about was clocking Travis in the jaw. It wasn't lost on him that Lacey's ex had a lot to offer. He was worldly, successful, and most importantly, her kids' real father. Garrett knew that living the highlife and luxury no longer really mattered to her, but security and stability did. And that wasn't lost on the guy who'd just returned from battling cartel assassins down in Mexico.

Hoping to change the subject, Garrett was just about to bring her up to speed on the earlier debacle with Talon when she brought it up on her own. "Did you hear the great news? About the new company that just moved into the area?"

"Talon Corporation," Garrett offered up begrudgingly.

Lacey frowned. "You don't look thrilled."

"Trust me." A smile broke across Garrett's face. "Got a few good reasons."

"Well, you're the only one in the Panhandle that's not dancing for joy. They say Talon's going to save us. Hundreds of jobs. *Good* jobs. A whole new world for all of us just trying to eke out a living. For everyone like me who lost their job after Mescalero went under."

Talon should've hired Lacey to deliver the news. Her pitch and enthusiasm nearly had him on board. And it made Garrett think that maybe he was being selfish, that by impeding this project on the ranch he was taking bread from the mouths of others. But he also felt a deep desire to protect the land that he loved.

Being a quarter Comanche on his mother's side, this subject had come up around her family's dinner table over in Lawton, Oklahoma, plenty of times. And he now knew, to a small degree, what it was like to lose your home and way of life in the name of *progress*.

Instead of railing against Talon like he'd planned, he decided to wait and see what she knew. "So, what's the good word on our savior, Talon?"

Lacey looked like she was bursting to tell him the news. "Well, their Texas division will be headquartered in Borger where the Kaisers' Mescalero refinery was located. Even took over their old Carbon Black plant on the west side of town. Talon is supposed to offer competitive pay, full health benefits, and a matching 401K."

Nearby Borger, located north of a hundred-thousand-acre division of the Four Sixes Ranch and on the south side of the Canadian River, had become an energy industry hub, in large part due to Phillips Petroleum. It was also home to several other petrochemical facilities that process oil and natural gas, to include one of the largest of these type of refineries in the world.

Garrett knew he should be formulating a rebuttal to Lacey's news, but he was starting to wonder if he should apply. "Kind of sounds like you're interested."

"Dropped off my résumé three days ago." Lacey's eyebrows raised in anticipation of Garrett's excitement. "They said I'd get an answer within the week."

That's just great. Not only was Garrett about to put the brakes on an opportunity for everyone in ten counties, but he was ruining his girlfriend's hopes and dreams as well. There had to be a middle ground.

With nothing to do about it for the moment, Garrett hoisted his Shiner Bock in a toast. "Well, then here's to you." He nearly choked out the rest, "And Talon Corporation, I guess."

Face beaming at the prospect, Lacey returned the toast. With her satisfied and himself ready to celebrate the victory over the Garza Cartel, Garrett allowed himself a moment not to worry about the ranch. He'd talk to his lawyer brother first thing in the morning. Bridger was a loophole mastermind, particularly when it came to mineral rights. He'd know just what to do.

13

Garrett assumed Bridger had gone over that mineral lease a thousand times, but maybe this was the eureka moment, the one in movies where the attorney suddenly remembers an arcane law school case that saves the day. So far though nothing had emanated other than a bunch of tsk-tsks and disappointed groans.

Nervous with anticipation, Garrett got up from the chair in front of Bridger's desk and wandered around the small law office in downtown Canadian. The place looked more like a museum of the American West than a place you'd tend to any real legal issues, but that hadn't hurt the practice. In an old-school town like Canadian, getting litigious was as uncouth as farting at the supper table or taking the Lord's name in vain. It was the last place locals wanted to be, particularly given his brother's ungodly fees.

Among the photos of the ranch was Bridger's favorite roping horse and a few action shots of him back when he was winning buckles during his rodeo days. To the right was a framed article of a case involving a wildfire he'd litigated a few years back. He'd helped to settle a claim as local counsel against a negligent power company responsible for a blaze that killed several local residents and destroyed nearly five hundred square miles of ranchland.

While the Texas Panhandle maintains an elite team of volunteer firefighters, the sheer size and speed of the inferno made it difficult to contain, particularly with wind gusts topping fifty-five miles per hour and changing directions frequently. The land and its inhabitants eventually bounced back, but it wasn't an easy recovery, particularly given the devastating loss of both human and animal life.

Thinking on how hard it would be to lose loved ones in such a horrible way, Garrett was nearly startled when Bridger spoke up from behind. He turned to find his brother was still staring down at the lease. "What'd you say, Bridge?"

"I said, I'm sorry, but there's nothing we can do." Bridger looked up from the document. "The lease is tight as a drum."

Switching mental gears, Garrett moved back to the desk, sat again, and stared at his brother, hoping his show of indignation would prompt something better than a *nothing we can do*. It wasn't what Garrett wanted to hear, and it pissed him off that Bridger was rolling over and giving up so easy. "What do you mean? We can fight."

"Fight what? The Mescalero lease was terrible back in the fifties and it's terrible now. Left us wide open for something like this."

"For drilling," Garrett argued. "Not mining. Says nothing about that."

"You're right." Bridger gave a nod. "That's why it's brilliant. It gives the lease holder carte blanche to do whatever they want when it comes to *any* minerals underground."

"But surely we have the right to keep them from destroying the property."

"*Mining* the property," Bridger corrected. "Destroying is in the eye of the beholder."

Garrett sat back stunned. "Sounds like you're defending them."

"I'm talking to you like your lawyer, right now, not your brother."

"Then don't." Garrett was almost shouting. "Talk to me like a guy who's about to lose his family home. Like a guy who cares about the land where his mother is buried."

Invoking their mother in a similar argument had caused a rift so deep the brothers didn't talk for three years. Garrett didn't want to go there again, particularly when they were finally back on good terms, so he backed off quick. "Look, I didn't mean to throw that in your face."

"Yeah, you did," Bridger shot back. "And you have every right to. But I just want you going into this thing eyes wide open." He pointed out the window to Main Street. "People here are ecstatic about this, Garrett. You're not just fighting Talon. You're fighting your neighbors. Hell, your own damn girlfriend. The community needs this. *Desperately.*"

Bridger was right and Garrett hated it. He sat quiet before delivering a halfhearted rebuttal, "Well, if folks are so thrilled with it, they can do it on their own property."

"You know that's not how it works." Bridger shook his head. "Look, I've seen Holloway's mineral maps, and Kohl Ranch is smack-dab in the fairway. And just so you know, we're not the only one they're mining on. They've got several other sites here as well."

"Let me guess," Garrett added. "No one else has a problem but us."

"Some are absentee landowners, who could care less." Bridger rubbed the tip of his thumb with his index and middle fingers. "And some want the money. As far as I know, we're the only ones making a stink."

"What about our reps? State and local politicians. Surely somebody's thinking about property rights issues."

"Nope." Bridger waved him off. "They wouldn't even return my phone calls. For them, it's all about the tall green. Voters with money in their pockets are happy voters. Voters who contribute to campaigns. Barking up the wrong tree thinking Austin or Washington's gonna jump on team Kohl. Hell, the county judge has plans for the funds he thinks are coming in. Last time I saw him and the mayor, they looked like kids on Christmas morning. City council is already talking about expanding the courthouse."

Bridger was right. They couldn't blame politicians for wanting to better the lives of many at the expense of a few. Still, though, keeping the High Plains from being pilfered and polluted had to count for something. Garrett decided to throw his Hail Mary. "Well, these strip mines aren't exactly without environmental impact, you know. I've been doing some research."

"You and me both. But for every concern you raise, Talon's got an answer." Bridger chuckled. "This Holloway's a helluva sharp landman."

"Humph." Garrett crossed his arms. "Claims he's *not* a landman."

"Well, whatever he is, he knows his business. And this ain't his first rodeo. Came at me well prepared, that's for sure. He's got a whole team of lawyers up in Chicago backing him up."

"Maybe we get our own team? You know legal experts in this area, right?"

Bridger leaned back into his chair and smiled. "Bucky, Talon is coming to the ranch and they're coming soon. And they've got every legal right to be there. Any lawyer who's being honest about it will tell you the exact same thing."

Conceding this Talon project might be inevitable, Garrett turned to the best alternative. "What about payment for surface damages?"

"We'll be paid at market rate." Bridger picked up the contract, flipped a couple of pages and focused in on a section. "Water too. And they'll be needing plenty of it."

"Yeah." Garrett gave a defeated nod. "That's what Holloway said."

Destruction of the property was one thing, but the thought of a major drawdown on the water table had kept him up all night, tossing and turning. Operationally, it'd be devastating. Financially, it'd ruin him. If it actually came to that scenario, Garrett's whole plan to return home for good and make the ranch a viable moneymaking enterprise had just bit the dust.

PART TWO

Who led thee through that great and
terrible wilderness, wherein were fiery
serpents, and scorpions, and drought,
where there was no water . . .

–Deuteronomy 8:15

14

Asadi had come to look forward to the morning horseback rides more than anything in the world. When he and Butch first began them, months before, they were an intense affair, lesson after lesson of basic instruction, most of which he couldn't understand. But over time both his command over the English language and sureness as a rider had improved by leaps and bounds.

Whether with Garrett or Butch, it was a time to bond. Sure, it was work. They were training young colts that they would eventually sell. But it was so much more. It was the thousand colors of a sunrise, the wafting aroma of juniper, and the sight of pronghorn antelope bounding across the plains. Except for the occasional jet streaking across the sky, the place was a time machine to a magical land where adventure abounds, and the Wild West was as wild as ever.

Kohl Ranch could never replace the home where he was born, but mostly because of his family. Asadi missed them every day and always would. But in the quiet of early morning, with only the steady cadence of hoofbeats, he heard his mother's heaven-sent voice on the breeze and in the rustle of swaying grass. Her whisper was clear as the sky. *I'm okay, son. And you will be too.*

Butch stood in the stirrups and turned to Asadi. "What in the world is that?"

Asadi raised up too but got little better vantage. "What you see?"

Butch didn't answer immediately, still staring. His answer came out more like a question. "Damned if I know."

Asadi climbed atop the saddle, moving to the seat's cantle to get as high as possible. He finally saw what had gotten Butch's attention, about a hundred yards ahead, a line of more than a dozen semitrucks hauling heavy machinery and equipment on their backs. A few even pulled houses behind them.

Blocking their path was their neighbor, Kate Shanessy, her giant diesel pickup parked crossways on the road. Standing before the convoy stood the little redheaded woman, one hand on her hip the other raised in a halting motion like a crossing guard.

"Uh-oh." Butch turned to Asadi, looking a bit nervous. "We better get over there before this turns ugly." He gave a palatal click and Skip rumbled into a trot.

Asadi had just nodded in agreement when Grizz lurched without warning. Not yet in the stirrups, he nearly tumbled off backward, which would not have been the first time. In seconds, Asadi caught Butch's buckskin and pulled up alongside them. They rode at a quick clip, trading the earlier soft clop of lazy hooves for the three-beat pattern of urgency.

Butch eased back in the saddle to bring Skip into a lope. Asadi followed suit when he saw exactly why. On the other side of the halted convoy was the sheriff's white four-by-four pickup with flashing red and blue lights on top. A deputy's SUV was parked wonky in the bar ditch to the right. Both drivers took cover behind their doors, guns drawn and aimed at Kate.

Butch thrust his weight into the stirrups to bring Skip to a halt. He put his palms up before addressing the armed men, "Whoa, whoa, what's going on here, boys?"

It was Kate who piped up first. "Told this sumbitch the other day I didn't want no damn giant crater on the place."

Asadi recognized the one sitting in the passenger seat. He was the same silver-haired man who was at the house the day before. He yelled something out of the window as he opened the door and stepped outside. Behind him in the backseat was a pretty blond woman—dressed much too fancy for a hot dusty ranch. The man raised his hands and eased to the front.

Butch cupped his hand and put it beside his mouth. "That you, Holloway?"

Holloway turned to Butch wearing a look of anguish. "Mr. Kohl, can you *please* try and talk some sense into her?"

Kate stepped toward the front of the SUV and whapped the hood with her right palm. "Screw you! We're past that now!"

"You don't even own the property anymore, Mrs. Shanessy." Holloway seemed to have grown some courage with Butch's arrival. "The Kohls do."

"Yeah, but I own this house and the porch that wraps round it. And I intend to kick my feet up here until I die."

The sheriff spoke up. "Kate, nobody's saying you cain't do that."

She turned her ire on him. "Put up an oil derrick, I don't care. They come and go in a month. But I've seen on *the Google* some of them big ugly holes this company's done dug. Dump a bunch of chemicals and pollute the aquifer!"

"Not us," Holloway countered. "Those were other companies, I can assure you. Talon has an outstanding record on environmental safety. There won't be any issues with your water."

Butch directed his gaze at the fat sheriff in the wide-brimmed cowboy hat. "What's with the guns, Sheriff? That really necessary for dealing with an old lady?"

Kate turned to Butch looking sour. "Who you calling *old*? You're as senile a coot as there is in the county!"

"*Dammit*, Kate! I'm as pissed about all this as you are, but I'm trying to help."

"Don't need no help from a man who'd insult me like that."

"I wasn't trying to—" Butch stammered as he worked to calm down. "Listen, all I'm trying to do is tell Sheriff Crowley and Mr. Holloway, there ain't no need for guns."

Crowley spoke up, his pistol still trained on Kate. "Tell *her* that, Butch. She's the one making threats. Said she'd shoot us if we drove another inch on the property."

"Well, she's not serious, Sheriff. You and I both know—"

"The hell I ain't!" Kate turned, revealing what looked like an Old West six shooter on her left hip. "Meant every damn word of it."

Butch shook his head and turned back looking hopeless. Of course, Asadi didn't know what to do either. Kate had been as kind to him as a grandmother. He didn't like to see her so upset and certainly didn't want to see her get hurt.

Butch looked to Crowley. "Sheriff, if Kate meant business, she'd have sniped you with her .270 before you crossed the cattleguard a quarter of a mile back. If she can take down pronghorn on the run at three hundred yards, your fat ass wouldn't stand a chance."

Crowley bristled and turned his glare on Butch. "Is that right?"

Asadi didn't know the full story, only that the Kohls hated Crowley. It all had something to do with him being a crook and ties to the ruthless Kaiser family. The sheriff was *slippery*, Garrett had said. *But his day was coming.*

"If Kate really wanted to shoot you," Butch stated flatly, "you'd be shot."

Crowley turned his glare to Kate, his gun still leveled at her. "Talk her down, Butch."

Just as Kate looked to be softening, a seething truck driver, who had been leaning against his rig, broke into a sprint. She had just turned to him when he slammed into her, knocking Kate off the road and tumbling in a dust cloud into the bar ditch.

Butch spurred Skip toward the driver and Kate. As she tried to rise, her attacker lunged again, but the old man had already wedged his horse between the two of them. As he fought off the driver, Crowley rushed in to grab Kate's pistol and knocked her back into the ditch by accident. She struggled to her feet, with the help of a deputy, after stumbling on the first attempt.

Kate's voice cracked, as she faltered on wobbly legs. "Get your hands off me, dammit!" She was teary-eyed and red-faced, partially due to the intense heat, and partially from what Asadi assumed was embarrassment. Covered in dust and dried grass, she tried to pat herself clean, but it did more harm than good, spreading the dirt all over her tattered old blue jeans.

The truck driver, still enraged, charged again, but Butch and his buckskin were an impenetrable wall. Wherever Kate's attacker went, so did Skip. The cutting horse did exactly what it was trained to do. But instead of preventing a calf from getting back to the herd it stopped this foaming-at-the-mouth thug from attacking a woman half his size.

This went on a few seconds then Asadi saw Butch smile. The old man lined up his horse with the giant, gave a squeeze of the knees, and Skip lurched forward. The driver's eyes widened the moment he knew what was about to happen. It was a look of both fear and remorse.

Butch and his buckskin had just bulldozed the driver and sent him tumbling into the ditch when Crowley moved in and aimed his pistol at Butch. "That's enough! Stop right there!"

Butch did as commanded and brought Skip to a halt. The only

thing that didn't change was his smile. "If you're so big on keeping people safe, Sheriff, then do your damn job. Then maybe I won't have to do it for you."

"That's exactly what I'm doing." The sheriff kept steady aim. "Now get on down from there. Real slow."

Butch raised his hands but didn't drop his grin. "Making a big mistake."

"You're the one made the mistake by interfering."

Butch scoffed as he looked at the truck driver, sitting dumbfounded in the weeds by the side of the road. "Seems to me you needed some *interfering.*"

As soon as Butch dismounted, Crowley slipped on the shackles. The awful sight made Asadi's heart race. "What I do now, Butch?"

The warmth in Butch's eyes covered Asadi like a blanket. "Don't worry one bit. We'll be fine. Just lead Skip back to the barn, get him and Grizz watered and fed, then go to the house and call Garrett. He's in town with Bridger. Anything this *stupid*"—he eyed Crowley— "will be taken care of in about two seconds." Butch turned back to Asadi. "You good with that, sonny?"

Asadi could only nod his response, feeling as though he might cry if he tried to speak. He stayed until Butch was driven away in the SUV, then watched as the trucks rumbled by. They left grit in his mouth and eyes burning as he fought back tears that dried in their dusty wake.

15

Garrett sat across the table from Butch and Kate at The Bucket restaurant in Canadian after bailing them out of jail. With Bridger there to explain the seriousness of their legal situation, Garrett hoped the duo might come to their senses and be ready to repent. But neither possessed a lick of remorse. They'd even demanded breakfast before heading back to the ranch.

When Kate excused herself to go to the restroom, Butch let his bravado slip. "Asadi okay? He didn't seem scared or nothing, did he?"

Garrett was tempted to lay into the old man but held back. "He's fine, Daddy. Sent Lacey out to look after him. But he *was* scared. That's for sure. Where he's from, folks picked up by the authorities were sometimes never heard from again."

Feeling the heat on his neck at the thought of what must've gone through the poor boy's mind, Garrett worked to cool his temper. "But Asadi's a tough kid. Did exactly what you told him. Took care of the horses before calling to let me know you'd been locked up. Still don't understand that part."

"*Responsibility.*" There was unmistakable pride in Butch's voice. "That's why he took care of the horses first. Taught him, you finish the job no matter what." With a nod he added, "Good life lesson."

"Good life lesson," Bridger scoffed. "How about not getting thrown in jail? How's that for a life lesson to teach a kid?"

Butch slammed his fist on the table. "I told you! I was doing a good deed. They were manhandling Kate!"

Garrett looked around at the other patrons, who either didn't notice or had become accustomed to Butch's trademark outbursts. "What the hell were they supposed to do?" He leaned forward and lowered his voice. "She had a gun and was threatening to use it."

Butch batted off the notion. "Oh, she's just talk."

"*No*, she's not," Bridger argued. "Kate shot at a damn airplane that was flying over her barn just because she said it stirred up her horses."

"Yeah, well, it was a cartel plane dropping off drugs. Turns out, she was right to do it."

"But *she* didn't know that." Bridger was turning red with exasperation. "You said it yourself, she just thought it was an oil company."

"Even better," Butch retorted with scorn.

Garrett had to keep himself from laughing. It was nice to see Bridger taking up an argument that usually fell on *his* shoulders. But his brother had a serious point. He loved Kate and hated to think she was losing it. But she was getting quick to the trigger. A little too quick. And this time it had come back to bite her.

Garrett was about to back up Bridger, not that he needed it, when Kate returned and sat. She scooped the napkin off the table and dropped it in her lap.

"Every time I get back, I always wish my food was sitting there waiting for me." Kate added with an assured nod, "You know? Like on *Pulp Fiction*."

Garrett felt Bridger's elbow beneath the table and knew exactly what his brother was thinking. How could a frontier woman like Kate, who'd never even owned a television, come up with that one? He'd dig on it later since there were bigger fish to fry.

Garrett fumbled for a response, still sidetracked by the Tarantino movie reference. "Yeah, well the judge is treating this a lot more seriously than you are. Says Talon can press charges."

"I'm taking it serious," Kate shot back. "Fighting these bastards the only way I know how. With a gun."

Bridger interjected. "Yeah, I'm glad you brought that up, Annie Oakley. Any fighting you do from here on out needs to be of the *legal* kind. Talon will let this go if you promise to behave." He turned to Butch. "Same goes for you. But they did get a temporary restraining order."

Butch looked more worried than Kate. "What does that mean?"

Bridger continued. "A TRO means you're not allowed on the property for a while."

Butch pounded the table again. This time it got the attention of the other patrons. "My own damn ranch?" He immediately settled himself down, not because he cared about who might hear but because their food arrived. As soon as the waitress left, he continued, albeit slightly more docile with hash brown in hand. "Ain't no piece of paper gonna keep me off my own property."

"You bet your ass, it will," Bridger answered, a mouth full of pancakes. "But not forever. This one lasts two weeks. But my guess is if you lay low, the judge will reconsider. You'll have to stay out at my place until then."

"What about me?" Kate hadn't touched her eggs, just poked at them with a fork. "What am I supposed to do?"

When Bridger didn't reply, Garrett spoke up, not really knowing what to say. "Same goes for you, Kate. Might have to bunk with one of your daughters until this thing blows over. Isn't Beth Anne over in Sunray?"

"Yeah, but she won't have nothing to do with me these days. Neither of my girls will."

"Why not?" Bridger asked.

"On account of me selling my land to your family."

Ah hell. Really? Garrett hadn't done anything wrong, but damned if he hadn't made a good case for her selling the land. And as his dad had said, she wouldn't have sold it to anyone but him. Hoping to assuage his guilt, he offered up a solution. "What do you say, Bridge, ya'll got room for one more?"

Garrett felt the elbow in the ribs again, this time it wasn't playful. His brother's awkward silence was followed by a response so fake it wouldn't have fooled anyone in the world but Kate.

"Well, of course, we do." He jabbed Garrett's ribs twice more, with a force that might have inflicted internal bleeding. "Cassidy and the twins are down in Corpus Christi for cheerleading camp this week, so we'll be roughing it. Living off venison sausage, borracho beans, and Lone Star beer. Think you can handle it?"

Garrett scooted his chair out of Bridger's elbow range. His dad looked less thrilled than Bridger at the thought of his new bunkmate. But the old man had made his bed by running over that truck driver with a Quarter Horse. Actions have consequences and Butch was reaping the reward of his *good deed*.

Bridger turned the topic back to the case. "In the meantime, I'm working on the legal side of things to see what can be done. Or at least, see what we can do to make sure this thing is a little less painful. Maybe get Talon's mine moved to somewhere out of the way."

The news brought Garrett a little hope. "But I thought you said you've seen the maps and we're right in the middle of what they want."

Bridger nodded as he finished up a bite. "Yeah, not surprisingly, Holloway keeps Talon's research close to the chest. We won't get access to that. But I've got a geologist buddy down in Amarillo working on it now."

Garrett was hoping maybe Talon would get out there, dig around, and come up empty. That happened all the time in the oil business. Geologists get excited looking at seismic data, until they drill a dry hole. Of course, rare earth minerals were different. Sounded like there was a lot more certainty in their research.

Bridger continued. "Obviously, this isn't my geologist's specialty. He was skeptical of a big find around here, but said it wasn't impossible either. Gave me a science lesson on ash deposits across the plains following some volcanic eruptions in the Rockies over two million years ago. Kind of like oil and gas, you don't know if it's really there until you start drilling. And given the demand for rare earth minerals, the whole world is starting to look."

Not the answer Garrett wanted. "So, he thinks it's legit?"

"Common sense," Bridger said with a nod. "Talon Corporation is here to make money. They wouldn't be out here spending a fortune without a damn good reason."

It occurred to Garrett that just like Kate, he hadn't eaten a bite of his own breakfast. Having a greater craving for answers, he pushed back from the table and rose. He wasn't a geologist, but that didn't mean he couldn't do some digging of his own. And there was no better place for it than at the dive bar to end all dive bars. If his buddy Ike Hodges didn't have answers, nobody did. It was time for a trip out to Crippled Crows.

16

Garrett was surprised to find Crippled Crows vacant of patrons when he walked inside, especially given the fact that there were at least a dozen pickups scattered about the parking lot. Standing in the middle of the concrete dance floor, he turned in a full circle, baffled by the quiet solitude of the normally raucous honky-tonk. The dilapidated dive, constructed mostly of cedar fence posts, corrugated tin, and particleboard, was bathed in an eerie blue tint from the fluorescents above the pool tables and neon beer signs on the walls.

Wondering if *he'd* missed the rapture when Ike's cronies had somehow made the Good Lord's cut, Garrett had to laugh. His mother always said you'd find Jesus in some strange places, but she'd never been here. At least, he sure as hell hoped not. About to leave, Garrett turned suddenly at the sound of boisterous laughter coming from the back.

Instead of retreating, Garrett marched across the dance floor to a party room and knocked on the door. When nobody answered, he said a quick prayer for safe passage, twisted the knob and barged on in. It was hard to tell which odor hit the nose harder, the plume of cigarette smoke or punch of rotgut whiskey. Either way, it was a full-scale assault.

If Ike cared about Garrett interrupting his poker game, he sure didn't show it. His face lit up as he waved him in. "Get our boy a drink, Crystal!"

Ike looked unusually haggard, even for a man who wrecked his health at an Olympic level with Wild Turkey, unfiltered Camels, and a never-ending rotation of trailer park hussies. To Garrett, Ike always looked a bit like a coyote, even in the way he ambled with a sort of sideways gait. The rangy barman, who usually kept a week's worth of stubble around his gunfighter handlebar mustache, had worked it up to a full beard. His salt-and-pepper locks, usually short shorn, had grown over his collar.

As he strode over to welcome Garrett, the wild-haired blonde in cutoffs and a red tank top moved with a sexy slink to Ike's makeshift bar, an overturned fifty-gallon drum covered with liquor bottles. Crystal didn't take his order, just dispensed into his glass a brown liquid that didn't look fit for disinfecting a flesh wound, let alone human consumption.

Ike chuckled. "I'd have offered you a barley soda or the good stuff, but these boys drank us out of house and home a couple of hours ago."

The barman always kept a sixpack of Shiner Bock beer and a bottle of Still Austin bourbon around just for Garrett. But apparently, they'd broken into his hidden stash of reserves.

Garrett didn't fuss, just gave the obligatory nod. "This'll do the trick. And do it quicker, I reckon. Hit me."

Crystal brought the glass over, sloshing it onto the concrete. After handing it over, she stared him down like he was a perp in a lineup. "Hey. I know you."

Garrett shook his head. "Nah, I don't think so." He wasn't actually sure, but Crystal didn't look like the kind of gal you wanted to hear those words from. *Ever.*

Her face scrunched as she studied him. "Yeah, you're one of them Kohl boys, ain't you?"

Yep. She knew him. But it wasn't until the busty barmaid threw her hand on her hip that it all came flooding back to him. *Nurse Knockers.* At least that was the nickname Bridger had given her when she'd waited on them several months prior. How could he forget? Crystal was exactly how Dolly Parton would've turned out had she stayed in Pigeon Forge and joined the carnival.

Before Garrett could acknowledge his error, she gave him a good scorching. "Yep. You're the one tore this place up and left a big old mess that *I* had to clean up. Didn't even leave a tip."

Garrett thought back on the incident where Bridger had broken a beer bottle over a guy's head and slammed his face onto the table. It was well-deserved for sure. And bloody for certain. But Garrett knew he'd left a tip. Of course, his dad had always told him never argue with a woman scorned, in any way, shape, or form.

Taking Butch's counsel, for probably the first time ever, Garrett yanked a crumpled twenty-dollar bill from his front pocket and handed it over. "For your troubles with interest, ma'am." He smiled wide, considering the matter resolved. But apparently, it wasn't.

Crystal took the money with a scowl, then walked away without a word of thanks. Garrett considered himself lucky that was all she did or didn't do.

Having watched the scene play out, Ike just laughed. "Can I deal you in?"

Garrett shook his friend's hand and surveyed the players around the table. It was a ragtag assortment of cowboys, truckers, and a gang of outlaw bikers, none of whom you'd ever willingly join in a game of poker. All Ike needed was Clint Eastwood leaning against the bar and he'd have created his own modern version of *Hang 'Em High.*

"Better take a raincheck." Garrett snuck a peek at the crowd around the room who were waiting their turn. The ones at the table went back to their game but those against the wall didn't look thrilled to see an interloper. "Looks like you've got a few antsy to double their paychecks."

Ike looked around. "They'll wait if I say wait."

"No doubt they would, Ike." Garrett checked his watch. It was just after noon. "A bit early to get a game going, isn't it?"

"*Early?*" Ike looked thrown for loop. "We've been going since two o'clock this morning. And it's just now getting good."

That explained the dour faces and bloodshot eyes. And maybe it had something to do with the burr under Crystal's saddle. Of course, she'd probably never be a debutante. Garrett suspected that had her boss been absent, she'd have introduced her knee to his crotch.

"Well, I hate to interrupt, but I had a few questions if you got a minute?"

"Got more time than that for a friend." Ike turned to Crystal. "Keep an eye on things."

She gave a nod, took a slow lap around the table, and the rowdy players got noticeably quieter. Had she a billy club to whack on her palm, Crystal could've been a Depression-era railroad cop trolling the tracks for a hobo to beat.

"Let's step outside." Ike led Garrett back into the bar and to a nearby table. "I was wondering when you'd show."

Garrett dragged out the metal chair that screeched across the concrete floor. He took a seat, marveling how fast Ike got intel. He referred to Crippled Crows as the Redneck JIOC, a Joint Intelligence Operations Center, where Texas High Plains gossip was procured, analyzed, and distributed to friends at his own discretion.

Garrett hoped like hell Ike had something of value. "Guess you heard the good news about what's going on out at the ranch."

"If it was *good* news, I doubt I'd have heard it. Bad news travels like greased lightning." Ike chuckled. "Human nature, I guess."

"What do you know, so far?"

"About Talon digging a big crater in your backyard or your daddy using one of their drivers as a doormat for his horse?"

"Both, I guess."

Ike lowered his voice, which was rare, even when dishing out the juiciest intel. "What I know about all that won't be as much use to you as some of the other stuff I've heard. Like what's going on behind the scenes that lead up to all this."

Leave it to Ike to stoke the embers of suspense like a Wild West Alfred Hitchcock. Garrett looked around and leaned in. "This about who's behind the Talon deal?"

Ike gave a single nod. "There's a reason you hadn't heard anything about this until now. And the reason isn't all that surprising. Politicians view money and votes as one and the same. From the county courthouse to the White House, this Talon Corporation deal is a no-brainer."

"Must be something wrong with my brain because I don't see it."

"You would if it wasn't your place being destroyed."

Garrett shrugged. "If you say so."

"Well, it's *all* for the greater good, you see." Ike chuckled. "Gotta think like one of them swamp rats in Washington."

The word *progress* had been thrown in Garrett's face earlier and now it was *greater good*. He couldn't help but think back again to his Comanche ancestors, booted off their land for the sake of achieving both. He thought about digging more into the politicians behind it but what was the point. As Ike said, it was a no-brainer on their end.

Upset a few for the sake of many. But what got his curiosity up was Ike's comment about *the other stuff.*

"Okay, Ike, that all tracks with what Bridger told me on how this happened so fast and why it was kept quiet until now. Legislators knew there'd be a stink. What else do you know?"

"Well, I've seen that symbol on the side of those Talon trucks before."

"The firebird?" Garrett asked.

"Yep. Saw it in Africa a few years ago when I was flying contract for an oil company. Well, a security detail for an oil company."

In places like Africa, Asia, the Middle East, and parts of Latin America, some *security details* were in fact just Private Military Companies. Garrett had been recruited by a few friends from the special operations community right before he got out of the Army. The paycheck was outstanding, but sometimes the work was sketchy, depending on the outfit. No money was worth some of the things you might have to do to earn it.

Ike, on the other hand, had a more tolerant conscience. He'd been highly recruited into the contracting world, even more so than Garrett. As a former pilot with the Night Stalkers, technically, the Army's 160th Special Operation Air Regiment, Ike was in high demand. He'd flown the AH-6 Little Bird helicopter and had combat experience when nobody else did before 9/11, notably the Battle of Mogadishu, more commonly known as Black Hawk Down.

Ike continued. "Saw that same firebird design. First in Nigeria. Then in Angola. First encounter wasn't a problem. Second time we had a whole lot of trouble."

"With Talon?"

"Not them," Ike clarified. "Whoever the advance security team was that paved their way."

"Who were they?"

"No idea. Always in the shadows." Ike's eyebrows raised. "That's why they're so good."

"Good at what?"

"Going toe to toe with some high-speed, heavily-armed American operators out in the jungle. And making sure they were never seen or heard from again."

17

As Smitty's rust bucket Chevy rattled down the caliche road, he couldn't help but think that working for Talon Corporation out on the Kohl Ranch was a bad idea. He'd figured himself rid of Garrett after Mexico and was content not to see him for a while. Making a fresh start was about cleaving off the past, and that meant everything that was tethering him to it.

Driving a bulldozer, of course, was a step in the right direction. Sure, it was a return to his old line of work, but there was nothing wrong with that. He just had to stay clean, mind his business, and work his damn ass off. Smitty could do that no problem.

With the ring of his cell phone, Smitty answered Crystal's call. She was no doubt wanting to wish him luck on his first day. He tapped the speaker button, to keep both hands on the wheel. Before Smitty could say hello, Crystal barked out, "You late?"

He shook his head, even though she couldn't see him. "Nope. Right on time."

A pause on the other end. "Got all your gear?"

Smitty knew he did but riffled through the items beside him for good show. "Yep. FR coveralls, hardhat, safety glasses, and steel toes on my feet. Got it all, babe."

Another pause on Crystal's end. "Get your supper?"

"Sitting right by me." Smitty crumpled the paper sack so she could hear it.

It wasn't much of a meal, truth be told, just deviled ham on a hotdog bun, and what crumbs were left over from a bag of stale FUNYUNS. But at least she tried. She'd done it all when she got home from Crippled Crows after being out all night. The gesture, for Crystal, was as close as it got to saying *I love you*.

"Okay then. Guess I'll let you go." It seemed as if she wanted to say something but held back. "Got a double shift tonight, so I'll see you in the morning."

Smitty was working up the courage to tell her something sweet when she ended the call. Part of him was disappointed, but realistically, she'd have only spat out a gruff response—maybe even an insult. He confessed it to the universe instead, "Love ya', Crystal."

No sooner had he said the words than he came upon the massive Talon compound flanked by a half-dozen trailer houses acting as offices. With its army of workers buzzing around and massive Caterpillar D10 bulldozers pushing dirt, it was clear the company meant business. Smitty couldn't help but smile. He needed work and they had plenty of it.

He pulled into a parking spot in front of the mobile office marked with a sign out front that read TALON CORPORATION MAIN OFFICE— ALL VISITORS SIGN IN HERE. Then he turned off the truck and went inside. Normally the first thing to hit you when walking into one of the trailers on a drill site is the stench of a place that should've been junked fifty jobs ago. It's a pungent combo, usually emanating from an endless row of sweaty work boots and a cauldron of coagulated Tuna Helper on the stove. But not this place. This one was Brand. Spanking. New.

There were guys who looked just like him sitting in folding metal chairs along the wall. They had the look of newbies, fresh to the job and anxious to get started before someone at the company changed their mind. A big ol' dude in a black Talon Corporation polo shirt with the badass firebird logo looked up from his computer. "You Ray Smitty?"

The guy had a weird accent. Foreign. Of course, that wasn't unusual in the energy business, particularly on seismic jobs. Over the years, Smitty had worked with at least one person from every hemisphere.

Smitty nodded, wondering how in the hell he knew it was him. "That's me."

"You're late," the guy growled. He picked up a clipboard with a stack of paperwork fastened on and handed it over. "Go sit with the others. This is your crew."

Smitty learned a couple of things in the exchange, the men beside him were his new best friends and *on time* meant *late*. *Must be Germans*. From here on out, he'd be the first to arrive. Smitty had just sat in one of the metal chairs when he realized they'd supplied no writing utensils. Looking up, he saw the foreigner was no longer at his desk. He called out *sir*, seemingly to no one around, then looked to his coworkers who didn't offer their own. They were already pissed off that he was *late*.

So as not to hold up the process any further, Smitty rose in search of a pen. Making his way down a narrow hallway to the door at the rear of the office, he broke the threshold to a throng of shouts. Before he knew what the fuss was about, a beefy hand clenched his throat and pinned him to the wall.

The giant doing the slamming asked in a voice as foreign as the one he'd just heard up front at the desk, "What you doing here?"

Smitty eked out the word *pen* through constricted vocal cords and raised the clipboard for proof. The brute let go and pointed with the same hand to the door. A sign Smitty had clearly not been able to see with it swung open posted a warning: NO UNAUTHORIZED PERSONNEL.

Around the giant, three men gathered stacks of papers, shoved them into a cabinet, and banged it shut. With the catch of a pen, tossed by the silver-haired man who'd hired him, Smitty turned on a heel and sped to his seat, hoping like hell Talon wouldn't hold it against him.

18

Garrett knew that he should've canceled his lunch date with Lacey given everything that was on his mind, but she'd just met with Doctor Travis for the court-ordered kid exchange and would need some cheering up. Losing her children to their dad, even for a weekend, always left her down in the dumps. What took her mind off things was meeting at the Coney Island Café, a little hole in the wall in Pampa that had changed little since it opened in 1933.

Given their uncomfortable relationship conversation the night before, Garrett didn't want to add fuel to the fire by calling off their date. And quite honestly, he didn't want to miss it either. Coney Island was *their* special place and a ritual he'd come to enjoy. The problem was that he couldn't shake his worries over the ranch, and what he was going to do to save it.

Ike's revelation about the Talon mercenaries didn't intimidate him, but he rested no easier either. And Garrett wondered if the company's ruthless tactics may be carrying over into the legal realm, which might be worse. He could hold his own in a toe-to-toe brawl with gun wielding thugs, but lawyers with politicians in their back pocket were an unstoppable force.

Lacey leaned over and put her hand in front of Garrett's eyes.

"You in there somewhere?" She smiled when she said it, but he could tell she was a little annoyed.

Garrett cleared his throat, trying to buy a little time to recall what she was saying. "Turks and Caicos, right? Travis wants to take the kids on vacation before school starts."

Lacey looked puzzled. "Yeah . . . but that's not the issue."

"Then what is?"

Lacey's hands flew from her sides. "The fact that he wants *me* to go with them."

How the hell had he missed that part? Garrett fought to keep calm. "What on *earth* for?"

"Same reason I told you. Travis says we're still a family, even if we're not married."

"This isn't hiking over at Palo Duro Canyon, Lacey, this is staying together overnight."

Lacey pushed what was left of her pecan pie to the side, having only taken a couple of bites. She'd clearly lost her appetite. "Obviously, we wouldn't stay together. He's offered to pay for a separate room."

Garrett could feel himself losing the fight to keep control. "That's even worse."

"How's that worse?"

Garrett would never admit it, but the thought of Doctor Travis paying for a lavish vacation for Lacey bothered him almost as much as the thought of her in his bed. He chose not to answer that question lest it reveal his jealousy. "Well. Are you going?"

Lacey looked hurt by the question. Her voice softened. "Absolutely not. I told him, no."

Of course, she did. Lacey was as solid as oak. Loyal as hell. Garrett felt guilty for asking.

Before he could apologize, she asked, "What's going on with you? With us?"

Those were two separate issues entirely. But both needed to be addressed. Badly.

"Look, I'm sorry, Lacey. It's just with everything going on with the ranch and the Asadi situation, my plate's kind of full right now."

Her brow furrowed. "Too full for me?"

Damn. It dawned on him how his answer must've sounded. All she wanted to know was where they stood, but he couldn't give her an honest answer, at least not until resolving his other problems. To hell with the ranch. He loved the land with everything in him, but it wasn't flesh and blood. Asadi on the other hand was. And he wouldn't let that kid go without a fight to the death. Unable to tell her or explain that he opted for doing what men do best. Deflect.

"We've both got complications. You with Travis and me with Asadi."

"My ex isn't a complication, Garrett. He's the kids' father. And despite all the horrible things he's done in the past, I have to give him a second chance. For *their* sake, not his."

No matter how she sold it to him, Garrett couldn't see it as anything other than Travis trying to weasel his way back into her life. And the fact that she was buying into it drove a wedge between them. With deflection a bust, Garrett turned the conversation to the ranch.

"Well, first things first, I've got to figure out a way to get Daddy back home. You know how he is about those horses. He'd have left me, Bridger, and Grace to fend for ourselves on Christmas morning if he thought his *real* family needed him."

Lacey smiled. "That's true. Nothing will ever compare to his horses." She shook her head. "Except maybe Asadi."

Garrett nodded in agreement. "Yep, he's the exception, for sure."

It was the perfect time to reveal he was thinking about making a run for it if they tried to take him away. Lacey would understand, he knew, and she'd do it for her own children without hesitation if circumstances ever came to that. But for some reason Garrett chickened out. It was still too early to lay that burden on her without knowing anything for sure. That conversation would have to wait.

"It's why I'm so worried about the ranch." Garrett looked deep into her eyes. "This Talon deal has everything in jeopardy. For dad. Asadi. Hell, the ranch *saved* me. You know that." Embarrassed to say it, but unable to hold back, Garrett confessed, "So did you."

Garrett knew those weren't *the three words* she'd been longing to hear, but they were close enough. Lacey loved him as much as he loved her. But he just couldn't say it. Not yet. Not until he could make the long-haul commitment and knew he was staying for good.

Lacey's face beamed. "Let's just say we saved each other." She reached out and took his hand into hers. "I'm in your corner. For better or worse. *Your* fight is *my* fight. Whatever's eating you up inside, Garrett, it doesn't have to. You've got a wingman right in front of you." She paused and added, "*If* you want one?"

Garrett couldn't help but chuckle at the thought of her using the term *wingman*. No girl but Lacey would've used that one to describe their significant other. But she knew who she was dealing with—a battle-hardened soldier looking for a partner to join him in life's trenches.

"That's exactly what I want," Garrett readily admitted, a smile rising at the thought of it.

"Then let me in." Lacey reached over the table and gently tapped him on the left temple. "Into that thick head of yours, so I can help."

Garrett sighed, feeling a weight lifted from his shoulders. "You really want to help?"

Lacey's eyes brightened. "I wouldn't offer if I didn't mean it."

Among the many qualities Garrett admired about Lacey, one that stood out above all others was the fact that she was a woman of her word. If there was a fight to be had, she'd be the first on the front lines. Lacey had proven herself more than once and he hated to press his luck. But with the Asadi situation being what it was, there was a good chance he'd put her to the test.

19

Lacey had almost forgotten why she was driving through Canadian's sleepy downtown when she glanced over at the deposit slip and an envelope full of cash from her mother's café. She'd been trapped in her head, not fully regretting the earlier conversation with Garrett, but wondering if she'd pushed too hard. The fact that her ex-husband *was* seeking to reconcile would turn a minor mess into a major morass and likely throw Garrett's trust issues into overdrive.

Lacey wanted nothing to do with Travis beyond what related to their children. She loved Garrett with all her heart. But she also knew that a rambler's gotta ramble and wondered if her hard-charging special agent boyfriend was really ready to settle down. She had just gotten her wits about her after parking the car and walking into the Happy State Bank lobby when she lost all semblance of composure. Seeing her old best friend from high school was like seeing a ghost.

The younger sister of the newly deceased Preston Kaiser could've been his twin. Vicky had the same blond hair, sharp patrician features, and slight raise of the chin, which must've been built into the family's DNA. She was in a white silk blouse, Fendi belt around her skinny waist, and handmade suede CITY Boots on her feet. Not a wrinkle. Not a frown line. Not a glimmer of anything other than monied perfection.

Vicky had either been living a carefree life or had a little help from Doctor Botox. Either way, she looked just like she did in high school. Everything about her telegraphed class and style, the way Lacey had been before her family lost their fortune. She only hoped the wafting scent of Vicky's Creed White Amber masked the stench of her own clothes reeking in crisp bacon and well-done hash browns from her mother's café.

Vicky's hand flew to her chest. "Oh. My. *God!* Lacey Mansfield. Is that really you, girl?"

Suddenly, Lacey was all too conscious of her own outfit, the uniform she wore on the breakfast shift—white V-neck T-shirt, faded Levi's, and New Balance running shoes. She was tempted to make up a lie but getting caught would be worse than caught in the couture.

"Vicky!" Lacey was brought into her old friend's embrace before she could get out another word. When Vicky let loose she struggled to come up with something, anything to minimize the awkward fact that her dead brother was involved with the cartel that'd tried to kill her.

Fortunately, Lacey didn't have to begin. "Actually, I go by Victoria now."

"Victoria?"

"Vicky wasn't exactly cutting it in the business world. Changed it when I got my MBA."

Lacey tried not to sound as impressed but failed. "You went to business school?"

"Wharton. Right after Vanderbilt. Oh, you know Daddy. Everything's gotta be the best."

Lacey didn't know anything about Wharton, only that it *was* one of the top programs in the country. Having dropped out of TCU when her father died, Lacey never finished getting her degree, even though she'd promised herself she would. Between lack of education and no way to upgrade her first name like her old friend had done, she was left feeling deflated and vulnerable.

Fighting off the panic from her insecurities, Lacey regrouped and turned the attention on Victoria, which was how her old best friend always liked it. "So . . . what brings you home?"

"After Preston's situation, the government pretty much came after every asset we had in Mescalero Exploration. Fortunately, our family's other companies were insulated. So I resigned from a venture capital firm in New York to come back and pick up where my brother left off. I was brought on as a partner by Talon to head up their mineral acquisitions. Lease and purchase lands for the company. Talon thought the Kaiser name might settle concerns about a group of outsiders moving in and taking over."

Lacey wrestled back a grin. With Victoria in charge of acquisitions, it was possible she could keep Talon from destroying Garrett's ranch. But before she could raise the issue, Victoria moved on.

"So, how's Travis these days?"

Lacey went from deflated to demolished. "Well, speaking of name changes. I'm back to Capshaw." She'd made the change immediately after the divorce, wanting nothing more to do with him beyond their shared custody of the children. She didn't want his prestigious name or the money. She'd not accepted a dime. "Travis and I split up. Couple of years ago, actually."

"Lacey, I am *so* sorry. I had no idea."

"No, It's fine Vic—Victoria. I mean, it's not exactly the kind of thing you advertise."

"No, of course not. Still, I'm sorry to hear it."

"It's okay. We make it work with the kids. That's the main thing."

Lacey couldn't help but think that Victoria looked at her a little differently. Travis was from an affluent family from the prestigious

Wolflin neighborhood in Amarillo. Lacey had once owned an art gallery there, where she displayed her work and ran in those elite circles. Now she was just a hometown girl with nothing but the prospect of an entry-level job with Talon.

Victoria seemed to brighten. "You dating anyone? Because I know a few single guys who would be—"

"Oh, no thank you. I guess, that's the good news. I *am* dating someone and very happy."

Victoria looked genuinely intrigued. "Anyone I know?"

"Yeah, you remember, Garrett Kohl."

Victoria's face screwed together. "Uh . . . Bridger's little brother?"

Despite the fact that she, Victoria, and Garrett were all in the same grade, she remembered Bridger first. Of course, *he* had always been popular and athletic, a real shining star in high school. Bridger was the dashing rodeo champ and quarterback, and their sister, Grace, was the homecoming queen. Garrett was the forgotten kid brother, who was either hunting or on horseback when everyone else was at the big party.

Lacey wanted to tell her that the scrawny kid she remembered was now muscled and handsome, the DEA badass that helped put her scumbag brother and his cronies six feet under. But she couldn't say that. For the sake of everyone, that story had been swept under the rug.

"Yep! Garrett's back in Canadian, working with his dad. You remember Butch, right?"

It was obvious by Victoria's deer in the headlights look that the awkward reality had set in. Her company was destroying his ranch. "Oh yes, I met him years ago through Grace and Bridger." She glanced down at her Cartier watch and eyed the door. "Look, I'm late for a meeting. But I'd love to catch up sometime. Can we have lunch, soon?" Before Lacey could answer, Victoria waggled her cell phone. "Oh, I'm getting pinged right now. Gotta run." She leaned in, gave Lacey another big hug, before moving out the door.

Lacey stood there in the bank lobby in silence, having forgotten again why she was there in the first place. It dawned on her in the moment that Victoria had not given her a card or told her how she could be reached. She wasn't sure of it but her old friend's mention of lunch was possibly an *un*vitation—something people say to minimize the awkwardness. There'd been plenty of that after the divorce.

It was sometimes easier just to pretend nothing was wrong. And the reality was that Lacey no longer belonged in Victoria's inner sanctum. But what bothered Lacey had nothing to do with society and everything to do with helping Garrett.

Victoria may not have anything more to say, but Lacey certainly did. If there was a chance that she could leverage her friendship to save the Kohl Ranch, she was going to take it, even if it meant losing what little pride she had left.

20

Garrett had just driven past Kate's ranch headquarters when he saw the dozers, graders, and dragline excavators belching black exhaust as they bit and tore into the earth behind his home. With the crust peeled back, the pounding sun zapped what moisture remained, leaving a hovering mirage on the horizon as far as the eye could see. What was once fertile acreage for grazing and growing his alfalfa hay was nothing but a wasteland of exposed soil.

They say that before you die, your life flashes before your eyes, but Garrett had lived his life with one foot in the grave and never had that experience. Watching his land be destroyed, however, in the dusty wake of the yellow machines brought the passing of time to a painful crawl. He relived every long walk, Sunday picnic, and trail ride across those once bountiful plains.

Recounting all the arrowheads he'd ever discovered, Garrett couldn't help but dwell on the ones still hidden, the ones Asadi would never find. They were scooped into iron buckets, dumped into semi-trailers, and hauled off to God only knows where.

Garrett prided himself as a man who never went off half-cocked, but the surge of bile could not be capped. Whoever had crushed the grove of trees where his mother was buried was in for the ass kicking of a lifetime.

Jamming his boot on the gas, Garrett gritted his teeth and jerked the wheel right, careening off the caliche road across the pasture. Laser-focused on the mammoth Caterpillar D10 bulldozer desecrating the Kohl family plot, he brought his GMC to up over fifty, nearly bouncing to the ceiling with every dip, dive, and chughole. Within fifty yards, Garrett was flanked by two white pickups, no doubt Talon security guards who'd been watching his approach.

Mashing the accelerator to the floor, Garrett left them in his dust and arrived just in time to reach the dozer which was heading for his mother's headstone. He swerved into its path and jammed on the brakes, skidding to a halt within feet of the grave. Garrett jumped out, fortunately with the wherewithal to yank the Nighthawk from his belt and toss it in the passenger seat, lest he lose what little self-control he had left and do something he'd regret.

With the passing seconds, Garrett worked to cool his temper and put the matter in perspective. He sprinted forward, grabbed the handrail to the dozer's cab and pulled himself up onto the first step. His back foot had just lifted when Garrett felt the tug that ripped him from the railing and slammed him to the ground.

Garrett scrambled to his feet and turned in a circle to find two beefy guards in tan tactical pants and black polos, with the Talon logo. They owned him collectively by a good fifty pounds. Both men had shaved heads and powerlifter physiques. The only distinction between the two was the one on the right sported a close-shorn Fu Manchu mustache. But both wore a smug look—the one that says *I dare you.*

Not one to disappoint, Garrett unleashed a left hook on the guy that grabbed him, followed by a right fist to Fu Manchu's solar plexus. Both hits landed with force but were easily absorbed—like punching a side of beef.

Garrett shuffled right to get from in between them and the dozer as the one massaging his jaw pivoted and tried to follow. He rushed Garrett on wobbly legs, but the clumsy blitz was easily dodged. As the guard's weight carried him forward, he tripped on a dirt furrow that sent him headfirst into the tilled soil.

Fu wasn't as reckless, nor as off kilter. He'd swapped his *I dare you* for an *I'm glad you did*, throwing out his arms before raising his fists. There's a look guys have who really know how to fight, and this guy wore it like Conor McGregor. It's not just technique, it was his swagger. It was more than evident by his ease that this dude was a real scrapper.

As Fu advanced, Garrett raised his fists but was a bit too sluggish to block the first jab. Fortunately, he'd dipped enough to make it only a glancing blow. A little dazed, Garrett backed to regroup as a fury of punches came flying in. He ducked one, blocked another, but took a solid left to the cheek that sent him backpedaling, off balance, and landing on his butt.

Fu's partner moved in from behind, but Garrett scrabbled to his feet and spun out of grasp, keeping a keen eye on the boxer, who kept a steady advance. With words of Joe Bob Dawson, always close to the heart, Garrett remembered his favorite philosophy on fisticuff fairness. He said *to the guy who's getting his ass kicked, there's no such thing as a fair fight.*

With two against one turning out poorly, Garrett remembered his only weapon, the Twisted X steel toes. Fu had just launched another onslaught when Garrett let loose a low kick to his attacker's leg, landing the steel tip of his boot on the kneecap. Mountain or not, the big man crumbled into a heap and grabbed his leg as he moaned in pain.

Garrett had just turned in search of the other when tackled from behind, landing in the dirt with his attacker beside him. Grappling in a plume of dust, he came out on top, cocked a fist, and smashed the guard's nose. Only feet away from his mother's sullied grave, the crunch of bone and cartilage beneath his knuckles felt good and it felt justified.

Raising his fist for another blow, Garrett felt his arm catch, body lifted in a state of weightlessness, as he was dragged backward and dropped to the ground about ten feet away. Spinning out of reach, he looked for Fu but found Holloway instead. The Talon landman was flanked by another guard, who was as big and pissed off looking as his friends. Garrett was about to rise when a guard unholstered his pistol and aimed it at him.

Hurt and enraged but smart enough to know when to stop, Garrett raised his hands, conceding it was time for a ceasefire. "Alright, Holloway. I know my limits."

Holloway smiled, seemingly amused, and offered Garret his hand. "Something tells me you don't."

Although winded from the tussle, Garrett turned down the help and struggled to his feet on his own. He dusted himself off, fighting to lower his temper before launching into Holloway. The standing bodyguard stepped toward Garrett, but their boss waved them off.

"No need for that." Holloway looked Garrett in the eye. "Right, Mr. Kohl?"

"So long as you get that dozer away from my mother's grave. Otherwise, you'd better call up every man you got."

Holloway turned to the grove of trees and studied the small headstone at the base of one of the cottonwoods. He turned back looking a bit contrite. "I didn't know that was there."

"Well, you would've if you'd asked. I thought we were in the negotiation process."

"We *were* in the process." The female voice that interrupted Holloway seemed to come out of nowhere. "Time to move on."

Garrett had been so blind with rage that he hadn't even noticed Vicky Kaiser in Holloway's passenger seat. Marching up, she wore that same smug look he remembered from high school. She'd been the quintessential *mean girl* snob, who'd lived to make everyone's life a living hell.

Before Garrett could reply, Vicky continued. "Surface damage payments were agreed upon years ago by our grandfathers. Market rate. Bridger should've told you already."

"And what about what you did here?" Garrett pointed at the bulldozed trees and his mother's desecrated gravesite. "What's the *market rate* for this?"

Vicky swallowed hard. "That wasn't—"

"Bridger didn't tell me anything about this happening today because I'm guessing he didn't know. Have to think that was intentional on your part."

Vicky shook off the suggestion. "Only thing intentional here is maximizing profit. Every second this equipment sits idle, we're losing money."

"Well, at least you're honest about it, Vicky. I'll give you that."

"You're no fool." Vicky stared him down. "A hothead maybe, like your father, but you've figured this thing out, haven't you?"

Garrett wasn't sure what Vicky was driving at, but assumed the whole nicey-nice, friend of the community garbage that Talon had been selling was all a crock. Kaisers cared about one thing and one thing only. Always had. "So, it *is* about the money?"

Vicky didn't miss a beat. "When isn't it?"

Garrett pointed to his mother's grave. "When it's about that."

Holloway, who'd been quiet for some time, broke into the conversation. "Look, fair enough, Mr. Kohl. We hear and understand your concerns, and this clearly wasn't our intent. But this is an active mining site. I can't have you making trouble for us out here."

Garrett gave a nod. "Then at least let me point out some of the places that are off limits."

Holloway studied the gravesite a moment before turning back to Garrett. "We'll fence this place off and clean up the damage we've done. But unless you've got an environmental or regulatory objection with where we're operating, nothing's off limits. I'm sorry about that."

Garrett couldn't believe it, but with the sudden appearance of Vicky Kaiser, he actually didn't mind Holloway quite as much. At least *he* was just doing his job, whereas *she* was doing it out of spite—a vendetta that had gone on for generations. Garrett was just about to turn his ire back on Vicky when a sheriff's deputy's Tahoe pulled up. There was a glare on the windshield but a shift by the driver revealed his best friend, Tony Sanchez, behind the wheel.

Garrett looked to Vicky and shook his head. "That really necessary?"

She eyed the two guards who were still on the ground nursing their injuries. They seemed to make an extra effort to look like victims. "I'm sorry to do this but Talon is going to have to file a temporary restraining order on you as well."

"You know why I did this, Vicky. You telling me you wouldn't have done the same if it was your father's grave?" Garrett knew she'd always been a daddy's girl. If she cared about nothing else, maybe that would hit home. When she didn't answer, he tried his luck with Holloway. "What about you?"

Holloway broke eye contact and looked off into the distance. "It's not up to her or me anymore. Went up the chain to Chicago. I'd do something if I could but I'm just the—"

"Landman." Garrett assumed Holloway was going to say *messenger* but as long as all their cards were on the table, he wanted the guy to admit that Talon Corporation was no different from any other oil and gas company in the world.

"That's right, Mr. Kohl. I'm just the landman."

Garrett couldn't believe it, but he actually detected a little remorse. He never imagined he'd have preferred dealing with Holloway, but with a witch like Vicky Kaiser as the alternative it made for an easy call. At least his role in this fiasco wasn't personal. With Vicky, on the other hand, everything was personal, particularly when it comes to family.

Sanchez called out as he marched up from behind. "What's going on here, Garrett?"

Garrett didn't turn. He kept his eyes locked onto Holloway. "Oh, we're just having a little meeting of the minds, that's all."

Sanchez surveyed the damage around the gravesite then eyed the busted-up guards, who were still nursing their wounds. It wasn't hard to figure out what happened. Garrett knew his friend was in a tough position and he didn't want to make it any harder for him.

Sanchez had always been there for Garrett, as much of a brother to him as Bridger. When Tony's father died and Butch was drinking and distant, they'd had each other. Preferring the ranch to prom and hunting season to football season, Garrett and Tony had the ranch. It was an alternate universe where they lived in a perpetual state of Old West purgatory, somewhere between the time of cowboys and Indians and the modern world.

"Yeah, Tony, it seems that Mr. Holloway and I have come to an understanding now. I was just about to leave."

Sanchez looked to Holloway. "Sounds like matters are resolved then."

Holloway nodded. "There'll be some paperwork I'll need to sign."

Garrett knew that had to do with the TRO, keeping him off his own property. He'd have put up a fight. But not with Sanchez there. His friend had no choice in the matter. And given the condition of the Talon guards, he was lucky to be leaving without handcuffs.

Turning to his mother's gravesite that was nearly destroyed, Garrett looked to the one responsible, the dozer driver who'd done the damage was standing slack-jawed at the top of the steps.

All Garrett could do was shake his head. Ray Smitty was like a bad penny. No matter how far you chucked him, he always turned back up.

21

Of all the things that should've occupied Garrett's mind leaving the ranch, it was the guard's pistol that had him stymied. He was packing a GSh-18, a Russian-made nine-millimeter that few Americans or Europeans used as their go-to sidearm. Every gunslinger has a preference, but most operators lived by the philosophy that *you dance with the girl who brung ya.*

Garrett, however, was the exception, opting for his Nighthawk over the Beretta M9A1 he carried in Army Special Forces or the Glock 17 he used with the DEA. Still, the GSh-18 was an odd choice for anyone other than former Spetsnaz, Russia's special operations forces. Those pistols weren't commercially available, making them nearly impossible to find.

Garrett let out a sigh when he felt the buzz of the cell phone in his front pocket and saw on his dash that the call coming in was from Kim. Last thing he needed was another problem. So as not to worry her, he mustered up a greeting that was all sunshine and roses. "To what do I owe the pleasure?"

There was a pause on the other end, which Garrett immediately took as a bad sign. He braced for impact as Kim launched right in.

"Got a little news on our situation."

A little news. That wasn't what he wanted to hear. She'd have said *good news* if it was anything other than bad. "Okay, lay it on me, I guess."

"On the positive side," she began, "it looks like we have more time than we thought until Asadi has to go back."

"More time is good," Garrett agreed. "But what does that really mean for a permanent fix?"

"Means I've got more time to work on that. To try and convince the deputy NSC director who's pushing this thing that there has to be another option. Got a meeting with him next week to see what I can work out."

"What's the bad news?"

"Bad news is I'm meeting some resistance here. Not a lot of support from my boss, which means he's getting pushback from upstairs."

Garrett knew that her boss was talking directly to the CIA director. There'd be no talking him into anything no matter how hard Kim tried. Getting an asset on board like Omar Zadran was a nice feather in his cap and a huge win for the Agency, which meant the chance of keeping Asadi in Texas was as good as gone.

"Look, Kim, I know why they want this to happen and I don't blame them. But Asadi's just a kid. He's already lost one family. I can't let him lose another."

"I know, Garrett. I know. Like I said, I'm working on it."

Garrett went silent. He was well aware of what the outcome would be. The CIA wasn't any different from the DEA in some regards. When leadership made a decision there was no going back. Bureaucratic wheels turn slow, but once in motion they were nearly impossible to stop.

Kim filled the dead air. "You okay?"

So as not to give away his plan to flee with Asadi, Garrett changed the subject. "Yeah, I'm fine. Just have some big problems going on around here."

"Asadi okay?" Kim sounded alarmed.

"No, he's great. Just something to do with the ranch."

"Anything I can help with?"

Remembering the Russian handgun and Ike's mysterious tale of trouble in Africa, Garrett launched a little salvo of misdirection to get her off his scent. "Ever hear of an energy company called Talon Corporation?"

There was a pause on her end. "Doesn't ring a bell. Why?"

"They've got a heavy hand, that's all. Ike mentioned he'd crossed paths with them in Angola and they weren't exactly the sort that plays nice in the sandbox, if you know what I mean."

"Few in Africa do." Kim chuckled. "They're drilling on the ranch now?"

"I wish. They're digging."

"*Digging?*" Kim sounded genuinely thrown off. "Digging for what?"

"Rare earth minerals."

There was an even longer pause on her end this time. "Talon, you said?"

Garrett could tell she was no longer making friendly conversation. Kim's intel ears were perked for a reason. But he doubted she'd tell him why. "Something jog your memory?"

"Had a few cables come across my queue on rare earth minerals lately. Becoming somewhat of a security topic given the fact that Beijing controls the bulk of the world's supply. The Chinese are even digging in Afghanistan now. Using the Taliban as security. Can you believe that?"

Garrett knew he was grasping at straws but had to ask. Maybe they could tie the company destroying his land to a terrorist organization. "Do the Chinese have any connection to Talon Corporation?"

"Not that I'm aware of but let me check. Maybe I can find something that'll help."

Relieved she'd taken the bait and forgotten about his plans to abscond with the boy, Garrett smiled as he pushed the gas and pulled back onto the road. He turned to his truck's open window and gazed out at the broad swath of Texas plains, as wide as the sky was tall.

Garrett was just about to end the call when she added, "And listen to me, cowboy, I haven't forgotten what you said the other day."

Dammit! He faked ignorance but knew deep down she'd never buy it. "Said about what?"

"I know you love Asadi. And I know you're in pain because I feel the same way. But don't do anything stupid. It won't end well." When he didn't answer, Kim pressed, "I'm giving fair warning, Garrett. You have to trust me."

Garrett ultimately agreed with her and promised not to do anything rash. But the truth of the matter was that nothing was resolved. And when the call ended, he was still left with one big question. *What the hell do I do now?*

22

Central Intelligence Agency
McLean, Virginia

Kim hung up the phone, wondering what Garrett was up to. If he fled with Asadi, there'd be a swift response from the seventh floor, where the CIA director and high-level officials pushed buttons and pulled levers that ended lives. Special Activities Center operatives were relentless, and at times merciless. Garrett was in a world of danger he couldn't fully understand.

Opening her desk drawer, Kim reached in and took out her favorite photograph of Garrett and Asadi, the one where they're wearing their Stetsons. They were both on horseback, sunset on the horizon, and smiles as wide as the open plains. The Texas cowboy and Afghan villager, though born worlds apart, had come together as a family. They were even starting to look alike.

Kim smiled, pushed back from her desk, and turned to the empty lobby of the Crime and Narcotics Center in the New Headquarters Building basement. Deputy director was as busy a job as it was solitary. Climbing the CIA's leadership ladder had left a wake of peers with bruised egos. And the ones who weren't jealous were often intimidated.

A sip of cold coffee from her green Dartmouth mug and she wondered how long she'd been sitting there daydreaming. Kim stared at the maxim of her alma mater and read it sotto voce, "*Vox Clamantis in Deserto.*"

All she could do was shake her head and laugh. Never had the phrase *the voice of one crying in the wilderness* felt more apropos. *Damn* it was lonely at the top.

Raised in Hartford, Connecticut, Kim had attended boarding school at Choate, did her undergrad at Dartmouth, and master's work at the School of Advanced International Studies at Johns Hopkins. She'd been top of her class from grade school. An achiever. A perfectionist. A career conqueror in every sense of the word. But the higher she rose the less she seemed to gain. It was one of those classic *Twilight Zone* ironies she was still trying to process.

Never one to wallow, Kim brushed off the self-sorrow just as CNC director Bill Watson flew through the door into her office.

Bill looked surprised to see her facing him. "You hear me coming?"

Rather than raise an unnecessary red flag concerning Garrett and Asadi, Kim pitched the rare earth minerals question. "Ever hear of Talon Corporation?"

If Bill was surprised before, he looked downright stunned. He pushed back a few dark strands of hair, which were always falling out of place. "Been talking to the seventh floor, huh?"

Realizing she'd stumbled onto something important Kim ignored the question and took the opening instead. "Thoughts?"

Bill was one of the old school intellectual Ivy League officers that never took off his suit coat. But with him, there was usually something askew. Sometimes he had missed a button, or he'd forgotten to shave. Today his tie was loose and tossed over his shoulder.

Bill wasn't necessarily a friend, rather somewhat of a confidant and professional ally. He'd hired her on as his deputy after serving as her second command in Afghanistan at Camp Tsavo. His promotion over her wasn't because he was better, but because he was better connected, a bureaucratic ladder climber who played the CIA's career advancement game ruthlessly well.

Bill let out a defeated breath, moved to the chair against the wall, and slumped into it. "My *thoughts* are that Talon has a few skeletons, and the administration wants somebody high up over here to give it the green light on U.S. operations. Looks like this company has been buying up energy assets all over the country." Bill shrugged. "Easy to do when they're worth pennies on the dollar. They'll make a fortune when prices inevitably rise."

Kim raised her eyebrows and nodded as if those were her thoughts too. Wanting to milk him further, she popped another question. "Why did the NSC director send it over here?"

"Just insurance." Bill shook off the notion. "Politicians need someone to blame if this blows up in their faces. You know how it goes. There are policy *wins* and intelligence *failures*. Amazingly, it never seems to go the other way."

"But you don't think there's a security angle to this do you?"

Bill looked at her curiously. "What are you talking about?"

Dammit! Wrong question. "I mean, why bother us. If it's a trade or export controls issue, it'd have State or DOE written all over it. Or if there's a tax thing going on then why not FBI?"

"It's all just a formality. The president and our director have been tight for years. My guess is they need us to run interference with the Senate. The press has been all over the fact that China is buying up ports around the world, including a few major ones here. Foreign investors were bound to raise some eyebrows from the hawks in Congress."

"Maybe their concerns are valid?"

"Well, I've learned those eyebrows tend to sag after campaign contributions start rolling in and there's a sudden interest in their *charitable* foundations and political action committees."

Kim took a moment to contemplate that disheartening reality before asking the question to which she already knew the answer. "Really think that'll happen?"

"According to my sources, it's already happening."

Bill was a wheeler-dealer on Capitol Hill, having influential contacts with big players on both sides of the aisle. She'd even heard his name bandied about for a White House position as national security advisor. Better him than her. Kim hated that world and most of the people working in it. She had enough information to go on until she tapped into her own sources.

"Well, Bill, you know more about what's going on over there than I do. And I'd like to keep it that way." Since Bill didn't make the connection between Talon and what was happening down in Texas, Kim figured she better let it go, particularly since there were political sensitivities involved. "I've got enough on my plate with the whole Garrett Kohl situation."

"Oh yeah." Bill looked amused. "How *is* the High Plains Drifter?"

"Not good, I'm afraid." She pursed her lips. "I just gave him the bad news."

Bill lost his smile. "You don't think he'll . . ."

"No, not Garrett. He's a rational loose cannon you might say."

Bill again looked amused. "Kind of an oxymoron, isn't it?"

"You just got to know the guy. He's different. Complex."

"*Complex?* We're talking about the same guy, right? The one who galloped his horse across Texas on a killing spree."

"Cartel *sicarios*, Bill." Kim felt her face reddening. "Vicious murderers and kidnappers. If anyone ever deserved a bullet, it was them."

"I'm just saying. Subtlety isn't in Garrett Kohl's wheelhouse. His tactics have caused a lot of problems for you." Bill narrowed his gaze. "And more importantly me."

"Didn't see you complaining about his tactics when we brought in Emilio Garza."

"No." Bill shook it off. "We got our trophy in the end. Made a lot of people happy."

"Then there you have it." Kim smiled with the satisfaction of getting Bill to admit that bringing Garrett into the fold was a good idea. "Kohl gets results. And he takes good care of Asadi. Which leaves me one less thing to worry about."

Bill paused as if in deep thought. "Well, *that* issue is about to be resolved."

Kim sighed involuntarily and immediately regretted it. Like her, Bill was trained to detect nonverbal cues, and her reaction was a huge red flag.

"What's the problem, Manning? You knew from the beginning there was a possibility that Asadi would return home for good."

"I know that, but things have changed. And Pakistan isn't really his home."

"Close enough," Bill shot back. "And he has family there. That's all that matters."

"He doesn't even know those people. And aside from that, Asadi has a family here now with the Kohls. It'll kill him if we take him away."

"You don't know that."

"I *do* know that." Again, her response was more forceful than intended. "Sending him to live with Omar Zadran is a bad idea."

"Bad idea for who?" Bill studied her the way CIA operations officers evaluate an asset under too much stress—the kind who get cut loose from the job. He leaned forward and stared her down. "You know what's riding on this. This deal with Zadran keeps us in the game. The NSC wants this, which means the president wants it. So, end of discussion. The kid goes back."

"Not if I can convince Conner Murray otherwise." The words slipped out so fast she hadn't even realized she was contradicting a direct order from the CIA director.

"Conner Murray?" Bill's eyes went wide. "Deputy director of the NSC Conner Murray? What makes you think you can change his mind?" Before she could answer, he focused in on the photo of Garrett and Asadi in their cowboy hats lying on her desk.

"Bill, I think if I can talk to him I can—"

"Forget it." His eyes went from disappointed to accusatory. "I think you're too close to this thing and it's clouding your judgment."

"What are you talking about?" The heat in Kim's cheeks was now fueled by his perception. Last thing operations officers wanted was to reveal any weakness. At the CIA, even among friends, you didn't want to give up any leverage, particularly if it was based on emotion. "Because I care about the situation doesn't mean I'm getting *too close*. I'm doing my job."

"Your *job* is to carry out the orders of our elected policy makers. And right now, ours are telling us that the boy goes back. End of discussion."

"Even if it's going to ruin peoples' lives?"

The only correct response was *you're right*. Their job was to steal secrets, and in some cases, carry out covert action missions at the behest of the president. She was a CIA case *officer*, not a case *worker*. If she wanted a career in child advocacy she was in the wrong profession. But before she could follow up her question to cover her tracks, Bill had made his decision.

"I'm pulling you off this, Manning. You're too close to it and it shows. The kid is going to Pakistan and that's final. Aside from that, we don't need Garrett anymore. He's served his purpose. Been a good asset. Now, it's time to move on.

A good asset? The term took her by surprise. Kim thought of Garrett as a colleague, not a CIA source. But the truth was he had never volunteered. He'd worked for her out of dire necessity to protect his family, and more importantly, so that he could adopt Asadi. Suddenly, she felt like a predator, stalking a wounded animal that's trying to protect its young.

Kim expelled a defeated breath, this time not caring what her boss thought. "I just don't want to wreck anyone's life because we gain an operational advantage in South Asia. It's selfish."

"It's selfish *not* to do it. Bringing Zadran on board is a matter of national security. And you need to make sure that whatever you do is for the good of the country. Not your own."

She was winding up for a counterargument when it hit her that the reason his words stung so deeply was because they were true. For the first time in her career, she was putting *emotion* over *mission*. But there was a part of her that felt the Agency owed her one. Her dedication to the fight had left her empty and alone, a realization that left Kim so deflated that she no longer felt like battling her boss. She just consented with a nod. In all reality, there was no good option.

If Kim took Asadi, Garrett would be devastated. And that was the irony. The only thing keeping a team of CIA Ground Branch operators from hunting him down and sending him to the forever hereafter *was* the mission. To save Garrett's life, she'd have to destroy him.

23

Asadi should have been nervous, maybe even a little afraid. But for some reason he wasn't. With Butch and Garrett kicked off the ranch, it was up to him to keep the operation running, or at least make sure the horses were watered and fed. He knew he was making a bigger deal out of it all than it actually was, but his family was in need and he wanted to prove his worth.

Bridger dropped Asadi off at the barn before heading into town, leaving him to tend to the horses by himself. With a little time to kill before his uncle's return, he threw a saddle on Grizz and led him out to the corral. Part of him knew that Butch wouldn't approve him doing this alone. But another part was certain it would make the old man proud.

Nothing thrilled Butch more than when Asadi did a job without having to be told. Working with the colt wasn't something that necessarily *had* to be done, but he didn't want to lose any progress, and knew Butch would feel the exact same way.

Asadi was opening the gate to the corral when he froze at a distinctive sound he'd come to know well. Before seeing the rattlesnake coiled against the fence post, Grizz must have sensed its presence. Asadi should have known by the sorrel's snorts and nervous bob of the head.

Anticipating what was sure to come, Asadi tightened his grip and braced for the struggle. But before he could get a good grasp, the reins ripped across his palm as the colt reared and shuffled away. Asadi made a grab for the leather straps, but they were just out of reach. He tried again, just as Grizz turned from the corral and bolted into the pasture.

Asadi's burning hand was nothing compared to the sting of his shame as the riderless horse trotted away. Not really knowing what to do, he looked down the road for Bridger, but there was no help in sight. Turning back to Grizz, he saw the jittery colt make a turn toward the mine, where growling machinery and rumbling trucks kicked up dust in their destructive wake.

Asadi sprinted to Grizz, who was at least fifty yards away and moving further and further by the second. Blood pumping and fueled by fear, he at first felt as if he could run forever, but the blazing sun quickly took its toll. Slowing to a walk, Asadi took a more measured approach. The colt had stopped beside the tall fence built by the new company and seemed to have tired out.

Asadi had not seen a fortress like it since the American army base in Afghanistan. The glinting razor wire was stacked in three separate coils, one atop the other, forming an impenetrable barrier at least six feet high. Knowing that a sudden fright could leave Grizz entangled and wounded, Asadi's approach went from measured to glacial.

He took a deep breath, raised his hand, and summoned a calm voice. "Come on, Grizz. Come on, boy." After a silent plea to his mother in heaven for help, he called gently to his partner. "No worry. No worry. Please stop, Grizz."

The colt's ears perked, turned forward, and his head swung around in Asadi's direction. Grizz took a couple of shaky strides closer to the fence and then stopped and looked back. After a skittish lunge, he slid to a halt. The colt stood rigid for a moment, then let out a snort and took a couple of timid steps forward.

Asadi kept an easy pace as he approached, moving steadily but cautiously, trying desperately to show enough confidence for them both. He kept his hand out, open and visible, rubbing the tips of his fingers, like he was bringing a handful of pellets. Within a few yards of Grizz, Asadi eyed the razor wire behind the colt, shimmering like diamonds in the setting sun.

Pretending they were in the safety of the corral, Asadi moved forward, his casual smile leading the way. He had just grasped Grizz's dangling reins when an engine roared from behind and the colt's eyes widened in panic. He stiffened, jerked his head, and shuffled backward, his rump nearly touching the fence.

With all his strength, Asadi held tight, his mind made up that he'd never let go, even if it meant being dragged into the razor wire along with Grizz. Digging his bootheels into the dirt, Asadi yanked the reins, but his strength was no match. A flick of the colt's neck in response to the truck's blasting horn launched him off his feet and landing face-first in the dusty ground.

A death grip on the leather straps, Asadi held on as the colt scuttled backward, dragging him through the dirt, and smashing over thorny bushes that scraped his forehead and cheeks. Barreling over a shrub, Asadi started to let loose, just as Grizz stopped. He tightened his hold, scrambled to his feet, and slid his palm along the reins until he got a firm grasp on the bridle.

A quick glance over the shoulder revealed the three uniformed men creeping up from behind. Only feet from the wire, Asadi began to panic as a terrified Grizz inched closer to the fence. It wasn't until Bridger drove up, flung open the door and marched to his pursuers spewing a slew of profanities.

While the guards turned their attention on Bridger, Asadi got a foot in the stirrup and swung into the saddle. With the razor wire to his right, he gave a palatal click and slight kick that got Grizz into first gear. Feeling his body unclench with a little distance, Asadi guided his colt to the flat, wide-open plains.

In that moment, Butch's words came rushing back. He'd said that horse and rider needed one another. They were *partners*. And Asadi knew it to be true. A cowboy finds no greater peace than in the saddle, and his horse no greater satisfaction than in harmony with his rider.

Asadi had just moved the reins left and begun a lazy counterclockwise turn when he saw Bridger on the ground about forty yards behind them. A man was kneeling on his back, and another restrained his legs, while a third delivered a kick to the head.

Remembering how Butch had put his horse between Kate and her attacker, Asadi spurred his colt toward Bridger in hopes of doing the same. They were only a few yards away when a man with a rifle stepped in between them and aimed. Asadi heard the gunshot, and he was thrown from the saddle as Grizz crashed forward and tumbled end over end in a cloud of dust.

Asadi scrambled to his feet and turned to find Grizz in an awful display of violent thrashing. He eased to his wounded colt, careful to avoid the fury of hooves that batted the air. "Easy, boy. Easy. It okay. Stay still, please. Just stay."

Grizz calmed a little at the sound of Asadi's voice, then rolled to his stomach, dug his front hooves into the dirt and launched his haunches off the ground, the way a newborn foal fought to take their very first steps. But halfway up his body shook, he collapsed forward, and again rolled onto his side. Grizz righted himself again and tried to rise but his front legs buckled, and his belly slammed to the ground. With a pitiful whinny, he looked to Asadi with desperate eyes.

Spotting the red wound on Grizz's neck, Asadi got down on hands and knees, crawled to the colt, and eased his hand beside the gunshot wound. Grizz's ragged breathing, nose to the ground, made little puffs of dust that caked on his bloody nostrils.

Asadi had just risen when he heard quick footsteps approaching. Hoping Bridger had broken loose and was coming to help, he turned to find the man with the rifle—the man who shot Grizz. He had been at the house the day before. It was the silver-haired man named Holloway.

By the time Asadi saw the rifle it was already too late. Dragged away by a beefy guard, he only heard the faintest of whinnies, two gunshots, a sad silence that told him his partner was gone forever and there was nothing more he could do to save him.

24

It wasn't hard for Lacey to track down Victoria. The Kaiser family was as close as it gets to royalty in Canadian, and royals can't pick their noses, under the covers in the dark, without everyone finding out about it the next day. What's more, Victoria's long absence only made the gossip juicier. She was either going to save the Texas Panhandle or bury them all. And given what was happening out at Kohl Ranch, Lacey wasn't quite sure of the outcome.

As she walked past the white Range Rover she'd seen in front of the bank on Main, Lacey slowed her gait to take in the beautiful grounds of the sprawling Kaiser compound. She couldn't help but think back on all the times that she and her friend, formerly known as *Vicky*, had sat out on the wraparound porch after cheerleading practice their senior year, talking about colleges, sororities, and the kind of man they wanted to marry one day.

One thing was for certain. Lacey had never imagined she'd be standing at the front door, hat in hand for a job, and begging Victoria to intervene on her boyfriend's behalf. As humble pie goes, it was only a slice. But it felt like she was eating the whole damn thing.

Spinning on a heel, Lacey decided to abort the whole humiliating mission when her old friend opened the door. Victoria's face registered a look that was somewhere between shock and joy, as she embraced Lacey with no less vigor than she had earlier.

"What a wonderful surprise!"

Once released from her friend's embrace, Lacey took a step back and thumbed over her shoulder to the car. "You know, I really should've called first. You're probably busy."

"Don't be silly!" Victoria batted away the notion. "Come in!" She glanced at Lacey's ten-year-old maroon Ford Explorer with the dented front fender parked in the driveway. "Just didn't recognize the car. Wasn't until I looked at the security camera that I knew it was you."

Just great. Had Victoria also seen the anxiety on her face and the fear in her eyes too? Lacey mentally collected herself and worked to match her friend's enthusiasm.

"Well, it's me again." Lacey followed Victoria through the foyer and into the newly redecorated living room that could've easily made the cover of *Southern Living*.

"Where are my manners?" Victoria stopped and turned. "Can I offer you a drink?"

"Nothing for me. I really can't stay long."

Lacey wasn't sure, but she thought her old friend looked a little relieved.

"Okay, well another time then." Victoria checked her watch, just like she'd done at the bank. "I've got a phone call with the Chicago office coming up anyhow."

"Oh, well, I'll get right to it then. There are a couple of things I wanted to talk to you about and the first one is a job. I've applied for an office manager's position with Talon, and I've got all the qualifications." She dug into her purse, pulled out a résumé and handed it over.

Victoria kept her hands at her sides, letting it hang awkwardly in the air. "I don't think so."

Lacey was stunned. "You won't even take a look at it?"

"Nope." Victoria gave a quick shake of the head.

Still surprised, Lacey wondered if this was because of her divorce with Travis. Could Victoria really be that petty? She was struggling for a response when her old friend smiled.

"Lacey, *you* are like family to me. Your qualifications begin with loyalty, which stands for a hell of a lot more than what's on that paper."

"Oh, well, that's great news. I was a little worried there for a second."

"Now, don't get too excited just yet. It would probably just be on a temporary basis to start. But I know I could sure use an assistant. Would something like that work?"

"Well . . . yeah." Lacey eased the résumé back into her purse. "Thank you."

"No need to thank me." Victoria's demeanor had changed in a millisecond from sociable to professional. "You're a good fit for Talon and we'd be lucky to have you."

"*Whew.*" Lacey wiped pretend sweat from her brow. "I had a whole speech planned and everything. You won't regret this. I promise."

Victoria's smile looked a little plastic. "I'm sure we won't."

Following an awkward pause, Lacey added, "Just one more thing."

Victoria glanced at her watch again. This time it was purely a signal, a reminder that she was very busy. Lacey was tempted to take the job and run but knew the victory would be hollow if she couldn't help Garrett as well.

"It's about the Kohl Ranch, Victoria. As head of Talon acquisitions, I'm sure you have a big say in what happens on that property. And I was wondering if maybe you could—"

"Let me stop you right there." Victoria's smile vanished. "I'm sorry about the Kohls' situation. I really am. But years ago, a contract was signed, people shook hands, and a sum of money was paid for the rights to those minerals. Because your boyfriend doesn't like it doesn't negate the fact that a deal's a deal."

"Okay." Lacey was struck by how quickly the conversation had turned. Victoria's response was so smooth it almost seemed rehearsed. "Well, if there's anything you can do to at least ease their burden it would certainly be appreciated."

Victoria's smile returned. "Best thing the Kohls can do to relieve their *burden* is obey the law, rather than attack my men who are out there just trying to do their jobs."

"*Attack* them? My understanding is Butch was just trying to protect Kate Shanessy from some idiot who tackled her."

"I'm not talking about that, Lacey. We fired that idiot driver on the spot. I'm talking about what Garrett and Bridger did out there. The whole family is out of control."

Not only was the news to Lacey out of the blue, it was so outrageous that she was tempted to call it a lie. But given what had happened with Butch, she knew better than to protest Victoria's claims just yet. "What are you talking about? What did they do?"

"I wasn't out there for the incident with Bridger, but I was standing right there when Garrett went berserk. Witnessed the whole thing."

"Witnessed *what*, exactly?"

"What I can only describe as a meltdown." Victoria shook her head looking confused. "He drove out there and attacked our guards. Tried to commandeer our machinery."

"*Garrett?* Are you sure?" Lacey couldn't believe what she was hearing. "He's so levelheaded. There must've been a reason."

"A reason to resort to violence?" Victoria scoffed. "Two of our workers had to be taken to the emergency room in Pampa."

"And *Garrett* did this?"

"Ask him yourself. We had to call law enforcement out there and everything."

Lacey was in a state of mind that was somewhere between shock and embarrassment. She wanted to argue but it was impossible without the facts. Naturally, she wondered why Garrett hadn't called. This wasn't like him. Of course, this whole situation had him stirred up. Maybe he'd been pushed too far?

With her mind racing, Lacey had almost forgotten that Victoria had made mention of Garrett's brother. "And Bridger? He was there too?"

"We're still trying to get the full story. Sheriff Crowley came out and took down everything that happened. There were multiple witnesses to the event. But it all had something to do with that little foster child that lives with Butch and Garrett."

"*Asadi* was involved?"

"Don't know all the details. Only that he rode his horse onto the site and started harassing our workers. Putting everyone in danger. Including himself. According to the incident report, he ran into our perimeter fence. Just know the horse was injured and had to be put down."

Lacey's hand flew to her face. "Is Asadi okay?"

"You mean the boy?" Victoria looked a little confused. "He's absolutely fine. Not a scratch. Thankfully, our security guards were there to help. He's lucky he wasn't killed."

"And Bridger?" Lacey asked.

"*He*, on the other hand, was a big problem. We may have to file charges, which could affect his law license."

Clearly, Lacey needed to talk to Garrett. Victoria's revelations were more than just embarrassing, they were troubling. She knew that what was going on at the ranch was unfair, if not devastating, but all this was hard to hear. Garrett and his family were tilting at windmills. Their issues and concerns weren't fabricated, but they were certainly delusional if they thought fistfights with a powerful corporation would solve any of their problems.

Victoria put her hand on Lacey's shoulder and leaned in. "Look, I hate to sound like a snob, but the Kohls—well, they're . . . of another sort. Garrett didn't grow up like us."

Of another sort?

If Victoria meant that the Kohls were men whose greatest ambitions centered on something other than wealth and power, then she supposed they were another breed of men. And she was glad of it. But rather than say all that, Lacey just gave a nod as solid as her answer.

"Yeah, Garrett is different from anyone I've ever met. Guess that's why I fell for him."

As she turned to leave, Victoria tried to stop her, but Lacey kept on the move. Despite her show of defiance, it was hard not to dwell on what had happened at the ranch, and why Garrett hadn't told her. It was yet another secret that was driving a wedge between them.

25

Kim took a seat by the window in the CIA cafeteria, a room filled with the low murmur of whispering intelligence officers, no doubt having a few *unofficial* discussions, just as she was about to do with Contreras. Her query on Talon had turned into a face-to-face, which meant he had found something big. And given the fact that he wanted to meet ASAP, it was likely urgent.

Contreras didn't have any more internal access than she did. In fact, he probably had less. But the Special Activities Center paramilitary officer and former Navy SEAL maintained an open line of communications with a tight group of black ops veterans, many of whom had gone on to earn the big bucks in defense and security contracting. Those positions, particularly ones in the private sector, opened them up to a whole different network of intelligence sources.

Seeing the smile on Contreras's face as he sat, Kim knew immediately that she and Garrett's mutual friend had hit pay dirt. "Take it your boys came through."

Contreras gave a quick look around before opening the folder even though everything he had was unclassified. It was mostly articles from obscure foreign media publications and blog postings. The one on top was from an environmental group in Burundi, featuring an article about government corruption, missing persons, and a familiar Russian private military company—the infamous Wagner Group.

Well beyond what American security firms Blackwater and Triple Canopy were doing in the early wild west days of Afghanistan and Iraq, Wagner's activities fell fully into the mercenary realm. Operating on Moscow's behalf in places like Europe, the Levant, Maghreb, and sub-Saharan Africa, their tactics in Ukraine and Syria were rumored to include atrocities such as beating their prisoners with sledgehammers and subjecting them to electric shock torture.

Kim thumbed through the articles, skimming similar headlines until coming to the last one from a media source in Malawi. There was a photo of three bloated bodies lying in a ditch, surrounded by gawkers from a nearby village. The headline above the picture read, *More Dead in Wake of Mine Dispute.* Wherever Wagner Group was rumored to be operating, it seemed there was a sudden change in environmental laws and national policy.

Contreras tapped his finger on the article. "Buddy from the teams told me Talon hires Wagner for contract security. And for their *special* jobs, they've got former Spetsnaz operators on the payroll, who can be as discreet or indiscreet as the situation calls for."

Kim stared at the not so discreet placement of the dead African men in the ditch, each with a bullet hole center forehead. She wondered how far removed the Russian government was from this, if removed at all. "Nobody's called out Talon for what's going on?"

"There's no direct ties. No way to link it to Wagner Group or to the company. Just sort of a coincidence. Wagner shows up and clears out any obstacles before Talon arrives to establish high-level government contact and make their deals."

"Coincidence, huh?" Kim had to laugh. "Given our history, you'd think we'd be watching this closer."

She couldn't help but be reminded that the race for energy resources was a factor leading up to Pearl Harbor. And hydrocarbons since then have been at the forefront of every major conflict in the Middle East. The scarcity of rare earth minerals in large finds could potentially pose the same big problem, particularly given America's heavy reliance on China.

Contreras chuckled. "Syria. Iran. North Korea. Those countries make big headlines. Not Malawi. Aside from that, we've had a lot on our plate. Taliban, Haqqani Network, ISIS, Hezbollah, Quds Force, Boko Haram, Al-Shabab. *Hell*, we've still got a damn shadow war going on in Afghanistan, whether our government wants to admit it or not. Rare earth minerals and Talon aren't at the forefront of anyone's mind."

"Well, maybe they should be." Kim looked up from the article. "Particularly if there's a possibility that a company like this is operating over here."

"That's Talon Corporation *International*. Talon Corporation *America* is a separate entity made up of U.S. citizens entirely. CEO and board of directors are as downhome as apple pie. Despite the similar names, TCI and TCA are separate businesses in no way connected. At least on paper."

Kim's mind raced, thinking about all the things she *didn't* know about Talon. "Yeah, but something still doesn't add up. I mean, why bother investing here, with all the red tape and environmental regulations when you can just go to some places in Africa, Latin America, and South Asia. Where you can bribe whoever you want. Blackmail whoever you want. Kill whoever you want. With no repercussions. I don't get it. Why take the chance?"

"Probably not as hard for them to operate here as you think." Contreras shook his head and laughed. "And who says our politicians won't take a bribe?"

Kim remembered what Bill had said earlier. Once the campaign contributions and money for pet projects started rolling in, concerns on Capitol Hill tended to disappear. It wasn't officially a bribe, but it wasn't on the up and up. She suspected a few key legislators were all too aware of what Talon was doing overseas and were just hoping no one else would find out.

"Alright, Mario, this is great stuff. I'll get this to Garrett and see if he can find anything else. We link Talon to Wagner Group or any of these atrocities and that company's done for."

Contreras gave a nod. "Just tell Garrett to give Talon a wide berth. From what I've heard from my sources, these guys aren't too keen on any opposition."

Kim pointed to the photo of the dead bodies. "They wouldn't try anything like this over here, do you think?"

Contreras shrugged. "I guess the real question is, what are they after down in Texas and how bad do they want it."

Kim thought a moment. "Don't know. But we've got a guy down there who can find out."

Contreras looked a little anguished, which was rare for someone who, like her, had spent most of his adult life living in war zones and grown accustomed to the dangers. "Just tell Garrett to watch his step."

Suspecting he knew more than he was letting on, Kim pushed, "You know something you're not telling me."

Contreras looked out the window into the cafeteria courtyard where a few other Agency staff were taking their coffee meetings out in the summer sun. "Like you, I've got my off-the-books Rolodex that I keep for special occasions."

Although Kim really wanted to know, she knew better than to ask. "And you think this is one of those *occasions*?"

Contreras turned back to her and smiled. "Don't know. But the fact that Wagner Group could be involved raises some big red flags."

He looked back to the courtyard. "Russians are getting more brazen all the time. If they'll assassinate someone on British soil, then why not here? They're always pushing boundaries. Seeing what they can get away with."

Kim couldn't think of a national security angle that would make Moscow risk an international incident with the United States. But over the years the Russians had used every trick in the book to turn Americans against one another, to tear down the country from within. The logical next step in the process was to capitalize on politicians' greed. Completely poison the already polluted well.

An operation on American soil wasn't completely out of the question. It was well known that Russian spies were active in the U.S. at any given time. Figuring out who they were and where they were operating was the problem. The CIA and FBI had been trying to figure that out for over a half-century. But after the fall of the Berlin Wall, Washington's focus was redirected. Moscow's hadn't. The U.S. was still enemy number one.

For Kim to prove Talon was connected to Russian intelligence, particularly given its powerful political ties in America, she'd need indisputable concrete evidence. And she couldn't lay that responsibility entirely on Garrett. She'd have to go down to Texas and find it herself.

26

arrett could feel the furnace within glowing red hot with fiery billows of seething rage. Butch's call had begun with the words *Asadi's okay*, but the following report of what happened at the ranch sent Garrett on the warpath. Talon guards had murdered Grizz, and beat Bridger within an inch of his life. It was the cherry on top after desecrating their mother's grave.

Marching down the Hemphill County Hospital hallway toward Bridger's room, Garrett rounded the corner to find Tony Sanchez guarding the door.

The sheriff's deputy threw up a hand, palm facing out. "Hold up there, buddy." When Garrett barged past Sanchez grabbed his shirt and threw him against the wall. "I *said*, hold on!"

There were only a few men in the world Garrett would've allowed to put their hands on him and one of them was Sanchez. "Need to see Bridger. Gotta find out what exactly happened out there."

"You will, but I want you to calm down first." Sanchez let go but kept pressure against Garrett's shoulders. "Okay?"

"I *am* calm." Garrett gave a nod. "Just want to see my brother. That's all."

Sanchez let go and patted Garrett's sleeves back down. "I know that, Quanah. But before you do, I want you to be prepared."

Garrett's heart sank at the thought of what that could mean. "Prepared for what, Tony?"

Sanchez grinned, just like he used to when they were kids. "Prepared for *Bridger* to be the ugly brother for once."

The fact that Sanchez could make a joke was a clear message. Bridger was bunged up, but he'd be okay. Garrett untensed and smiled also to let his friend know he was calming down. "I'm alright now. Really. I am. I just want to check on him and get the full story."

Sanchez let go and took a step back. He looked both ways in the empty hallway and lowered his voice. "What do you know, so far?"

"Just what Daddy told me. Asadi's horse got away. He went to get it and these guards chased him down. Shot that colt and beat up Bridger when he came to help."

Sanchez shook his head and laughed. "I'm sure that's exactly how it went down, but that's not the story Talon's telling Sheriff Crowley."

"What other way could it be told?" Garrett's temperature was on the rise again. "We're the ones with a dead horse and a family member in the hospital. And we're lucky that's the worst of it given Asadi was riding on top of Grizz when they shot him."

"I know, Garrett, but they're saying Asadi was out there harassing them, got too close to the mining operation and they went after him for his own safety and protection."

"*Really?*" Garrett was almost as furious as he'd been when he saw what they'd done to his mother's grave. "They were so worried about his *safety* they shot the horse out from under him?"

"Given what Butch had done to that truck driver, they said they were afraid they'd be trampled. And because you'd injured two of their guards earlier, they thought Bridger might do the same."

Ah hell. Talon was building a case against the entire Kohl family. Garrett knew exactly where this was going but asked anyhow, "So, now what?"

"Now Bridger's kicked off the ranch too. And Asadi."

Garrett crossed his arms. "For how long?"

"Long as Talon's out there."

"You're kidding! That could be months! A year! Longer! Hell, this won't stand."

"It *is* standing, Garrett. Judge ordered it less than an hour ago."

"What about the cattle and horses?"

Sanchez nodded, as if they'd already thought of everything. "Talon agreed to let you on the land with a sheriff's escort, which will, of course, be me. So, don't worry. The animals will be well taken care of. You can count on that."

Garrett thought about his friend's words: *Talon agreed to let you on the land*. In what circle of hell do you need permission from a corporation to set foot on your own damn property, land his family has owned for nearly a century, and his Comanche ancestors before that.

Garrett shook his head in disbelief. "The world is upside down, Tony."

"Preaching to the choir, man. But here we are. I'll do everything in my power to help, but Crowley has always been thick as thieves with the Kaisers. You know that. And Vicky has him eating out of the palm of her delicate little hand. Sheriff's on Talon's side. Not yours."

Garrett stared at the door leading to his brother. "Guess I better tell Bridger the bad news."

IT HAD TAKEN GARRETT A minute to get adjusted to his brother's cuts and bruises. The normally dashing Bridger Kohl was a swollen mess. On top of an injured kidney, he had two cracked ribs and a broken bone in his right hand. Apparently, he'd landed in a couple of good haymakers before the guards took him down in a rush. Despite the bad news Garrett delivered, Bridger took it all in stride, almost to the point of seeming laid back about it.

Nearly to the point of being pissed off at his brother for being so lax, Garrett had to ask, "Well, what kind of dope they got you on? Might need some of that myself."

Bridger smiled a groggy smile. "I don't know, Bucky, but it's damn good."

"Want to tell me why you're grinning like a guy who didn't just get his ass kicked?"

Bridger grinned wider. "Just thinking back to our conversation from yesterday. The one where you accused me of defending Talon Corporation, and not caring about the land where our mother was buried."

Now that Bridger was lying there beaten and broken, having defended the ranch, and more importantly, Asadi, Garrett felt the sting. "Look, I told you I was sorry about that. What more can I say?"

"You can say 'thank you.'"

Garrett's guilt was giving way to anger again. His brother was pushing it. "Well, kind of figured it goes without saying, but *thank you* for what you did. Don't think I gotta tell you this but Asadi means everything to me and—"

"Not for that, moron." Bridger picked up his cell phone lying beside him on the bed and winced as he tossed it over. "For this."

Garrett caught the phone, stared at it, and looked back at his brother. "For what?"

Bridger's eyebrows raised in delight. "Had the camera mounted on my dash. Video rolling the whole damn time."

Garrett pulled up the camera feature and played what it had recorded, which included every agonizing frame of the incident. From the rifle-toting guards chasing Asadi to Tom Holloway shooting Grizz. It also captured the ruthless three-man attack on his unconscious brother. Not a judge in the world could deny that Talon endangered the life of a child, murdered that poor colt, and had beaten Bridger severely and unnecessarily.

Garrett looked up to find his brother's swollen face in a full smile. "*Damn*, Bridger, if I'd have known whooping your ass would save the day, I'd have been whooping it for years."

"Think we need to set up another meeting with Holloway. This one on our terms. They can get their asses off our property, or we send that video to every news outlet in the country."

Garrett nodded, feeling positive for the first time in a while. "That'll get us broad public support, but we'll need buy-in from locals, the ones losing money. We need photos of the damage to the ranch. Proof that they're wasting water. We need to show all of it to make our case that what happened today wasn't just an isolated incident. We've got to show that Talon's image as 'savior of our community' is all just a farce. They're destroying it."

The only thing worse than trenching through the gravesite of a beloved local hero nurse was wasting water and bulldozing a grove of full-grown trees. In a land once known as the Great American Desert that was a sin of the blackest sort. For all the stereotypes of environmentally dispassionate Texans, the ones who called the High Plains home could hug a tree with the best of them.

To drive the final nail in Talon's coffin, Garrett needed visual proof of the wanton destruction taking place on the ranch, proof of the company's hypocrisy. But as persona non grata on his own property, he was going to need help. And the one to do it was the man who'd done all the damage in the first place. It was time to pay a visit to Ray Smitty.

27

Smitty knew it was bad when Garrett wanted to meet in person. In the run-up to the operation to capture Emilio Garza they'd had plenty of backroad secret meetings, never once discussing those details over the phone. Smitty had no idea who could possibly be listening, only that the DEA special agent took operational security damn seriously. Of course, this meeting had nothing to do with the cartel and everything to do with his dozer work on the ranch.

They had met at this location a few times before, a dried out old frac pit about a mile or so off the highway. Garrett claimed it was halfway between the two of them, but it sure didn't feel that way. He'd have argued but Smitty was in enough hot water already.

Smitty glanced over at Savanah who was sitting beside him in the truck, opened the door and hopped out. Turning back to his daughter, he ginned up a big smile. "Just gotta talk a little business with a friend of mine. Back in a jiffy."

Savanah looked skeptical about the whole deal, but she didn't argue. It'd been a blessing to have her along for the ride. Garrett might be pissed off at him, but he wouldn't hit a man with his kid there watching. At least Smitty sure as hell hoped not.

"Well, hello there, Garrett! I was hoping we'd get a chance to talk."

Garrett didn't look amused as he jumped out of the big black GMC and marched toward Smitty. In fact, he looked like he *was* ready to punch someone. Even if a kid was watching. Stopping dead in his tracks, Smitty cringed in anticipation of a beating. But when no fists came flying, he opened his eyes to find Garrett neither mad nor happy. Just somewhere in between.

"I'm not going to hit you, Ray. I know you were just following orders."

Smitty sighed. "Look, I'm really sorry about all that. They just told me to knock down them trees. I didn't know nothing about your mama's grave. Because you gotta believe—"

"Oh, I know." Garrett pushed the air. "Even *you* wouldn't sink that low."

The old Smitty might've bristled, but the new one took the insult on the chin. Better that than a fist. "It was an honest mistake, Garrett. Really. Nobody knew nothing about it."

"Yeah, well that's the problem. Talon is in such a hurry to dig that they didn't bother to ask us those kinds of questions. All this could've been avoided."

"For what it's worth, we fenced off that area now. Saw to it myself. Nobody's gonna get to her resting place now. I promise."

"Resting place? What kind of place is that to rest?" Garrett shook his head. "And how are we supposed to visit her if it's barricaded? Not a day's gone by that my dad hasn't been out there since the day she was buried. That old man may have the temperament of a badger but he's loyal as a Labrador. He won't be kept out of there for long."

"I don't know what to say." Smitty felt low, even if he wasn't entirely to blame for what happened. "What can be done about it now?"

"What can be done is the mining operation can be moved and the land restored. That's what can be done. But I need your help to do it."

"*My* help?" Smitty's pulse raced. "They won't listen to me. I ain't nothing but a hand to them folks. They'll cut me loose for even mentioning it. Made that clear right after it happened."

"Look, I don't need you to talk to them or anyone else. I just want some good pictures of the damage to the gravesite and the trees you knocked down. Maybe get a look at my water wells. See how much they're pumping out."

"If I do that, Garrett, they'll drop me like a hot tater. Photos get out and I'll get the blame. I can't lose this job."

"I don't want you to lose your job. I don't want anyone to lose their jobs. But Talon's up to no good and I've got to prove that."

A beat passed as Smitty thought on the words *up to no good*. Ever since he got shoved against the wall in the back office, he'd suspected the same. He started to say that but held back. More important than Garrett's request was Crystal's latest threat. *Don't screw this up. Or else.*

"You know something, Ray." Garrett's eyes bore into him. "What is it?"

Smitty had been involved in enough shady dealings over the course of his life to know when one was going down. "Well, maybe I saw something. I don't know."

Garrett took a couple of steps forward. His face was less angry now and more pleading. "Look, it's not just about the land anymore. They came after Asadi. Beat up Bridger and killed one of our horses. These people are out of control and need to be dealt with."

Killed a damn horse?

Growing up, his foster family kept a couple of swayback pasture ornaments around. The old mares were about two steps away from glue but that never bothered him. When he had no friends, the horses had been there. They were the only bright stars in a childhood of heartache and abandonment.

Smitty knew that if he lost his new job Crystal would kill him. But he also knew that this was an opportunity to make things right. He didn't know if you could buy your soul back from the devil, but if there was ever a goal worth the effort, skirting perdition was at the top of the list.

Smitty leaned in close, so Savanah couldn't hear him since the window was down. "Garrett, I think you're right. Not everything with Talon is on the up and up."

"Okay." Garrett gave a nod and lowered his own voice too. "What's going on?"

"No idea. But they've got some secrets, that's for sure." Smitty gave a quick glance at Savanah who was still staring daggers at him. "Whatever they're doing it's being kept in their main office on the ranch. I saw it the morning I first got there."

Garrett perked up. "Saw what exactly?"

Smitty shrugged. "Don't know. Something. A bunch of maps and papers. Just know they didn't want me seeing what they got there. That's for sure."

Garrett seemed to think hard on it. "Can you take a trip out there with me? Show me where you saw it go down."

Relieved he had an excuse to turn Garrett down, Smitty glanced back at Savanah. "Well, I'd like to help, but I've got my daughter to look after while her mama's at work. And have to be out at the dig site early in the morning. So, unfortunately, no can do, amigo."

Garrett leaned left, peered around Smitty, and stared at Savanah. "That's no problem, Ray. I can help you out with your little girl."

Smitty didn't like the slow smile that crept up on Garrett's face. It was the same one as when he'd told him about his pipeline ruse and Emilio Garza, the same one that nearly got him killed. And it was the very same one that just might lead to Talon completing the job that the Guatemalan mercenaries never got to finish.

28

Asadi sat across from Savanah Smitty at Bridger's dining room table, eating pizza, drinking Dr Pepper, and wondering what on earth he was supposed to say. The girl didn't look happy. Not one bit. But Garrett had told him she was just a little shy and would warm up to him once they found something in common. Apparently, junk food wasn't it.

Savanah had plopped down a sleeping bag and a ratty old stuffed teddy bear by the door when she first walked inside. They were the same items the twins brought with them for sleepovers out at the ranch, which gave Asadi good reason to be concerned. He wasn't the best at making friends because of his broken English. There was always an awkward pause in his answers, and he usually said something wrong.

While Garrett's and Savanah's fathers were *taking care of some business*, which Asadi had learned over the past few months was code for *not going to get the truth*, he pondered what they were up to, assuming it had something to do with what happened at the ranch. Truth be told, Asadi had hoped for a little time alone. He had shed quite a few tears over the loss of his colt, his *partner*, a reaction Garrett and Butch assured him was quite okay.

Asadi knew that his family would think no less of him for crying, but he also knew the value they placed on toughness. And he wanted so much to prove his emotional strength. More importantly, he wanted to prove it to their surprise visitor with the blue eyes and curly brown hair. Savanah seemed not to care what others thought, a trait that Asadi really admired.

He, however, always worried about the opinion of others, mostly Garrett and Butch, which usually had something to do with training horses or chores on the ranch. But sometimes Bridger's daughters, Sophie and Chloe, were the culprits. The twins had been kind and caring, treating him like a little brother. They'd even worked hard to make sure he was cool, keeping him fashionable and teaching him all the right things to do and say.

Asadi had made tremendous strides since moving to Texas, but he still had a long way to go. Middle school was only two weeks away and there was much to learn. With Sophie and Chloe moving on to high school, he was starting to panic about who would he sit with at lunch? And what would he wear on the first day?

The twins assured him both were a really big deal, but the seating arrangment was the most important. Your *entire* future, they'd said, depends on the table where you sit. Asadi couldn't imagine how that was possible but took their words to heart. The girls were his guardian angels and had been since the moment they met. They'd yet to steer him wrong.

While Savanah wasn't too friendly, she sure was pretty. *Real pretty.* She was maybe even as beautiful as the twins, and that was saying a lot. Ray's daughter had yet to communicate, unless you counted sighs and eyerolls, which were getting more frequent by the moment. Thankfully, Butch ambled over from the living room to check on them and break the awkward silence.

Butch looked down at Savanah's half-eaten slice. "I've seen boll weevils make a bigger dent than that. Not a pizza fan, huh?"

Savanah stared at it too. "It'll do, I guess."

Butch shrugged. "Well, I got you a cheese. Figured every kid likes a cheese."

She mumbled under her breath, "Ought to keep on figuring, old man."

Butch wore the same confused look he did whenever he had a conversation with their neighbor Kate. "Alright, then." He turned to Asadi looking defeated. "With Bridger in his condition and the girls still on the way back from Corpus, I reckon he'd be mighty grateful if you helped out with some of Sophie and Chloe's chores. Think you could manage that?"

Thank God! Never happier to take his leave, Asadi donned his cowboy hat, popped up from the table, and bolted for the door. He was almost home free when Butch cleared his throat. "You forget something, sonny?"

Asadi stopped and turned slowly, thinking how close he'd been to escaping Savanah's silent wrath. He didn't say anything back, just shook his head vigorously and looked to Savanah, who was no longer staring dead-eyed at the pizza, but glaring at him.

Asadi mustered up his kindest smile. "You want, go with me, feed steers?"

A couple of seconds passed while Savanah stared him down, then she tossed her slice on the plate and rose. "Why not? Curious to see if they eat any better than this."

As she marched to the door, Asadi glanced up at Butch, who just scratched his head and shuffled back to the living room. His favorite hunting show, *Bone Collector*, was paused on the screen of the sixty-five-inch television mounted to the wall.

Asadi crossed the yard out to the barn out back with Savanah in tow. The twins' hungry Angus show steers, Booger and Swole, were already waiting by the fence. Savanah stepped up to the behemoth bovines and took turns scratching each on the nose. The fact that she at least liked animals gave Asadi hope. He walked up beside her and greeted them himself.

Asadi turned to her as she scratched Swole's big forehead. "You have animal too?"

It took her a second to answer. "Not like this." She cut her eyes at him. "I mean, we've got dogs where I live. But most you don't touch unless you gotta whup-up on 'em or something."

He stared at her curiously. "Why you want, *whup-up* on dog?"

Savanah seemed a bit defensive. "It's not that I *want* to, necessarily. It's just some of the dogs where we live are a bit mangy."

"Mangy?" Asadi asked.

"You know, *nasty*," Savanah clarified. "And they'll try to jump in the car and get at your food when you ain't looking." She seemed lost in the moment. "I mean, I don't really mind it too bad. Kind of like their company when I go down to the river, because there ain't really no other kids around. But Mama's got a big issue with them eating out of the garbage."

Asadi looked at her in disgust. "The kids? They eat the garbage?"

For the first time, Savanah let out a chuckle. "No, silly. I'm talking about the dogs. One choked on a wine cork once and barfed it up on the couch."

Asadi's growing disgust must have registered in an even bigger way. She playfully whacked his arm. "Oh, it's not that bad. It cleaned right up the next day."

Wanting to change the subject, Asadi brought the conversation back to the steers. "No got pets like these?"

She registered her own look of disgust. "Daddy says showing livestock is rich man's game. Says it's all rigged. Rich get richer and all that."

Asadi didn't know if that was true, but he did know there was a lot of money involved. He remembered hearing that the grand champion steer from a show in Houston had once brought in well over half a million dollars. Knowing what could be made, he was tempted to give it a try. But Garrett had not been supportive either. At least he and Savanah had that in common.

Saying without really thinking, Asadi announced, "I like the horses best."

Her face brightened again. "Got any we can saddle up?"

On a roll now, Asadi kept it going. "Horses out at ranch. We got best. Quarter Horses." He pronounced the word *Quarter* slowly to make sure she understood the distinction.

"I know what Quarter Horses are," Savanah shot back. "I'm not an idiot."

"They the best," he said again proudly. Asadi didn't really know if that was true, but he'd heard Butch say it so many times that he'd come to believe it.

Savanah's demeanor softened. "Daddy says when we move out to the country, we can get some horses too." She looked embarrassed. "Maybe not *the best*, but at least ones we can ride."

Asadi felt a little bad that he'd made that comment, not wanting her to think he was boasting, or even worse, feel bad because she couldn't afford them. He would've tried to fix it, but his English was not quite good enough yet and would probably make it worse. Time for another subject change. "You go to school?"

Wrong subject. Asadi got the eyeroll again.

"Unfortunately" was all she said.

"You not like?"

"Oh, just wait. You'll see." Savanah turned to him, looking a little sad. "Some of the kids are alright. But then you got the ones who'll make fun of you."

"Make fun?" Asadi couldn't believe what he was hearing. The twins' friends had all been so kind and welcoming. "Why make fun?"

"All sorts of reasons. The way you dress. Way you talk. You name it. They'll find something wrong. You can count on that."

Asadi's heart sank. He had been worried about wearing the right thing but knew Sophie and Chloe could help him. The way he talked was another matter. He had not even thought about that problem. If a girl as pretty as Savanah could get made fun of, there was little hope for him. Plus, she dressed so cool. Since she walked through the front door, he'd been jealous of her T-shirt with the hilarious cartoon worm sporting the droopy mustache and sombrero.

Before he could ask where she got it, Savanah had already moved on. "Well, these big sumbitches look hungry." She gave Booger a scratch on the nose. "We're supposed to pour some feed, ain't we?"

Thankful for the reminder, Asadi smiled. Although her warnings about school made him nervous, he valued the advice. If the way you talk was that big of a deal, he'd have to work extra hard. From here on, he'd pay close attention to everything Savanah said, and more importantly, the way she said it. With only a couple of weeks left, he had to make every moment count.

29

Garrett lay prone in what was once beautiful prairie grassland now churned into upturned soil, a place he no longer recognized, like some Hollywood set for a movie about World War I. Even if he could get this no-man's-land back from Talon, restoring the ranch back to its original beauty would take an act of God.

Gazing beyond the razor wire barricade around the mining operation, Garrett monitored the grounds to make sure they were alone. The West Texas sun was taking its sweet time dipping below the horizon, so long that Smitty dozed off and was starting to snore. With the nightfall darkness providing just enough cover for their mission, Garrett roused his partner with a nudge.

"Get up, Ray. Time to go." Garrett felt Smitty shudder as he came back to life. "For someone who fought the idea of sneaking in here tooth and nail, you seem awfully at ease. Anybody this comfortable snoozing before a B and E is too damn lax for their own good."

"I ain't comfortable or lax," Smitty argued. "I get too still for too long, I just fall right to sleep. Doctor says I got the heartrate of a possum. It's a medical condition, you know."

Garrett studied Smitty, who didn't appear to be joking. "*Possum heart*, huh?" A pause and a chuckle. "Yeah, think I read about that in a medical journal somewhere."

Garrett grabbed Smitty by the sleeve, yanked him up, and sprinted toward the fence. He checked to confirm his partner was behind him, then hit the gap beneath the razor wire, careful to suck in and make himself as small as possible. Smitty was no less cautious, easing underneath it in slow-motion, a careful eye on the bladed coils above.

Once inside the perimeter, Garrett surveyed the Talon compound, which included a half-dozen doublewide mobile offices about forty yards ahead. Heavy machinery and fleet vehicles were parked in neat rows around the back. But for the glow of halogens in the caliche parking lot, there was little light other than what was provided by the stars.

Garrett turned to Smitty who had just crawled up beside him. "Which trailer has the documents and maps?"

Smitty pointed to the second one on the left. "That one. Back office. Why?"

"Think I'm going to need to see what these guys are hiding."

Smitty let loose a string of profanities under his breath. "*Why?* You already got the video Bridger took. And we can read the meters on the wells to see how much water they're wasting. Between all that and photos of the busted-up gravesite that should be all you need."

"That's just bad publicity. It'll only slow them down. To get their asses off this place for good, I'll need something better. Something illegal."

"What if it's nothing and we get caught?"

Garrett thought for a moment. Smitty *was* prone to exaggeration. But something was off about Talon. Something big. If there was hard evidence that could take them down, then it was worth the risk. He pulled his wrist to his face and checked the glowing hands on his watch.

"Look, Ray, we'll be in an' outta there in five minutes."

"What do you need me for?"

"You saw where they put the maps, right?"

Smitty looked like he was going to be sick. "Yeah, so what."

"Then I won't waste a bunch of time looking all over the place." Garrett pointed ahead. "Nobody's even here. It'll be quiet until morning."

Smitty rose and studied the grounds. "In and out? You promise?"

Garrett jumped up, grabbed Smitty by the sleeve, and dragged him along in a sprint to the portable office. At the side of the building, he threw his back against the wall and eased to the corner. He peered around, saw no one, and dashed to the front door. The quiet of the night was only shattered by two gravelly barks from Smitty, battling it out with his smoker's cough.

Garrett slipped on a pair of leather work gloves and tried the front door. Finding it locked as suspected, he pulled the stowed rubber mallet from his Mystery Ranch backpack, raised the tool, and brought it down with a jab. It was so swift that half the doorknob busted off with a *ping* and shot across the deck. Garrett turned the hammer around, jammed the handle in the hole and gave it a pop. The rest of the apparatus ejected from the back and banged on the floor inside.

"Why'd you do that?" Smitty grimaced. "Now they'll know we been here for sure."

That was true, but Garrett didn't care. If they found something good, it wouldn't matter anyhow. Talon would have a helluva lot bigger fish to fry. Garrett stepped inside and kicked the other half of the doorknob out of the way. With Smitty behind him, he pulled the door shut and clicked on a red-lens flashlight.

Smitty took the lead, moved to the back-office door, and used his sleeve to cover his hand before giving the knob a try. He'd barely gotten a verdict when Garrett whacked it with the mallet and followed up with a front kick that crashed the door inward. Smitty made a beeline to a cabinet at the back of the room.

Garrett handed off the flashlight, reached to his belt, and unsheathed the Moore Maker Tactical Clip Point knife from its nylon scabbard. A quick flip of the blade downward and he jammed it into the space between the cabinet door and the opening. A couple sharp taps to the handle and the lock popped open.

Smitty shook his head. "And you call me a criminal."

Garrett took off his pack, opened it wide and shoved every document he could from the cabinet into it. There were files, maps, and spreadsheets. Nothing that looked incriminating as far as the eye could tell but there was no time to study it. He had just gotten the last file into his bag when headlights flashed across the wall.

Ducking as he moved to the front window, Garrett peered over the window's edge to find a white SUV and a Talon pickup swinging into parking spots right out front of the trailer.

A near paralyzed Smitty asked in a voice just above a whisper, "Now what?"

Good question. At the sound of slamming vehicle doors, Garrett moved across the room, keeping his head low until he reached the back window. Gliding up with his shoulder to the wall, he flicked the latch open and slid the pane up at a painfully slow pace. Turning back to the front window, Garrett watched as four silhouettes crossed the parking lot, heading to the front door. He swore he heard a woman's voice among them.

Smitty hopped onto the windowsill, hung over the side, and dropped to the ground with a louder thud than Garrett liked. But given the rising voices and fast beat of footsteps down the hall, the jig was up anyhow.

Garrett ducked under the window and hurled himself outside. Landing with his own clunk, he scrambled to his feet and sprinted after Smitty, who was already nearing the fence. With angry shouting and heavy footsteps close behind, Garrett turned on the afterburners, legs pumping like pistons, as he fought to catch up.

With his pursuers bearing down on him, he lost sight of Smitty, who dove in and burrowed through to the other side. Garrett slowed his speed with the glinting razor wire only ten yards ahead. He had just slowed his pace when the supersonic *snap* of a bullet zoomed overhead. A closer second sent him ducking and a third headfirst into the hole.

Halfway into the burrow, a burst of light filled the tiny cave, and a *crack-crack-crack* of pistol fire from behind. With freedom in sight, Garrett's spirits rose until his pants leg caught. He kicked like a mule and dug in his elbows, but the freshly churned soil gave him no traction.

His hopes were nearly dashed until Smitty's bony hand reached down and clutched onto his sleeve. Another jerking yank came from behind but Garrett's partner in crime held on tight. With a solid back kick as Smitty yanked, the tug-of-war was over and Garrett broke free. He lunged, scrabbled to his feet, and tore after Smitty, who was a good twenty yards ahead.

Jogging back to his truck on the backside of the ranch, Garrett didn't worry about getting caught, or even gunfire that echoed from behind. He was worried what would happen if his gamble didn't pay off. Whatever he'd stuffed into his bag better amount to something huge. If not, he had just gotten himself into a helluva lot more trouble than he was already in.

PART THREE

If you're scared of wolves,

don't go into the woods.

—Russian Proverb

30

Smitty sat in the passenger seat of Garrett's GMC Sierra staring out into the nighttime nothingness of the flat rolling plains. He couldn't help but wonder how he kept managing to heap one bad decision on top of another. Thinking back on it now, part of him wished he would've died down in Mexico, or at least pretended he'd died. Things were about to get real bad for him and his family.

Garrett jammed the accelerator as they peeled off the county road and launched onto the highway back to Canadian. "You're awfully quiet." He glanced over. "What's going on?"

Smitty let out a sigh. "What's going on is that I'm going to lose this job at minimum, and maybe go back to jail."

"Not gonna happen, Ray. They didn't see you. If anyone should be worried, it's me."

Smitty turned from the window to Garrett. "*Well*, are you?"

"Nope." Garrett shook it off. "Not at all. Long as we got something we can use, we're in the clear." He quickly corrected himself. "I mean, *I'm* in the clear. They don't even know we're acquainted. You're safe, man. Trust me."

Smitty wasn't buying it. He could see the worry etched on Garrett's face. "I can't mess this up or it'll be the last straw with Crystal. I'm gonna lose my family and a whole lot worse."

"Nothing's messed up. I promise. Just show up tomorrow like always and nobody will be the wiser." Garrett turned to Smitty, clearly to drive home the point. "But if you miss work, someone's going to come looking for you. And they'll have lots of questions. Understand?"

Smitty nodded, even though Garrett had already turned back to the road. He was to the point of not caring whether he lived or died. Crystal had put up with enough of his mistakes and he doubted she'd put up with any more. Garrett's optimism wasn't buying him any more chances.

Smitty patted the pack full of documents. "What are you going to do with this?"

"After I drop you off, I'm going over to the hospital to meet with Bridger."

"Visiting hours are over," Smitty countered.

"They're going to have to make an exception. My guess is that even if Talon can't prove who broke into their office, they'll point the sheriff in my direction. That means, if we're going to find something, it'd better be fast."

"And you think Bridger will figure it out?"

Garrett gave a nod. "He's pretty much a mineral rights expert on top of being a lawyer. If anybody can find a way to shut down Talon, it'll be him."

Realizing what this could mean, Smitty turned and asked with venom, "So, you don't just want to shut down the operation on your place, you want the whole damn company down." When Garrett didn't answer immediately, Smitty filled the void. "Why did I even help you then? Whole time I was just putting myself out of a job."

"It's not that bad, Ray. There's plenty of jobs out there."

"Not for a guy like me there ain't." Smitty let out another sigh.

"Man, this was going to get us out of that RV park and on a piece of land of our own. That was the dream."

A few seconds passed until Garrett finally spoke. "Yeah, I guess I didn't think about all that." He turned again to Smitty looking genuinely concerned. "If this Talon deal falls through, you and your family will be taken care of. I promise I'll help you find something."

Suddenly, Smitty felt a sense of relief. A family like the Kohls vouching for you meant something. Even for a guy like him. "Oh yeah, like what?"

Garrett looked a bit hesitant. "Well, with Asadi heading to school in a few weeks and me going back to the DEA field office in Amarillo, we're going to need some help on the ranch. If you can drive a dozer, I'm *assuming* you can drive a tractor."

"Better believe it! That's what I learned on." Smitty tried hard to hide his excitement but found it nearly impossible. "My first job out of high school was cutting grass on the highway. And did some silage work too for a dairy down in Hereford after that."

Garrett nodded, although he still looked reluctant. "Sounds like you got some skills then."

"Can you match what Talon's paying?"

Garrett winced. "Unfortunately, I doubt that."

"What about medical and retirement?"

Garrett shook his head. "Definitely can't do any of that. At least not right now with that debt I'm in with the land bought and the new irrigation system."

Smitty was feeling low again when Garrett offered up something even better.

"But you said you wanted a place in the country, right?"

Smitty turned and smiled. "Like I said, that's our dream."

"Well, we got a little hunting cabin on the back side of the ranch."

Garrett wore a sheepish smile. "I mean . . . it's pretty basic. Just a deer camp, really. But it wouldn't take much to get the place up to snuff. And of course, there's the horses."

Smitty's curiosity was further piqued. "*Horses?*"

"Riding. Grooming. You got any experience with that?"

"Better believe I do." Smitty threw out his hand to lock in the deal. "Garrett, I promise, I won't let you down."

"Hold on. Hold on." Garrett laughed. "We're still in the discussion phase." He shook Smitty's hand anyhow, probably to be polite. "But I like your enthusiasm."

"I got that and a whole lot more. I know farming. Can help you tend to that alfalfa hay you got out there. You won't be disappointed, I swear it."

Garrett pulled his hand back and placed it on the steering wheel. "Alright, alright, we'll see where all this goes." His face turned gloomy again as he patted the pack beside him. "Unless we find a miracle here somewhere among these papers, there won't be much of a ranch at all."

For the first time in a long time, Smitty was starting to feel like his luck had turned. He even felt better than when he got the offer from Talon. Working on the Kohl Ranch wouldn't just be a job. It'd be a way of life. Every dream he had for his family was on that land. And the thing to make that dream a reality might be sitting in the backpack right beside him.

31

Asadi lay in bed, staring up at the ceiling, unable to sleep. He was tired for sure, borderline exhausted, having cried until he could cry no more over Grizz. The murder of his sweet innocent colt unlocked feelings he'd not felt since the slaughter of his own family in Afghanistan, leaving him to wonder if he should ever have let his guard down all.

He remembered his earliest moments with Grizz. From feeding him sugar cubes to slipping a hackamore over his nose for the very first time. Every moment was memorable because every moment was special. Grizz wasn't just any colt. He was *his* colt. And as Butch had told him the other day, Grizz was his partner.

Love was a dangerous thing—lost in the blink of an eye. And Asadi just prayed it would never happen again.

Forcing himself to think happier thoughts, Asadi went from brokenhearted to his heart racing. He'd seen lots of beautiful girls since arriving in Texas. Bridger's twin daughters, Sophie and Chloe, were the prettiest he'd ever met. But the twins were like his sisters now, so that didn't count. Savanah was different from the other kids he'd met.

Although she hid her insecurity under a layer of orneriness, Asadi knew she was timid, like a skittish colt. And he knew that because he felt the exact same way. Asadi loved his new life in America, but there had been one big challenge after the next. New to the culture, it seemed there was always a test before him. Some he had passed. Some he had failed.

His worst fiasco yet was peeing in front of everyone in the Dairy Queen parking lot. Nobody was mad about it. In fact, everyone just laughed, chalking it up to him growing up in a small village. But what frustrated him was that his upbringing wasn't the reason he did it. He had seen Garrett and Butch do it out on the ranch about a million times before and nobody had a problem. There was so much to learn and so little time to learn it.

In his prayers, Asadi always focused on Garrett and Butch, but tonight, his words were for his new friend Savanah. Aloud, he spoke to his mother up in Heaven in their native tongue, "Mama, I don't need help not to be sad anymore."

Asadi felt a little guilty, worried that it might hurt her feelings. But Garrett told him that she was content with her life and was probably friends with his own mother, who had died also when he and Bridger were just kids.

"I'm happy here, Mama. So you don't have to worry about me. I'm okay. The ranch is my new home and I love it."

Asadi wanted her to hear some good news so she wouldn't worry. But didn't want her to think he was happier now than he was with her. It was a careful balance. Garrett had also told him God knows our hearts, so we can't really hide anything. He figured the rules probably applied to her as well, but who really knew. Better play it safe.

"Mama, I'm nervous about school, about the way I talk, where to sit, and fitting in." Asadi wondered if those things were too trivial to bother people up in Heaven. He'd have to ask Garrett. "But if you can help me to be ready for it all that would really help."

Garrett told him if you're asking something from God, then

it couldn't hurt to end on a note of gratitude. "And thank you for bringing Savanah, a new best friend when I needed one."

With that off his chest, Asadi closed his eyes, feeling at peace. And with a smile he ended the prayer in the way Butch ended all of his own. "And a big *amen* to that."

32

Kim boarded the Cessna Citation a little before midnight and took off shortly after. The random memory of her first trip on one of the CIA's jets came to mind. The jitters. The excitement. The feeling of importance. It was the embodiment of knowing she'd arrived in her career. But as Kim sat there in silence, an important truth rose from somewhere deep within. It was only a mode of transport, a way of getting around. And really nothing more than that.

In retrospect, she wished she would have flown commercial—just to hear some voices, even if they weren't speaking to her. She longed for conversation—laughter—anything other than the whine of those twin jet engines—the loneliest sound in the world.

Sinking into a pit of her own making, Kim thought back to her meeting with Contreras in the CIA cafeteria. There was something about his demeanor that didn't sit quite right. The fact that the undaunted former SEAL was so worried about Garrett's safety made her wonder if she was playing with fire. Kim had just pulled up her laptop to do some more research when she got the call from her boss, Bill Watson. She had only texted him her last-minute plans, in part because she knew he was asleep, but more importantly because she thought he might say no.

Kim answered and hit the speaker button. "Hey Bill! Hope I didn't wake you."

"Had to let the dog out and saw the message." Bill cleared his throat, which made him sound only slightly less groggy. "You're going to see Garrett? Everything okay?"

"Yeah, everything's fine." Since they were on an open phone line, Kim was careful to speak in vague generalities. "Remember the conversation we had about Talon Corporation?"

Another pause as he yawned. "What does that have to do with Kohl?"

Wanting to leave Contreras out of this she fibbed, "Nothing really. It's just that I looked into it after we spoke and found out they might be dirty. And since they have an active dig site on Garrett's ranch, I thought I would go have a look and see what I can find out."

"What do you mean dirty? Dirty how?"

"Dirty corrupt, maybe. I don't know. That's why I'm flying down."

"Oh." Bill cleared his throat again and ginned up a more serious tone. "Kind of got the impression from the seventh floor that this was a rubberstamp sort of deal. I'd leave it alone."

Kim stared at her phone in disbelief. "Since when do we rubberstamp anything when it comes to our country's security?"

"That's not what I said."

"Then what *are* you saying?" Kim shot back.

"I'm saying Talon is a multibillion-dollar company with extremely powerful political ties. Ties with a direct line to our director. Our *boss*. Understand?"

Kim fumed at the thought that this all went back to Bill's opportunity to move on to greener pastures. Guys who rock the political boat don't get appointments to the National Security Council. She was about to call him on it when he called her out first.

"Kim, you haven't told anyone about this, have you?"

"No. Not yet," she lied.

Of course, she had Contreras beating the bushes for everything he could find. But Bill wouldn't know that. In the world of intel sources, they dipped from two different personal contacts: for her boss, political operatives on Capitol Hill with ties to powerful multinational corporations; for Kim, a former Navy SEAL with sources in special operations all over the world.

"Good. Keep this quiet." Bill sounded less pissed and more relieved. "Aside from upsetting a lot of people around here for no reason, you know the rules. I can't have you doing some investigation on U.S. soil."

"Well, that's where Garrett comes in. I'll have a federal law enforcement chaperone along with me. It's all on the up and up."

Check and mate.

Bill groaned before speaking. "Just don't do anything before talking to me first. And I mean every step of the way, Manning. This can get ugly in a hurry."

Kim wanted to call him out on the spot for being more of a political hack than an intelligence officer but refrained. She got what she wanted and that was good enough.

"You have my word, Bill. We find out anything, you're my first phone call."

She was hoping that would end the discussion when Bill added, almost as an afterthought, "While you're down there, go ahead and pick up Asadi and bring him up here." He cleared his throat again. "Longer he stays with Kohl, the harder it's going to be to separate them. Just rip off the Band-Aid. Easier that way."

Kim was winding up for rebuttal when Bill hung up. Her temporary joy over leaping the Talon hurdle was trumped by a new major one involving Garrett and Asadi. She'd done a lot of unpleasant things in her career but nothing like this. It would emotionally demolish them.

Devastated at the image in her mind of having to rip Asadi from Garrett's arms, she closed her laptop, and leaned back in her seat. The burn of new forming tears was just beginning when the phone rang again. Her pulse was racing at the thought that Bill had reconsidered when she saw it was Contreras.

Perking up a little at the prospect of some juicy intel, she answered with some hope in her voice. "Tell me something good, Mario."

"Got something." Contreras chuckled. "Not sure if it's *good*."

Kim brushed a tear from her cheek with a knuckle and cleared her throat to get the frog out. "Give it to me anyway."

"Hit up a buddy of mine over at TigerSwan. Former team guy who did some contract security work over in Ukraine a few years back. Said the guy who was behind the Wagner ops in Africa was a dude named Alexi Orlov. He came up in the GRU after serving with Alpha Group, smoking Chechens back in the day. Made it sound like he's a real pipe hitter."

Just great. While it was worrisome enough that a former Russian military intelligence officer might be involved, his ties to the country's elite counterterrorism unit known as Alpha Group was even more alarming. These highly skilled soldiers were hardened killers who used extortion, torture, and targeted assassinations as part of their repertoire of tactics.

Noteworthy Alpha Group lore includes kidnapping the family members of a terrorist group that took four Russian diplomats as hostages. When the radicals murdered a captive, Alpha operators severed a body part from one of their prisoners that most men preferred you didn't. It was delivered to the radicals with a not-so-subtle message— release our people or there's more to come. The diplomats were freed, and the Russians had little such trouble ever again.

While Kim admired Alpha Group's ruthlessness in dealing with terrorist thugs, she hated to think one of these guys might be operating in Texas near Garrett and Asadi. She shook her head in disbelief. "How has all this slipped under our radar?"

"I don't know, Kim. Maybe for the same reason as everywhere else in the world. All comes down to money."

Kim paused a second to think. "In developing countries, sure . . . I get it. But not here. Too many watchdogs."

Contreras chuckled again. "Watchdogs get lazy when their masters don't really care if they're watching. I mean . . . look at China. We know what they're up to and nobody in Washington gives a rat's ass. As long as the money flows in, it's *see no evil, hear no evil, speak no evil.* Until, of course, they take out a carrier group with hypersonic missiles. Then it will be the largest intelligence failure since 9/11. And then they'll say *we* didn't see it coming."

Contreras was right. The fact that it seemed impossible that Russians were carrying out a major operation on American soil made it even more likely because who'd believe it. Before September 11, 2001, who'd have thought you could start a war with boxcutters.

Had the lesson not been learned? If no one else was seeing what didn't want to be seen, then maybe she'd better take a harder look.

33

Garrett knew he shouldn't have put too much stock in Smitty's wild tale of forbidden back rooms and secret documents. Nearly four o'clock in the morning and he and Bridger hadn't found jack squat. There were reams' worth of mineral maps, environmental permits, and geological surveys but no evidence of anything other than a large-scale mining operation.

No corruption. No broken laws. And no smoking gun. Their B&E was a complete bust.

Of course, Smitty had only reported what he saw and nothing more. Garrett had only himself to blame. It was *he* who had hoped there to be more to the story. And in this hope, he'd jeopardized the future of a husband and father—a man who was genuinely trying to clean up his act and hold down a steady job.

Garrett had just finished going through a stack and was damn close to giving up when he saw his brother sit up straight in his hospital bed. "Find something?"

Bridger furrowed his brow. "Think maybe . . . I did."

Garrett stood and moved to the bed where Bridger had several stacks of reports, each highlighted in multiple fluorescent colors. "Just looks like you marked a bunch of minerals."

"Might be something to it." Bridger picked up a heavily marked-up spreadsheet and waggled it at Garrett. "Like I told you before, this Holloway guy is sharp. He's not going to leave anything incriminating lying around, even if it is under lock and key. So, after a first pass, I didn't find anything. Nobody would unless they knew exactly what they were looking for. So, I went back again and searched for anomalies."

In his eager anticipation, Garrett could hardly keep from yelling at his brother to get to the point. "So, what'd you find?"

"Nothing."

"Nothing?" Garrett repeated.

"Nothing irregular anyhow. Then I started to look for trends. Anything consistent. And the only thing consistent was the minerals they're focused on." Bridger raised the sheet with multiple items underscored in blue pen. "Yttrium. Terbium. We've got a lot of that out on the ranch, and so do a few other landowners who are all under the old Kaiser leases. It's pinpointed on these maps. Maps nobody had access to but Talon." He grinned wide. "Until now."

Garrett picked up the mineral list and studied it. "Have any idea what these are used for?"

Bridger held up his iPhone, tapped the screen. "Didn't until I typed them into my trusty friend Google and found a Congressional Research Service report. Says these minerals, along with quite a few others that are plentiful here, are critical to the Pentagon. Used in Predator drones. Tomahawk missiles. F-35 fighter jets." He swiped the screen. "And according to this *Forbes* article each jet carried about a half ton of these strategic elements, many of which are found on our place and on other Talon mining locations across the United States."

While this news didn't strike Garrett as particularly odd, it would explain why Talon operations had gone through so quickly and under the radar. If there were major U.S. security implications for this mining project, then there was nothing they could do to stop it.

It would also explain the secrecy, strong-arm tactics, and heavy-handed security personnel involved. The U.S. government could be downright draconian in dealing with its own citizens. When the government had decided to build the nearby Pantex nuclear weapons facility during World War II, they uprooted the farmers that had worked that land for generations.

Garrett, however, also remembered Ike's stories about mercenaries in Africa and Kim's revelation of Chinese mines guarded by the Taliban. "Anything about any foreign ties?"

"Interesting you mention that." Bridger picked up another stack of papers and held it up for Garrett, this one marked in neon green. "A company called Scepter Trading out of Dubai came up a few times. I looked it up and didn't find much. But I dug into a database I use running title searches and found a connection to a Russian company named Orlov Energy Consultants."

Garrett shrugged. "That supposed to ring a bell?"

"No, but this might." Bridger showed Garrett the Orlov website, which had on its masthead the same firebird emblem used by Talon. Even if far removed, a Russian company involved in importing American minerals vital to the U.S. defense industry was at the very least disturbing.

"Bridger, could you tell what their roles are in all this?"

"Best I can tell is that Scepter is an import company. So, I'm guessing it takes the handoff of at least some of the refined minerals mined by Talon."

"And Orlov?" Garrett pressed.

"Hard to say by looking at the website. Typical consultants, you know. Vague about what they do. But looks like they broker deals between energy companies and foreign government. Procurement issues. Legal counsel. That sort of thing." Bridger chuckled. "Basically, do what I do as a landman and oil scout but on an international scale."

Garrett wasn't an expert on U.S. export controls, but he knew enough to know that somebody in Washington had to be following this. And if they weren't, they should be. Of course, part of him was wondering if this was just a bureaucratic oversight. Russians were sneaky as hell.

Talon's intentions could have less to do with using the minerals and more about denying vital components to American armed forces. That technique was a major part of drug policy and exactly what Washington did in places like Latin America and Afghanistan.

While interdiction efforts, notably high-level busts with photos of mountains of cocaine and heroin, made headlines, drug enforcement efforts were more involved than that. Denying traffickers the resources they needed to grow, process, and move dope in the first place was the best way to stop it. That's why efforts to freeze bank accounts, disrupt weapons flows, and seize precursor chemicals were so important. It didn't stop the drug trade, but it did make it a hell of a lot more complicated, time-consuming, and expensive.

Could the Russians be taking a page from the DEA playbook? If they were, they'd be severely kneecapping the American military without ever even having to fire a shot. When future global hostilities arose, China would control the lion's share of these minerals with Russia hoarding the rest. It was more of a scorched-earth policy. If Moscow was preemptively depleting vital resources under the radar, their plan was brilliant.

Garrett immediately reached for his phone to call Kim but stopped short. It was already five a.m. in Virginia, which meant it could wait a couple of hours until she was awake. He looked to his brother with an even better idea than bothering her.

"Okay, Bridge, I'm thinking there's enough to wrap up Talon in so much bureaucratic red tape with Commerce, Treasury, Homeland

Security, and the State Department that they may just pack up and leave."

Bridger looked hopeful. "Think this'll get someone's attention?"

"If there's straight-up collusion with Russia, then it'll do more than that. We're looking at treason." The thought of nailing both Tom Holloway and Vicky Kaiser as enemies of the state was too good to be true. He'd settle for just getting them the hell off the ranch.

Bridger perked up, wincing as his swollen face stretched with his smile. "Well, at the very least, this should be enough to get an injunction against Talon and shut down operations."

Garrett gave a confident nod. "We've already got the video of them shooting the horse and kicking the crap out of you. That alone is a PR nightmare. But with the minerals and a Russian company involved, we have a scandal with national security implications. They're done."

"Well, we haven't proven anything yet," Bridger countered.

"Burden of proof lies on them to explain this Russian connection to the FBI, and everyone else who jumps on board to investigate."

"Don't know." Bridger grimaced. "Every politician from here to D.C. and every state in between with money riding on this will want to keep Talon digging. A lot to be lost if it stops."

"In Washington, there's *money*, and there's *influence*. Believe it or not, the latter is usually more important. The politician who rids America's heartland of the big bad Russians will get both the media spotlight and the resources to make things happen. For policy makers, always reaching for the next rung, this is manna straight from Heaven. Ticket to the job they *really* want. For some, that's president of the United States."

Bridger found his smile again. "By your way of thinking, an opportunity to grandstand trumps the almighty dollar." He shook his head and laughed. "Find that kind of hard to believe, but D.C.'s your world. And you know it a hell of a lot better than I do, thank God."

Garrett shook his head, imagining the firestorm to come. "Well, my hope is that it won't come to any of that."

Garrett would pass the evidence to Kim when the time was right and let the CIA pick Talon apart. But all that would take time—time they didn't have with dozers peeling the flesh of the earth and hauling off their precious topsoil. With Talon's team of lawyers, it could take weeks, if not longer, to halt operations. Every second they waited left their home marred forever.

Garrett picked up Bridger's phone and tossed it over. "Give Tom Holloway a call and let him know it's time to talk."

"Are you crazy?" Bridger looked mortified. "They'll suspect it was us who broke in."

"Trust me, Bridger, they already know that. I'd wait if we could, but there won't be anything left of the ranch if we don't move now." Garrett pointed to the phone. "Just send him the video and let him know we've got a whole lot worse on them. Holloway may be a snake oil salesman but he's no fool. He'll be ready for another meeting. And this one will be on our terms."

Garrett leaned back and closed his eyes, knowing it would be hours while Holloway scrambled for a response. Playing fast and loose with a few assumptions, Garrett just prayed like hell that he wasn't stirring up more trouble than he and his family could handle.

34

Asadi was beyond thrilled to be picked up by Tony Sanchez, who drove him and Savanah out to the ranch in the sheriff's SUV. With his broad shoulders and big pistol on his hip, the Stetson-wearing cowboy cop had the look and manner of a real Old West lawman. He would have been scary were it not for his ear to ear grin, a permanent fixture that always put Asadi at ease.

Judging by Savanah's wide eyes when she first walked into Butch's horse barn, she was impressed with what she saw. And Asadi couldn't have been more pleased. He was well on his way to securing a lunch buddy for the first day of school, which was a big reason why he wanted her to go along. If she liked the horses, then maybe she would like him too.

Pulling up on the saddle's cinch, Tony turned to Asadi. "Sure am sorry for all your family's been going through, but I've never had better duty in my life." He smiled wide before reaching up to the saddle horn and giving it a tug to make sure everything was snug.

Asadi didn't get the joke but assumed it meant he was enjoying his time out on the ranch. He thought he better clarify. "You miss ride horse?"

Tony looked up from beneath the big palomino named Ringo, where he was adjusting the stirrups. "When Garrett and I were your age, this is pretty much all we did." He chuckled to himself, as if remembering a fond memory. "Butch would tell us all the stuff we were doing wrong. And I mean *everything*. So, we'd come out here real early, just to be left alone."

This made no sense to Asadi. All he ever wanted was to ride with Butch and to soak up his knowledge on horses. "Why you not like him learn you?"

Tony shook his head. "Wasn't that at all. Butch taught me everything I know about cattle and horses. In fact, he was probably more of a dad to me than my own ever was." He moved to the front of the horse and adjusted the bridle. "My pop worked in the oil field down in the Permian, so I never saw him much. At least not until it was too late to really matter."

"But Butch was always there for me. Rough as a cob but always kind." Tony stopped what he was doing and looked over, his eyes a little sad. "Problem is that kids of a certain age don't want to be told what to do. And that was me and Garrett. Thought we didn't need any looking after. Just the way it is when you're young."

Asadi couldn't imagine feeling that way but nodded anyhow. "Bridger same?"

Tony chuckled again. "Bridger never liked to be told anything by anyone. Still doesn't. But he always had a lot more going for him than us. He had his cheerleader girlfriends and keg parties. We had hunting, horses, and the ranch. That was *our* fun. Our life. That's why this place means so much to Garrett. And me too, I guess."

Worried that he'd brought up a topic that made Tony sad, Asadi decided to change the subject. "You ready go ride?"

"I'm ready." Tony pointed to Savanah, who was still struggling with the cinch. "Why don't you check on your friend over there first? See if she could use a hand."

Asadi had learned Tony was the type to make sure everyone

looked after each other, particularly when it came to his own four children. There was one that Garrett had described as *special*, who never left the deputy's side. It was an odd description since the boy seemed no different than his siblings. But Tony doted on him the most.

Asadi unwrapped Skip's reins from the fence and led him over to the hitching post where Savanah was working up a good sweat. "Need help?"

Savanah made a half-turn, somewhere between startled and annoyed. "No, I got it."

Asadi eased up and grabbed the leather girth with her. "We both try."

She looked as though she might slug him, but then relented with a nod. Asadi gave a three count and they pulled up on the cinch together, got the girth to the right notch, and passed the latigo through the latigo keeper.

Savanah smiled wide at their accomplishment, letting her guard down for just a moment, but quickly found her scowl again. "I can do the rest myself."

Asadi led Skip a few feet away and watched from a distance. "Where you learn?"

"Some of it on YouTube." Reaching between her horse's front legs to snap the breast collar to the girth ring, Savanah displayed an air of confidence. "But Daddy taught me, mostly. His old boss used to have some good horses." She turned to him with an inquisitive look. "Ever heard of Preston Kaiser? That rich oilman who got himself killed in a helicopter crash."

Asadi was struggling for an answer when Tony rode over on Ringo wearing a big smile. "Oh yeah, we know *all* about that." The deputy's eyebrows raised. "Tragic accident."

Asadi guided the toe of his left boot into the stirrup and pulled himself into the saddle. He was wondering if Savanah could do the same when she made the same move with ease. With Savanah and Tony trailing behind, Asadi rode out to the back of the barn and looked up at the caprock cliffs behind them. His plan was to stay as far as he could from the mining operation.

Asadi aimed Skip toward the cutback oil-field road that would get them atop the ridge. He had just turned back to Tony, who was riding as tall as his smile was wide, when the deputy looked as if he'd smacked right into an invisible wall.

Tumbling backward off the saddle, Tony landed with a thud on the dusty ground. Startled and confused, Ringo shuffled left and circled around the deputy, who was curled into a ball and writhing in pain. The echoing *crack* of the first gunshot was followed by another.

Asadi looked to Savanah, whose face showed her terror. She worked to calm Moxy, but the chestnut mare pitched and bucked in a fit of panic. Asadi's more experienced buckskin, Skip, held still but his ears flicked forward on full alert. The gelding nickered and snorted as his eyes found the danger beside the corral.

Asadi had expected to see the beefy guards from the day before, but the two men in front of him were less thuggish and cleaner cut. Both were tall and muscular, one with blondish hair, a chiseled jawline, and icy blue eyes, the other with dark hair and olive skin.

Fearing Savanah would be thrown, Asadi spun Skip in a tight circle and raced toward her. He'd just leaned over and grabbed Moxy's bridle when he saw a white SUV easing down the caliche road about a quarter of a mile away.

35

Driving onto the Kohl Ranch, Kim replayed the conversation with her boss over and over in her head, wondering if she could have said or done something that would have talked him out of his order to retrieve Asadi. But the reality was that the seventh floor had made their decree and there was nothing she could do to stop it. Whether it was her or a team of heavily armed Ground Branch operators charged with the task, the boy was going to Pakistan and that was that.

As Kim pulled up to the house, she saw that the destruction to the ranch was far worse than she'd imagined. And her heart sank at the loss of its rugged untouched beauty. While she had the career that she'd set out to get, nothing nourished her soul like the trips down to West Texas. Sitting out on that back porch with Garrett, Asadi, and Butch gazing out over that endless horizon, she'd never felt so free, so able to leave behind everyone's expectations and just—*be*.

Kim had been so focused on the devastation caused by the mining project that she hadn't even noticed the scene playing out by the barn. What seemed to be a morning ride, an everyday occurrence on the Kohl Ranch, had turned into a horrifying nightmare, with a bloodied sheriff's deputy lying motionless on the ground. A turn of the steering wheel right left a break in the sunrise glare, revealing two armed men by the corral who had turned their aim on Asadi.

Jerking the wheel left, Kim aimed her Chevy Suburban at the attackers and mashed the accelerator to the floor. She ducked, just as two bullets *thwacked* the windshield and drilled the headrest behind her. The shooter on the right took a glancing hit from the fender, the other too slow, reaped the brunt of the grill.

Kim didn't hit the brakes, nor did she take her foot off the gas, even after her Chevy exploded through the oak beams of the corral that splintered inside the arena. It wasn't until her SUV slammed into the massive railroad tie fence post that it crashed to a halt in rhythm with the explosion of the air bag. Between the bone jarring crash, and the surge of adrenaline, Kim was light-headed and woozy, battling to stay upright as she swayed in her seat.

Groping at the side panel, Kim found the handle and yanked. With a bang on the door using her shoulder, a waft of dust flew inside the cab. She stumbled out coughing, fell to her knees, and looked to the front of the SUV, where the gunman she'd hit was trapped between her bumper and the fence.

Struggling to her feet, Kim choked, spat, coughed, as she wiped away the blood that was trickling from her broken nose. She made a pass over her torso with shaky hands to check for bullet wounds as she stumbled around in search of the kids.

Kim had just moved past the back bumper when quick footsteps moved in from behind. There was a flash of steel, a whack to the head, and she went face-first into the dirt. Ears ringing, eyes clogged with tears and dust, she tried to scrabble away but the attacker clutched a fistful of hair and yanked her back.

With the second blow that fell between her shoulder blades, Kim's vision went from a misty brown to hazy dark gray, until eventually everything was black, and she saw nothing at all.

36

Garrett had just driven past the Stumblin' Goat Saloon on his way to Bridger's office when the call came in from Lacey. He was tempted to kick it to voicemail, unprepared to field any questions but he answered against his better judgment. "Hey there!"

"Hey yourself! Never heard back from you last night."

Damn. There'd been five missed calls from her when he got back to the truck after his B&E. Garrett had meant to at least send her a text, but the whole getting shot at and escaping with a bag of Talon documents had consumed every bit of his mental and emotional energy.

"Really sorry about that, Lace. Ended up staying with Bridger at the hospital all night."

"*Hospital?*" There was genuine worry in her voice. "Is he okay?"

"Yeah, he'll be fine." Garrett checked his watch. He was supposed to meet Holloway in less than a minute. "We're just trying to work out the whole Talon problem, that's all."

"Well, that's why I wanted you to call me back. I had this crazy conversation with Victoria Kaiser yesterday."

"Why were you talking to her?"

The question came out way more accusatory than Garrett had intended and it registered in Lacey's voice. "Thought maybe she could do something about the ranch. She's Talon's head of acquisitions. A partner in the company. Worth a shot, right?"

There were so many thoughts running through Garrett's mind he didn't know where to start. At the forefront was the possibility that Vicky Kaiser was at the root of everything bad that was going on and she was the last person in the world that would help.

"I've already had a face-to-face with Vicky, and trust me, she has no intention of doing anything other than kicking us off our land."

"Yeah . . . about all that. What's going on? She said something about you and Bridger had attacked her guards."

"She said that *we* attacked them. Did she tell you why?"

"No, Garrett. That's why I called you half a dozen times last night. I was trying to find out."

"Where did you even see her?"

"Since I had applied for a job with Talon, I thought maybe I could use that as an opportunity to talk to her. So I went over to her house yesterday and—"

"A job?" Garrett knew she needed work and he couldn't blame her for looking wherever she could to find it. But approaching anyone in that murdering clan was a bridge too far. "After all they've done to my family. To *you*. How could you stoop so low?"

As soon as the words left his mouth, Garrett regretted it. He was tired. He was stressed. He was at the absolute end of his rope. But that was no reason to take it out on her. Lacey was just trying to help. He was about to launch his apology when she cut him off.

"I didn't just go to her for a job. I went to her to ask for a favor on your behalf. And by the way, I had to swallow what little pride I had left to do it. Vicky used to be one of my best friends. *Remember?*"

How could he forget? Something about her comment struck him wrong. Maybe it was a reminder that he'd never fit into that crowd.

Or maybe it just was asking someone with the last name *Kaiser* for help. Whatever it was, it fueled the misplaced building anger he was heaping on the woman he loved.

"I know she was your friend, Lacey. Long before you knew I even existed. Back when you had money and thought it was just fine to walk all over families like mine."

And *poof*, there it was. His old insecurities came out so suddenly he hadn't even realized they were there. It'd been festering all these years. The Doctor Travis situation had spurred Garrett's worries about providing the kind of life he knew Lacey deserved—the kind she'd never even asked for. This was his problem. Not hers. He had a chip on his shoulder the size of a sequoia.

If there was a lower son of a bitch in the world, Garrett didn't want to know him. Living in the Kaisers' shadow since his mother's death had left a darkness inside that still haunted him. But that had nothing to do with Lacey and everything to do with his own demons. He could blame it on his current situation, his worries about the future, but it all went back to the past.

Garrett let out a sigh, dropped his guard and prepared to deliver the *I'm sorry speech* of a lifetime. He could tell by Lacey's lack of response that she wasn't mad. She was hurt. Which made it even worse.

"Look, Lace, I really shouldn't have said that. I just haven't slept and now I've got this meeting with Talon, which I assume Vicky will be a part of. And the truth of the matter is that I don't even know what I'm going to say yet. Or if my plan is even going to work."

When she didn't answer, Garrett pressed, "Can we meet later? I'll explain everything. It's been a tough couple of days, that's all. You just got caught in the crossfire and I'm really sorry."

Another moment of dead air passed, then Lacey spoke in a voice so soft he could barely hear her. "I know it's been rough. But that's what I signed up for. What do I have to do to prove that? Thick or thin. For better or worse, I'm there for you. *And* your family. Don't shut me out."

To her rhetorical question, Garrett knew the answer without a doubt. There was nothing more she could do than she'd already done. It was time to turn loose his insecurities—his inhibitions—something he should've done a long time ago.

"Lacey, you don't have a thing in the world to prove to me. Not a damn single thing." Garrett knew nothing in life is certain. Not for him. Not for the ranch. And certainly not with Asadi. Only thing he did know was that he loved her, and it was time to come clean on that.

Turning off Main, Garrett nosed into the parking spot in front of Bridger's office, mustering the courage to tell her those three little words he'd been so scared to confess. And he'd just come up with the right way to say it when the text message from Tom Holloway popped up.

Change of plans. Now we have something that belongs to you.

A cold chill ran through Garrett as he thought about what this could mean. Consumed with a million horrible thoughts at once, he stumbled for a reply. "Lacey, I uh—I got to let you go. Call you back later."

There was a pause on her end. "What's wrong?"

"Yeah, I don't—" He stammered for an answer as he stared at the text. "I just—I got to go. I'll call you back in a bit, I promise."

Garrett ended the call without waiting for her reply, struck with the awful thought that Asadi might just be the *something* that Holloway was referring to.

37

Smitty looked down at the screen on his cell phone to make sure he was talking to Garrett. The abrupt, "where the hell you at?" greeting was highly out of character. The DEA special agent, unnervingly calm during the direst of situations, sounded unusually panicked. Smitty stopped the mammoth Caterpillar D10 bulldozer he'd affectionately nicknamed Big Yeller and looked around, suddenly feeling like he was being watched. Other than the other excavators around the dig site, there was nothing around him but the wide-open dusty plains.

"I'm right where you told me to be, Garrett. *Remember?* You said come to work like normal or Talon would think something was up."

Garrett's voice held an edge. "You near the house?"

Smitty looked around to get his bearings. "Sitting on a dozer about a quarter mile behind it. Why?"

"Sanchez is supposed to be with Asadi and Savanah. Can you see his truck up there?"

Smitty strained his eyes at the Kohl house. "Yeah, I see it. Parked up by the barn."

"Everything look okay, then? No problems?"

Smitty glanced over at the corral by the horse barn, just beneath

the Caprock where he saw the crashed SUV. "Holy hell. What's going on, Garrett?"

"What do you mean?"

"Someone drove through your corral and busted out the other
side."

"Drove through it?" There was a short pause on Garrett's end.
"What are you talking about?"

"All the damn boards are busted to pieces and there's a white
SUV crashed up inside against the fence post."

"Is it a Talon vehicle?"

Smitty strained his eyes. "Don't know. Can only see the back."

"Anyone around it?"

"My little girl is over there, right?" Smitty's blood ran cold at
the thought of what might be happening. "Dammit, Garrett! Do I
need to be worried?" With Garrett's long pause, he started to panic.
"What *the hell* is going on? Tell me!"

"I don't know, Ray! I don't know!" Another pause. "How quick
can you get over there?"

"I'm driving a damn eighty-seven-ton dozer, so not too fast."

"Heading over from Canadian, right now. Just hightail it up to
the house and let me know what you find."

Smitty's heart sank at the thought of Savanah in danger. It
sank even further thinking it was all because of what he'd done. He
scanned around the dig site, at all the dozers, maintainers, and the
massive earth-hauling trucks. The only thing between him and his
little girl was a razor wire fence, and that wouldn't contain Big Yeller.

Throwing every bit of hope for a better life out the window, he set
a direct course for the barn, where his *darlin' girl* was supposed to be
riding horses. Smitty knew he'd be fired, arrested, and maybe even
shot. But if Savanah was in trouble, he'd be there. The only thing *off*
the table was failing Savanah when she needed him most.

38

Lacey glanced around her mother's café now teeming with customers and let out a groan, zapped of the energy she'd need to
take on the crowd of hungry farmers and ranchers after another
disappointing conversation with Garrett. She'd call it a pattern, but
it was getting worse.

Turning back to the kitchen, Lacey discovered that orders were
piling up because her mother had forgotten to signal. Recognizing
her memory slip, a pattern that was getting more frequent with age,
Helene dinged the bell and mouthed the word *sorry*.

Lacey let out a sigh, and moved to the plates, heaping with
eggs, bacon, and hash browns to gather them up and distribute. "I
got it."

Before she arrived, Helene stepped in between and gently placed
her hands on Lacey's shoulders. "What's going on, girl? I can tell
something's up."

Lacey shook it off. "Nothing. Just tired, I guess."

"I'm your mother, Lace. So don't hide it, just—"

"Spill it. I know." Lacey didn't feel like getting into the whole
Garrett thing. She was sure her mother was sick of hearing about it
anyway. "Mom, folks are out there waiting."

Helene leaned left, looked out at the dining area then turned back to Lacey. "Trust me. Those fat old men can keep from stuffing their gullets for two damn seconds."

Lacey glanced out too. A few of her patrons, heads swiveling, were clearly searching for a coffee refill or to place an order. "Really, I gotta get out there. Customers are—"

"Who the hell cares? They can go elsewhere if they don't like it."

Lacey had to laugh. Henry's Café was the only restaurant in town. "Okay, Mom, it's Garrett. We got into another fight." She backtracked a little wanting to tell the story correctly. "Well, it wasn't exactly a fight. More of a . . . disagreement."

Helene cocked an eyebrow. "What'd you do?"

"*Me?*" Lacey knew she shouldn't have said anything. Her mother always took Garrett's side. "I didn't do anything but try to help him." She clucked her tongue. "But I might've overstepped. Just . . . a little."

"*Well*, did you?"

That was just like her mom. She didn't even want to hear what happened, knowing that if she just dug further, Lacey would come up with her own answer. "I don't know. *Maybe?* I went over to Vicky Kaiser's to see if she could help with the Kohl Ranch situation."

Helene looked skeptical. "And?"

"And it blew up in my face. With Vicky *and* Garrett." Lacey was preparing for a lecture on butting into other people's business when her mother threw her a curveball.

"Look, Lace, men can be ambitious. And men can be strong. But they're proud to a fault, and emotionally they're just plain stupid. Put all those traits together and you've got problems. Holding everything inside makes them as prone to self-destruction as a kamikaze. Your father was like that, and Garrett is too."

"So . . . you think I did the right thing?"

"Not saying that." Helene wagged her finger at Lacey. "Just saying that you've got one of the good ones. A keeper." Her face scrunched in disgust. "Not like that other one."

Her mother hated Travis and adored Garrett. So maybe her encouragement to make it work shouldn't have been all that unexpected. But it wasn't just that. Lacey's father had lost his fortune and taken his own life as a result. Although she never said it, Lacey knew that Helene regretted not doing more for the man who was the center of their universe. The guilt had weighed on her mother for years. It was even heavier than her own.

Helene grabbed each of Lacey's shoulders, leaned in and smiled. "Do you love Garrett?"

"It's complicated, Mom. There's a lot to consider."

Her mother pressed, "Do—you—love—Garrett?"

Lacey let out a huff. "*Yes*, you know I do."

"And does he feel the same way?"

"I don't know. He's never said it."

Helene batted her hand at Lacey as if she'd just spouted the biggest load of crap she'd ever heard. "Men don't always say that kind of thing. But in your heart, deep down, you know."

Lacey smiled and shook her head. "So, what do I do? If I keep pushing on all this, it might drive him away."

Helene smiled back. "I can't tell you what to do. But I can tell you that there's nothing worse than regret. You have someone you want to give your heart to, then you hold on tight, with everything you've got, and never let go." She pulled Lacey into a hug. "When it comes to love, never ever leave anything on the table."

Lacey could feel the tears welling in her eyes and it wasn't just because her mother's words hit home. It was the revelation that Helene was still heartbroken over what she thought she should've done for her husband.

Garrett was a different situation, but if there was a fight to be had then she'd fight it tooth and nail. He might get away, but she'd not make it easy. There were worse things in the world than giving all you've got. Lacey may have her regrets, but Garrett wouldn't be one of them.

With her mind made up and soul determined, Lacey snapped out of her trance with the ding of the bell and an *order up*. That sound was one she'd heard a thousand times before. But for some reason, she knew she'd remember this moment for the rest of her life.

39

Racing to the ranch, Garrett tried to call Sanchez for the tenth time, only to again get voicemail. Of course, cell service was spotty to nonexistent, especially if they were away from the house. But with Smitty's report of a crashed SUV Garrett was borderline panicked. He'd just brought his GMC up over ninety when the call from Holloway came in.

Garrett hit the answer button and tried to sound calm. "Want to tell me what's going on?"

It was clear from the smoothness of Holloway's voice that his show of confidence wasn't just an act. He was very much in control. "I take it you're eager to talk."

Garrett had to smile. If this is how the prick wanted to play this thing, then so be it. "We had a meeting this morning, Holloway. Or did you forget?"

"Oh, no, I didn't forget. It was just overcome by events."

Garrett wanted to reach through the phone and strangle the son of a bitch, but he kept his composure. "Does it have anything to do with the video of *you* shooting a horse out from under an eleven-year-old boy? Or your thugs brutally beating an unconscious man? Or does it have something to do with the minerals you're extracting and Talon's connection to companies with ties to Russia. Because those are pretty big events. The kind that might end up on the front page of every newspaper in the country."

Holloway's retort following a brief pause was less than calm. "I don't know what you *think* you know. But I can tell you that this will not end well."

"Couldn't agree more, Holloway. And I think that's what's got you rattled."

There was a pause on Holloway's end. "Maybe it's time we have that meeting."

Garrett smiled again, this time feeling the power of the upper hand. Of course, the earlier text message indicated otherwise. And since there'd been no confirmation that his friends and family were safe, he figured he'd better hold off on the victory lap. Garrett took his foot off the accelerator in anticipation of turning around and going back to Canadian for a meeting at Bridger's office. But before he could confirm, Holloway threw him a curveball.

"Know the old Carbon Black plant on the west side of Borger?"

"Sure do. But I don't see that happening." Garrett prepped himself mentally to stand his ground. "Why don't you—"

"As I mentioned earlier, we have something that belongs to you. And if you want it back, I suggest you get here as soon as possible. Be sure to bring what you stole from us."

Garrett was desperate to know what Holloway was up to, and with every second that ticked by without hearing from Sanchez or Smitty his apprehension grew. He couldn't help himself, he had to ask. "Not a big fan of guessing games. How about you lay your cards on the table?"

A moment of silence passed then a panting female cried out in a desperate voice. "*Garrett!*" He was about to answer the cry when she screamed, "Don't come! It's—" Her muffled plea was followed by the commotion of a struggle that ended with the echoing clank of metal on concrete.

Silence preceded Holloway's smooth-as-silk voice. "Ready to make a trade now?"

Garrett immediately thought of Lacey, but before he could demand to speak to her, Holloway confided, "Your CIA friend has proved to be quite spirited. Hard-shelled. But every shell can be cracked. It's just a matter of finding the right spot."

At the mention of CIA, Garrett immediately recognized that it was Kim's terrified voice. Although she would have gone through Level-C SERE, the most brutal and intense Survival, Evasion, Resistance, and Escape training course in the U.S. military, there was a certain level of torture that will break anyone. In the wrong hands, the knowledge she possessed could jeopardize intelligence operations all over the world and put dozens of lives in danger.

It was abundantly clear that whoever Garrett was dealing with was well-connected, potentially to a mole inside the Agency who had ratted her out. Kim carried no identification revealing her CIA affiliation and wouldn't have confessed it on her own.

Garrett took a breath, checked his attitude, and put all of the ranch business out of his mind. It was time to get serious about saving his friend's life. "Okay, what do you want, Holloway?"

"You know what I want, Special Agent Kohl. Do you have the documents?"

There it was. Garrett's cover was blown also. But he'd not give Holloway the satisfaction of acknowledging it. Clearly, he had a well-placed spy. Talon's ties to Moscow and the guard packing the Russian GSh-18 pistol were all the clues Garrett needed to solidify his hunch.

Garrett eyed the pack of Talon documents on his passenger seat. "Yeah, I've got them."

There was a muffled conversation before Holloway continued. "Then let's make a trade."

Garrett knew it wouldn't be that easy. There was no letting bygones be bygones after kidnapping a U.S. intelligence officer on American soil. If these were the men Ike Hodges had warned him about then he'd be killed and so would Kim. He needed a plan and he needed it fast.

Garrett checked his watch. "I'm about forty-five minutes away. Just leave her alone and you'll get what you want."

"I'll get what I want either way. And if you continue at ninety-one miles per hour, you're only thirty-eight minutes from here. Show up a second later and I'm liable to get bored. Start cracking at your friend's pretty shell."

Before Garrett could plead with Holloway, the call ended. Apparently, they'd LoJacked his truck and were watching him close. With Bridger out of action and Sanchez out of pocket, his next call was to Trip. If his friend had agreed to one suicide mission, then why not another?

40

sadi pulled the reins and slowed Skip to a trot, riding along the bottom of the steep caprock escarpment, scanning the barren plains ahead. He turned to Tony, whose khaki shirt was ripped at his abdomen where the bullet had torn through and embedded in his protective vest. A second round must've grazed his temple, as the left side of his head and face were covered in blood.

At the roar of distant engines, Asadi turned to find two white trucks about a hundred yards out and closing in fast. Not far ahead of him was the switchback trail to the top of the ridge, too narrow and rough for a pickup to climb.

Asadi turned back to Tony, whose eyes were unfocused, and he sat wobbly in the saddle. The deputy yanked a handkerchief from his pocket and dabbed his wound. Blood was trickling down to his collar and soaking through his shirt. With a few inaudible words he tipped forward and nearly fell off.

Asadi watched helplessly as the deputy was losing consciousness. "You okay, Tony?"

Tony stiffened, forced his eyes open, and sat rigid. "Just a scratch, kid. I'll be alright." With those slurred words, he tilted sideways like a falling timber.

Asadi leapt from the saddle, dashed to the palomino, and caught the deputy before he hit the ground. Guiding him down, Asadi was careful to brace Tony's head, protecting the wound. Looking back at the approaching trucks, Asadi was left with a difficult choice—leave Tony behind or stay and take their chances.

Savanah rode Moxy around beside them. "They're almost here!" She kept her eyes trained on the pickups. "We have to go!"

Asadi couldn't believe it was up to him to make the call. His every instinct told him to run, but his heart sank at the thought of it. He had just looked up to Savanah to tell her to go on without them when Tony struggled to rise.

Garrett had always said that jarheads were *too stubborn to die* and maybe he was right. Although Asadi never fully understood exactly what that meant or how it could be true, it turned out that Tony wasn't done just yet. Unfortunately, they were too late to make it up the ridge. Their only hope now was to find a place to hide.

SMITTY HAD HAD THIS NIGHTMARE his entire life. He'd be trapped in mud and his legs didn't work, or he was in a gunfight for his life but he had no bullets. There was always something out of his control, preventing him from getting where he desperately needed to be. Every situation was different, but one factor remained the same. He screamed with a voice that carried no sound.

As his mammoth yellow dozer rumbled across the dusty plains, Smitty could see it all playing out before him. The trucks. The horses. And the riders that for some damn reason didn't get up and run. He yelled at them to move, but it was no use. All he could do was pray like hell that he made it in time.

Of all the horrible thoughts running through his mind, the worst among them was telling Crystal that something had happened to their *darlin' girl*. She'd never forgive him and he wouldn't blame her. He'd made yet another bad choice in life and now Savanah was going to pay.

Maybe everyone was better off if he was back in jail, locked behind bars forever? Or maybe they'd be better off if he was just dead. Smitty hated to think this way, to sink so deep, but it was the God's honest truth. There was a peace in the thought of moving on to the next world. But there'd be no rest until Savanah was safe.

Straining his eyes, Smitty watched the two on the ground rise to their feet. The bigger one, who must've been Sanchez, looked a bit wobbly as he stood. With the inevitable fight coming, Smitty reached behind his back and pulled out the *other* souvenir he'd brought back from Mexico—the one he told no one about. Emilio Garza's Cabot Diablo pistol was locked, loaded, and ready to go.

Despite Garrett's guarantee that everything would be fine, Smitty knew better. And he knew that because things were too good. *Too good* was an alarm bell for guys like him. It was a surefire sign that his whole damn world was about to burn to the ground.

41

Trip had taken his pontoon boat out to Lake Meredith and, true to his word, he'd gone by himself. It wasn't that he didn't enjoy Garrett's company. His brother in arms from the wild and wooly days in Afghanistan was always a pleasure to have around, even if he *did* drink all his beer. But at a certain age you know what you need to unwind, and for Trip it was solidtude. As an only child, he valued his *me time*, needing a day to just chill and be left alone.

His love of isolation was yet another thing he and Garrett had in common, in addition to their love of good horses. But unlike his DEA buddy who lived to fish, Trip's draw to the lake had nothing to do with angling and everything to do with the calm of the water. In fact, he'd been tempted to cast out an empty hook if it wouldn't have made him look crazy. And he got enough curious looks as one of only a handful of Stetson-clad, spur-jangling Black cowboys in the Texas Panhandle.

Trip cared little what anybody thought regarding who he was or who they thought he should be. Never had. His father, an avid hunter, was the exact same way. He'd grown up helping to cull deer on the Briscoe Ranch near Uvalde and had fostered Trip's love of the great outdoors. Rodeo, however, had not been welcomed into the Davis home by either his mom or dad.

Trip's passion for bull riding was born on his first ever visit to the

Top O' Texas Rodeo. From team roping to saddle bronc, he loved it all. But the men who climbed atop beasts hell-bent on stomping them into the ground was what intrigued him the most. And it all began with the Professional Bull Riders emblem—the image of a cowboy, arm raised high, just hanging on for dear life atop the meanest-looking animal you ever saw.

Latching onto these beasts was like harnessing a tornado or riding a hurricane—the perfect metaphor for life. Grab on tight, hang on with all you got, and pray to the good Lord you don't get killed. There was no equivalent to the rush of eight seconds on the back of a bull. And he'd tried like hell to find it. Not his combat experience with Special Forces. Not border ops with Ranger Recon. Nothing could touch being inside the arena.

With the guilt of his early-morning beer consumption fading with the crack and sip of a fourth Carta Blanca, Trip leaned back and closed his eyes, letting the lap of the waves carry him off to a place between the real world and limbo land relaxation. With the ringtone blasting from his front pocket he remembered that he needed to put his phone on silent.

Trip pried a heavy eyelid open to discover it was Garrett, and was smacked with a shockwave of guilt. He'd planned to have him out later, after a little solo decompression, which had always been his process after a deployment, or more recently, nearly getting gunned down by a team of Guatemalan assassins. Knowing that Garrett was probably just securing his reservation for dinner at the Davis house, he let it go to voicemail.

At Garrett's immediate second attempt, Trip was about to just turn it off. But when the guilt intensified, he pulled it out, praying he'd come up with a good lie in that split second between accepting the call and saying *hello*. But his wits weren't quick enough to save him, as Garrett launched in first.

"Where you at, Trip?"

"Uh . . . fishing out at Meredith." Trip braced for the inevitable ass chewing. "Spur of the moment kind of thing, you know."

"Really need your help, man. How quick can you get out of there?"

Trip first assumed that some of Butch's cows must've gotten out on the highway, but it was clear by the urgency in Garrett's voice that this was no small favor. Something was wrong. "What's happening? Everybody okay?"

"No, not really. Kim's in trouble unless we do something fast."

Trip's first thought was that the Garza Cartel was seeking reprisal. The wheels in his mind immediately started to turn as he formulated a plan to get down to Mexico ASAP. "Say the word, buddy. When do we leave?"

"She's in Borger," Garrett stated flatly. "Old Carbon Black plant."

Borger made no sense whatsoever but the Carbon Black plant made even less. Trip had a million questions, but all of them could wait. A lifetime working in the military and in law enforcement had taught him there's only one question that mattered when seconds count. And judging by Garrett's tone, this was one of those situations. "Where do you need me?"

"You know my friend Ike Hodges?"

"Know *of* Ike. Never met him."

Trip hadn't ever been to Crippled Crows. His mother was a staunch Southern Baptist and a card-carrying teetotaler. Her only vice was wrath, a sin she'd honed to ruthless perfection. She doled out discipline with an Old Testament style and flare. To her, Ike Hodges was the Texas High Plains version of King Herod. His den of iniquities was strictly off-limits.

"I'll shoot him your number to give you a call. He's got a Hughes 500, like the Little Bird choppers we used in Iraq. You got your gear?"

"*Gear?*" The sudden switch temporarily threw Trip for a loop.

"Got my pistol and AR in the truck. Threw in a little extra ammo for some hog hunting later on." Fortunately, he'd packed his Lone Star Armory TX10 rifle chambered in 6.5 Creedmoor.

Garrett's voice seemed to lose its edge. "Alright, that's good. I've got something these folks want. And in return, they say they'll turn Kim loose."

"And you believe them?"

"Nope. If I did, I wouldn't need you there watching my back. My plan is to make sure the exchange happens out in the open. Somewhere you got a clean shot."

Trip took a deep breath. "I'm there for you."

"I've gotta get off and call Ike. Is it clear what we're doing?"

Nothing had ever been *less* clear. But Garrett needed him and that's all that mattered. On the battlefield, as soon as the first shot is fired the plan goes out the window anyhow. But this wasn't even a plan. It was a "just be there in case something happens." And to hear Garrett tell it, something was going to happen.

Trip had been on missions with worse intel than that. And with people he trusted a whole hell of a lot less. "Tell Ike I'll be at the west side of the lake in fifteen minutes. Silver Dodge dually."

Trip tossed the pole, jumped into the driver's seat, and cranked the motor. Within seconds, the boat pointed toward the shore, he was racing toward the dock, and wondering what in the hell Garrett had roped him into this time.

42

Kim sat erect, back against the wall as she stared down at her bound hands and feet. The memory of being pistol-whipped, beaten, and dragged up the stairs flashed through her mind. Her heightened senses caught the stale stench of dust and the sharp chemical punch of rat poison. It was the kind of place where screams are born in defiance but die in whimpering defeat.

In a shadowy corner to the left, a man spoke to her in a booming voice, his words reverberating through her concrete cell. "You don't look surprised to be here, Ms. Manning."

Kim had been trained to keep her identity hidden at all costs. And she expected this man was aware of that too. His use of it was a calculated move—said to make her wonder what else he knew.

Interrogation works best when the inquisitor has good information on the detainee. It allows them to ask questions they already know the answers to and get a baseline of the subject's level of cooperation. The fact he used her name immediately told her that time was a factor. Had it not been, he'd have started with that first. This man was getting to the point for a reason.

Kim mustered the most defiant voice she could summon. "Who the hell are you?"

He stepped over to her casually and leaned in close. "You can call me Holloway."

His answer told Kim what she already suspected. Even if it was an alias, he'd told her because it no longer mattered. She'd never utter the name *Holloway* to another living soul.

"Well, if you know who I am," Kim answered, "then I expect you understand the seriousness of what you're doing."

Holloway wasn't phased in the least. "Killing an American intelligence officer is, in fact, a serious offense, as is killing a DEA agent." He paused, seeming to want her to grasp the fact that Garrett was also in danger. "Challenge is not drawing suspicion. But there are ways around that."

With Holloway's cards on the table, Kim decided to lay down her own. "You've done a great job of hiding your hand, so far, but this isn't Malawi. Federal officers don't just fall off the radar here. People are going to want answers. And they won't stop until they find them."

Holloway smiled and slicked back his silver hair. "That's the good news, I suppose." He raised a finger. "For us. The ones who will be asking those questions are on *our* side."

"This isn't one of your backwaters," Kim scoffed. "You don't have enough money to buy your way out of murder."

Holloway chuckled as he turned and paced the room. "This is already the land of prosperity, particularly for the ones in charge. We don't win them over with money. We win them over with a place at the table. The opportunity to feel important." He added as almost an afterthought, "And they'll lap it up like thirsty dogs."

With this cryptic confession, Kim knew that an insider was involved. It was someone with detailed knowledge of the highly compartmented Special Access Program (SAP) involving Garrett and the Agency's use of him as an off-the-books operator. And the only one who came to mind was her boss, Bill Watson. The big question was *why*.

The rage that burned inside at the thought of being sold out by one of her own superseded her fear. "Must've snuck past us on the inside." She forced a smile, hoping to keep it light, keep him talking and buy some time. "Anyone I know?"

Holloway marched over to her and smiled. "For someone who has been in this business as long as you have, I'm surprised I have to tell you how this works." He bent over and leaned in close. "I will be asking the questions. And *you* will be providing the answers."

43

Asadi looked to the south and eyed the massive crag in the earth about thirty yards ahead. It was the place he called Lion's Canyon because of the cougar he'd battled there when he first arrived in Texas. The two-mile-long stretch of ravine looked like a giant had cut a three-story-high trench in the middle of the plains and then filled it with mesquite brush, tiny boulders, and felled trees.

At the far end of the gorge was a natural spring that kept the grass lush and green, the cottonwoods full, and gave every critter on the ranch, from deer and antelope to cattle and horses a fresh drink of the coolest crispest water around. Especially during the drought, when everywhere else was the color of dust, the oasis was Asadi's favorite spot on the ranch.

Both Butch and Garrett assured him that mountain lions like the one that had stalked them last winter were few and far between and very rarely did they want anything to do with humans. But the event had made an impression, and very rarely did he venture into the canyon alone.

With escape over the caprock too far away, the canyon was the only option. Once inside, they'd be trapped inside its sheer walls. But the Talon guards would be unable to follow in their trucks and there were plenty of places to hide.

Asadi looked up to Savanah. "You help me get Tony?"

Savanah didn't respond, just spun in Moxy's saddle, dropped to the ground, and dashed over. With the two revving Talon pickups racing up from behind, Asadi and Savanah each grabbed one of Tony's arms and pulled with all their might. His muscles tensed with his strain to stand, but he rose no more than a few inches.

Asadi yanked again, groaning in fear and frustration. "Please! We have go! They coming!"

Asadi had just begun a desperate prayer when Tony put his palms flat on the ground and pushed himself upright. He rocked forward a couple of times for momentum and got to his haunches. With Asadi and Savanah on each side shoving, he labored to his feet.

"Over there!" Asadi pointed to the canyon. "Over there we hide!"

Tony nodded and took several clumsy steps toward the crag, faltered, and stumbled to a knee. But before Asadi could reach him to help, he was already back up and lumbering toward the canyon. First to arrive, the deputy plopped down on his rear, threw his legs over the lip of the ridge and pushed, sliding down to the bottom, with a dust trail wafting up from behind.

Next in line was Savanah, who eased to the side of the escarpment, dangled her legs over and took the plunge. Asadi had just turned back to see the two pickups busting around clumps of mesquite brush when a bullet snapped overhead. Not a second to spare, he dropped to his rear and pushed himself from the edge. There was a moment of freefall until the slope evened out and his heels caught the crumbling dirt, slowing his descent until he reached the others.

Turning back and looking up, Asadi saw the first of their armed pursuers at the ledge, just as the deafening *crack* of Tony's pistol came from behind. As the guard crumpled and tumbled headfirst into the ravine, the deputy fired at the next one in a tit-for-tat exchange.

Asadi grabbed Savanah's arm and pulled her behind a jagged tree stump. They had just ducked for cover when multiple reverberating gunshots rang out—the source of them were two men with pistols, who had eased into the crag and were maneuvering in their direction. Asadi spun around to find that Tony had killed the second shooter but taken another bullet in his protective vest.

Amid the flying bullets that *buzzed*, *whirred*, and *popped* all around them, Asadi dashed to the deputy and rolled him over. Searching for an escape route, he looked back and eyed the wooded area fed by the spring. They'd find good cover in the brush and could make their way up the embankment on the backside where there were plenty of places to hide.

Asadi wondered though if it was already too late—if Tony was even alive. His chest didn't move and his grip on the gun was no longer tight. It was as if both he and Savanah noticed it at the very same time. Their eyes met and registered their mutual fears.

Asadi turned to Savanah. "You ready run?"

The pain of leaving him visible on her face. "We can't just go without him."

Asadi studied the deputy's ashen face, hoping to find a glimmer of life. He swallowed hard and turned to Savanah. "We get help and come back. Okay?"

As she gave a reluctant nod, Asadi looked down at the pistol, tight in his grasp, and peered around the serrated stump. He took Savanah by the hand and helped her to her feet. But just as they were about to dash, a *buzz* of angry rounds came flying overhead and pinned them to the ground.

44

Trip got into the prone position under the cover of a salt cedar about fifty yards from the plant, recollecting the layout from a fieldtrip he had taken there back in high school. It was the same as most industrial facilities in the area—a hodgepodge of cooling towers, storage tanks, and smokestacks flanked by buildings, all within the perimeter of an eight-foot-high security fence.

It wasn't Fort Knox, but there wasn't a big welcome mat out front either. The soot-covered structure with its rusted-out spires, cauldrons, and railroad cars made for an unsettling sight—the picture of some post-apocalyptic hell, where the thorny vegetation surrounding it was no less ominous than the barbed wire barrier. Drop the toxic waste plant from the movie *RoboCop* into any spaghetti western ever made and you had the Carbon Black plant in Borger.

Humming the theme song from *The Good, the Bad and the Ugly*, Trip scanned the outer buildings, painted arctic blue, and stained with a coating of residue waste. There were two guards in khaki tactical pants and black polos, standing outside the main office. They were kitted out in chest rigs, with CZ Bren-2 carbines in single-point slings around their necks.

Trip had no idea what to prepare for, only that it was as serious as it gets given Garrett's uncharacteristic unease. Breathing a sigh of relief when his phone buzzed, he reached to his ear to activate the Bluetooth. "Hope that's you, Quanah."

"Sorry it took me a while." Garrett must've been anticipating that comment. "Had to get Daddy and Bridger up to speed."

"No sweat. Just do what you gotta do."

"Ike get you in place?"

"Guess so." Trip clamped his eyes shut, feeling a bit woozy from the oppressive heat and earlier beers. He opened them again and focused on the facility, which sat in a dusty section of ranchland surrounded by a natural hedgerow of cactus, yucca, and mesquite.

"You guess?" There was a brief pause on Garrett's end. "You're either there or you aren't."

"Oh, I am. Just wasn't an easy hike after four Carta Blancas." Trip swatted at a fly that kept buzzing by his ear. "Nothing but a bunch of ravines full of every damn thing on earth that'll scratch, sting, or bite you."

"It's rattlesnake country for sure," Garrett replied.

Trip hadn't even thought about that. He glanced around, swearing he could feel one of the slimy bastards slithering across the back of his thighs. "How long's this gonna take?"

"Hopefully, just a few minutes. My plan is to meet them out in the parking lot in front of the main building. I've got the pack. They've got Kim. Done a million undercover drug deals just like it. They get what they want, and I get what I want. Over and done."

Sounded too easy. Trip winced at the idea. "Really think it's going to go down like that?"

"Think you'd be here if I did?"

Trip had figured as much but had to ask. "Alright, what do you want me to do?"

"I'm going to keep you on speaker while this thing goes down. If I draw my pistol," Garrett continued, "do what you can to buy me some time. But if things go sideways, get the hell out and go for help." He paused then added, "If you're able."

For some reason, Trip thought that Garrett was miles away, so it surprised him to see the black GMC three-quarter-ton turning off the main road pulling into the complex. Trip expected a longer farewell, that *just in case we don't see each other again conversation*, but it was too late.

Garrett started in with the goodbyes. "Thanks for being there, buddy. I owe you one."

"First Mexico and now this." Trip chuckled. "You owe me two."

"Remember what I said, Trip. This gets ugly, you haul ass. Okay?"

Trip put eyes back on optics and watched as the Talon guards hopped to attention and moved through the parking lot. "Yeah, sure thing."

It wasn't a convincing reply, but it was as good as he could do under the circumstances. Plus, Garrett wouldn't buy it anyhow, and not just because it didn't sound genuine. They'd made a pact in Afghanistan that no matter what happened, they'd never leave each other behind.

Trip would've liked to hear his old friend argue, but since there were no objections, he eased his thumb to the selector and clicked it from SAFE to FIRE. Something bad was going down and there was nothing he could do but be ready when it happened.

PART FOUR

O death, where is thy sting?

—1 Corinthians 15:55

45

Ike Hodges eased the stick right and lowered the collective as he circled his Hughes 500 helicopter over Bridger's house. There weren't
many details to go on other than that Asadi, Sanchez, and Crystal's
daughter had gone out for a ride and hadn't been heard from since.
Between the crashed SUV and the kidnapped CIA officer things
didn't look good for the ones who'd gone missing.

Swooping around the barn, Ike found a nice piece of flat pasture
and dropped the skids down into the buffalo grass. He raised the
collective slightly, pushed the cyclic left, and hovered over closer to
his ragtag crew, who ducked, darted to the helo, and piled in like a
couple of experienced commandos.

Ike had expected to see Butch waiting, but was surprised to see
him clutching the lever action Marlin. And he certainly hadn't anticipated Kate Shanessy beside him with a deer rifle. Their *search-and-
rescue* mission looked a helluva lot more like a *search and destroy*.

With their rifles pointed outside at the nothingness of the prairie,
Ike yanked the collective, and gave it some right pedal. They had just
made the turn and were on the way to the ranch when Kate chimed
in first over the headset from the backseat.

"Cain't this thing go any faster?"

Ike's parents had taught him to always be kind to old folks, but they'd never met a woman like Kate. He'd taken her out a few times over the years to go after feral hogs that were rooting up her alfalfa. The old gal was a pain in the ass, but paid like a slot machine. She was a helluva good shot to boot.

Ike turned to her and smiled. "Kate, we're going a hundred and forty miles per hour. Only way we're going any faster into this headwind is if you get out and push."

All Ike heard over the intercom was a long and dragged-out *smart-ass*.

From the passenger seat, Butch jerked a thumb over his shoulder. "*Ah*, don't listen to her. She's as big a backseat driver as God ever put on the earth."

Kate had just launched into rebuttal when Ike reached to his controls and silenced her microphone. There was too much at stake to get roped into one of their asinine quarrels.

Knowing they had twenty-six square miles to cover, Ike turned to Butch for a plan. "Alright, navigator, where do we start?"

Butch seemed to be looking ahead, his eyes sweeping back and forth over the horizon, as if thinking out a strategy in his mind. "Well, they were supposed to go up on the caprock, but that's out in the open. I'm guessing if someone's chasing them, they'll look for somewhere to hide."

Ike knew the Kohl's place well enough to figure it out. There was a ravine that ran from the caprock south, about two miles. There was enough foliage around a natural spring to get in there and hunker down.

Ike gave it a little left pedal and aimed in that direction. "Butch, you really think these Talon folks would go after a couple of kids? Seems a bit heavy-handed, even for the kind of sorry ass folks that'd shoot a horse."

"I don't know." Butch kept quiet for a moment, his eyes dead ahead. "Just know Garrett found something big. Something that's got Talon awfully worried. And you know how people can get when they're backed into a corner. Anything can happen."

Ike couldn't agree more. Glancing down again at the big bore 45-70 in Butch's hands, he couldn't help but wonder what they were getting themselves into. And more importantly, could they get themselves out of it. If they were up against the same nasty bunch that his security team tangled with over in Africa, they were going to need more than a worn-out old chopper pilot and two elderly ranchers to counter threat. They were going to need a damn miracle.

46

Lacey had just cleared all the tables at the café and begun the arduous task of scrubbing dishes when she heard the bells on the front door jingle. She let out a breath, pulled off rubber gloves that she'd literally just put on, and wiped her brow with her forearm. On her way out of the kitchen, she grabbed a couple of clean menus that she always kept handy for her late arrivals, assuming they'd still want breakfast since it wasn't quite lunch.

Expecting a couple of farmers or a lone oil-field pumper, Lacey was shocked at the sight of who'd walked in. Thinking it must've been a mistake, she let loose with an unfriendly *can I help you* instead of her customary *sit anywhere you like.*

The blonde in cutoffs and a red tank top threw a hand on her hip. "You can start by telling me where my child and husband are."

Lacey was so thrown by the comment that she didn't even know where to begin. Why would *she* have a clue about anything to do with this woman's family? Her thoughts racing, she bounced from the idea that the lady was drugged out of her mind, to the possibility that Garrett had a secret wife, and this was Asadi's mother.

Quickly dispelling that as ridiculousness, Lacey took the logical step. "Why don't you have a seat, and I'll see if I can help." She gestured to the table closest to the door in case it got ugly. "Can I get you a coffee, Coke, ice water, or something?"

The woman stood firm, fire in her eyes. But the crack in her voice was that of a desperate wife and mother. "Don't want nothing but to know if my family's okay."

Lacey moved to the table and pulled out a chair for her guest. "Is your husband a regular here?" She looked over her shoulder to see if her mother was nearby. "My mom knows just about everybody that walks in the door. I can ask if—"

"No, he don't come in here or nothing." The woman took a few shaky steps to the table and eased into the seat. "He knows your boyfriend."

Lacey nodded, wondering if all this had to do with Garrett's mysterious behavior and earlier rush to get off the phone. "Is your husband with him now?"

"Don't know." The blonde gave a shake of the head. "When I got back this morning nobody was home." Her eyes filled with tears. "Ray left me a message saying that an emergency came up at work and he had to take Savanah over to Bridger's place for a sleepover."

Lacey took a seat across the table. "Did you say, *Ray*? Is Ray Smitty your husband?"

The woman pulled her hand from her lap and thrusted it at Lacey. "I'm Crystal. Work over at Crippled Crows." She glanced down at her skintight red tank top looking a little ashamed. "Guess you figured that out by now."

"I'm Lacey." She shook the woman's hand. "Well, your get-up certainly has a lot more pizzazz than mine." Lacey looked down at her white T-shirt, blue jeans, and running shoes. "Maybe if I was wearing what you had on, I wouldn't be sitting in an empty café right now."

The joke must've struck a chord because Crystal laughed. "Maybe." She glanced at her own attire again and shrugged. "Look, I know you got work to do and I don't want to interrupt. But I keep calling Ray and he don't answer. I even tried Bridger's place, but nobody'll pick up over there. Thought maybe you could get ahold of Garrett and see if he knows something."

Of course, Lacey knew Bridger was in the hospital and his family was driving back from Corpus Christi, but she couldn't explain anything else. She pulled her cell phone from her pocket, waggled it at Crystal, and smiled. "Spoke with Garrett not long ago, so I'll just give him a ring. There's probably a simple explanation and he'll help us sort everything out."

Crystal drug her index finger beneath each lower eyelid to brush away the tears. "I'm sure you're right. I'm sure it's nothing." With a smile and a nod, her words held hope. "If you could just get ahold of him, I'd feel better. Ray and my darlin' girl are all I've got."

As a mother and a woman in love, Lacey didn't need any justification. She pulled up her phone and tapped Garrett's number. As it rang, Crystal leaned in, her face eager, eyes hungry for answers in anguished anticipation. Although Lacey would never reveal it, her guest's strange story, on top of Garrett's secretive behavior, had her almost just as worried.

47

Garrett saw the call from Lacey pop up on his screen but there was no way he could answer. Aside from having already crossed into the Carbon Black compound, he still had Trip on the line. He hit the IGNORE and spoke to his friend out on overwatch to make sure he hadn't lost him. "You still there, buddy?"

Trip's voice came over the speaker. "Where the hell else would I be?"

Doing his best to get a handle on the threat before him, Garrett panned the inner perimeter. In the rearview, he watched as the automatic gate closed behind him. "Uh-oh."

Trip spoke again. "Saw the gate?"

"Yeah, I saw it."

"What do you think?"

"Not good." Garrett knew his GMC three-quarter-ton with the Ranch Hand grille guard could bust through the barrier like a wet paper sack, but he didn't like their intentions to hem him in. "Don't think this is going to be an in-and-out kind of thing."

"I'm in position. Got a good line of sight." When Garrett didn't answer, Trip continued. "Just say *take 'em* and I'll drop these boys flat."

"I hear you, Trip. But we gotta make sure Kim's safe first. Not leaving without her."

Marching up to the truck were two guards in tactical pants and matching black polos, brandishing short-barreled CZ Bren-2 rifles. Unlike the beefy thugs from the ranch, these guys had a professional air—clean-cut, broad-shouldered, and narrow-waisted. They had the confident gait of experienced operators.

Garrett eased his hand to the handle, opened the door, and stepped out of the truck. He raised both hands, palms facing out, but kept them close to his waistline where his pistol was in the appendix carry position. He was itching to draw, but with Kim still captive, he couldn't take that risk.

The one on the right spoke with a heavy Slavic accent. "Hands up. Up. Up. High."

Garrett's chance to grab his pistol had come and went. "Hold on. Relax." He eased his hands above his shoulders and tilted his head to the pack stuffed with maps and documents in the passenger's seat. "Got everything you asked for right there."

The guard on the left veered off to the truck and the other moved to Garrett and lifted the front of his shirt. He knew exactly where to look first and didn't seem surprised. Of course, they already knew he was DEA and probably figured he'd roll up armed.

The guy by his truck unzipped the pack and riffled through the papers. He spoke in heavily accented English as well. "This all of it?"

"That's everything." Garrett turned back to the one who'd taken his pistol. "You got what you want. Now how about what I want?"

The guard who'd disarmed him tilted his head toward the main facility of the plant. "You talk to boss first." He grabbed a handful of his shirtsleeve, but Garrett didn't budge.

Scanning the facility grounds, Garrett saw no one else, but he knew eyes were on him. Given the go-ahead, Trip would drill two lethal rounds into the Talon goons, but it'd be a death sentence for Kim. He couln't make a move until he played this thing out.

TRIP COULDN'T BELIEVE WHAT WAS happening. He had the crosshairs on the guard on the left, following the trio across the parking lot, ready for Garrett to give the signal. They were within yards, then feet, then inside the building. His chance was lost and there was nothing he could do.

Like he did in any other situation, he kept running the *what if* game, playing out scenarios in his head. He could hold tight, exfil to get help, or break into the compound and risk getting caught. Trip rose from his hide but kept low as he wound his way through the brush. His only good access to the plant was through the main entrance by Garrett's GMC.

Trip moved stealthily around the perimeter, keeping careful watch for any guards or cameras. Fortunately, there were a couple of abandoned railcars on the tracks in front of him which provided good cover from a frontal assault. Sprinting from the cover of mesquite to the cyclone fence, he skidded in, took a knee, and pulled the wire cutters from his pack. Clipping each wire, one by one, he looked up periodically to check for threats.

Like almost every solider who'd ever served, there were a few great war movies that stuck out in his mind. Not surprisingly, *Saving Private Ryan* was among his favorites. He always loved the line from the steely-eyed sniper who focused on a single window in an isolated tower and utters to himself *That's where I'd be.*

It was with that uncanny memory that Trip detected a flash of light in the corner of his eye. And he couldn't help but worry that it was already too late.

48

Smitty felt like it had taken an eternity to close the distance between his dozer and the canyon where his daughter had disappeared. He didn't know if she was dead or alive, only that the guards in front of him were going to pay either way. As they fired at him with their rifles from the pickup bed, three bullets pierced the windshield in quick succession. Smitty reached right, yanked a lever, and raised the blade. With the *ting-ting-ting* of lead on steel, he gritted his teeth as he rammed the truck and pushed it into the ravine.

ASADI LOOKED TO THE TOP of the ravine, certain he was living out the last seconds of his life when the truck slid sideways, hovered for an instant, then rolled over the edge. The echoing explosion of gunfire all around them was nothing compared to the crash and crunch of metal against rock when the Ford landed upside down on the canyon floor. The bloodied driver lay motionless inside, while another guard was crushed beneath the cab.

A third rolled clear of the wreckage in a dusty ball of flailing limbs, but still managed to grab his rifle and rise. He had just turned and aimed when another shot came quicker that killed him dead.

The silence was broken with an enthusiastic *daddy* that leapt from Savanah's mouth.

Asadi looked up to find their pistol wielding savior, Savanah's father, who dropped to the ledge, wedged himself into a narrow opening and slid down the canyon wall. Dirt clods broke loose beneath his heels and tumbled like an avalanche beneath his old work boots.

Ray Smitty had just made it to the bottom of the gorge when Savanah reached him, and they wrapped in a tight embrace. With the rattle of a machine gun, Ray scooped his daughter into his arms and sprinted back to the felled tree trunk where Asadi and Tony were taking cover.

Asadi could tell by the look in Ray's eyes that the outlook for Tony wasn't good, but he still had to ask. "He be okay?"

Ray gave a confident nod before leaning over the deputy and inspected his head wound. "He's going to be fine. But we've got to get him to a hospital. And we gotta do it fast."

Asadi wanted that, but he believed deep down there was little hope. "We get help now?"

Ray looked up the canyon ridge, pulled out his cell phone and stared at the screen. His look of disappointment only revealed what Asadi already knew. They were too far out to get a signal.

Ray turned to Savanah. "Sweetie, you okay? Can you run?" After a nod from Savanah, he looked to Asadi. "What about you? Think you can move real quick on outta here?"

"I run okay." Asadi pointed to Tony. "But him?"

Ray looked at Tony and shook his head. "We're gonna come back for him."

The news hit hard. In Asadi's mind, an adult showing up was as good as being saved. He reached for Tony's hand, held it in his own and was surprised to feel the squeeze. The deputy opened his eyes and struggled to push himself to his knees. He tried to speak but only muttered a few quiet words. Ray grabbed Tony's other hand, draped it over his neck and threw his shoulder under the deputy's armpit. With a groan, he heaved the deputy to his feet and got him balanced.

Ray turned to Asadi. "We ain't climbing out like this." He scanned the canyon ridge. "But Garrett knows we're here and he's sending help. We just need a safe place to hunker down."

Asadi knew just the spot. "This way! This way!" He pointed in the direction of the spring, which was only about forty yards ahead. Not only were there trees and brush to hide in, but there was a natural indention in the canyon wall. "There a cave!"

"Cave?" Smitty's eyes widened. He looked to Tony. "Make it a little further?"

Tony nodded unconvincingly. His knees were buckled, and Ray struggled to keep him on his feet. They'd just taken the first wobbly steps when a machine gun behind them roared to life.

49

After several calls that went straight to Garrett's voicemail, Lacey immediately phoned Bridger. It took some cajoling, but she eventually got the truth. Garrett had gone to make the exchange and hadn't been heard from since. With Crystal in the passenger seat beside her, Lacey raced to Canadian for another visit with Victoria. And this time she'd not come groveling, hat in hand.

Lacey had no idea what she was going to do or say, only that she wasn't holding back. As she pulled into the circle drive, Lacey saw the white Ranger Rover out front and parked behind it. She hopped out and marched up onto the wraparound porch with Crystal in tow.

Lacey was about to bang on the door when Victoria opened it. Her face immediately fell at the sight of Crystal. Apparently, her security camera had not caught the curvy blond waitress in Daisy Duke cutoffs.

Victoria eased out a hand as if picking up a roach she wasn't quite sure was dead.

"Don't believe we've met."

"This is Crystal," Lacey interjected. It wasn't lost on her that they'd not been invited inside. "Her husband works for your company out at the Kohl Ranch."

"Oh, how nice." Victoria strained to smile as she shook Crystal's hand. "Always a pleasure to meet someone in the Talon family." She said the word *family* with gritted teeth.

Crystal was clearly intimidated, and who could blame her. Even though Lacey had grown up as wealthy as Victoria, the opulence of the mansion still made an impression, as did the owner's beauty and style. She was impeccably outfitted in Chanel seersucker and Balenciaga heels.

Lacey had started to feel less than worthy again. *Started to*. But not this time. Not after what happened to Bridger, Asadi, and Grizz. "I don't know what the hell your Talon *family* is up to but it's not good. So why don't you cut the crap and tell me what's going on."

Victoria's look of surprise was as fake as the smile she'd greeted them with. "Look, I know you're not happy with the operation on your boyfriend's property but—"

"Not happy?" Lacey interrupted. "It's got nothing to do with my happiness and everything to do with Talon being out of control and dangerous."

Crystal's look of timidity had turned to thoroughly entertained. She was clearly enjoying a side of Lacey she had not expected.

"That's absurd." Victoria expelled a haughty laugh. "If we're so *dangerous*, then why did you come here begging for a job?" She scanned Crystal from stem to stern. "And it doesn't look like you're in a position to forgo any income. Which you're about to lose, by the way."

Lacey took a couple of steps forward and poked her finger at Victoria's chest. "Don't you bully her. You got something to say, then say it to me."

"I'm not *bullying* anyone," Victoria countered. "And before you go making any accusations you can't back up, you might want to think about how you're jeopardizing your future." She glanced at Crystal. "And hers."

"Our future has nothing to do with you or Talon and everything to do with the people we love. Which is something you'd know nothing about."

Victoria guffawed. "Oh, is that right?"

"Yeah, that's right." Lacey leaned in and stared Victoria down. "All you've ever done was look down your nose at people. You and your whole damn family. But at the end of the day, for all the money, and all the land, you don't have anything in your life that really matters. The Kaiser name, your reputation, it's all a joke. It started with your father, it continued with your brother, and it'll end with you unless you do something about it."

Victoria grabbed the edge of the door. "I think it's time for you to leave." As she was pulling it shut, Lacey stopped it with her foot.

"We're not going anywhere unless you help us." Lacey glanced at Crystal. "Her daughter and husband are missing, and I think Garrett is in danger. I don't know what's going on, but I know your company is behind it. Please, Victoria, you have to do something."

"What the hell am *I* supposed to do?"

"Make a phone call dammit! Throw around that Kaiser name you're so proud of and get some answers!" Lacey pointed to Crystal. "If not for me, then for a mother worried sick to death about her child."

Victoria looked to Crystal and her face softened, seeming to register a rare look of contrition. "I'm sorry, but I can't help you."

Lacey crossed her arms. "You *can't* or you *won't*?"

"I *can't*," Victoria stressed.

"Why the hell not?"

"Because I can't! I just can't! Don't you get it?"

"No! I don't!" Lacey matched Victoria's vigor. "Why *can't* you help us?"

"Because it's not my company anymore! *Okay*. I don't have any power over these Talon people. I barely even know them."

"What are you talking about? I thought you were the head of acquisitions or some crap. A big executive. A *partner*."

"No. I'm not a partner, Lacey. And the title is nothing more than that. I'm just a name to them. They just want me around to show my face. To put *Kaiser* out front to make it look like a local company, like nothing much has changed. But I don't even own this house anymore." She nodded to the Range Rover. "Or the car. It's all for show."

Lacey didn't know whether to laugh or cry. The one person she thought could help was nothing but a fraud. Before she could dig further, Victoria continued. "Talon bought all of our energy assets. The other Kaiser businesses, the bank, the ranches, the feed yards were all seized by the government. Our family lost it all."

"Then why did you leave a wonderful job in New York for this?"

"I didn't leave any wonderful job." Victoria looked away. "I was living off a trust fund." She turned back. "But since it was connected to my brother, the government took that too."

Lacey didn't even know where to begin. "So, you're—"

"Broke. I got nothing." Tears welled up in Victoria's eyes. "I don't even have what you have. I don't have anyone anymore. My friends vanished as quick as the money."

Lacey couldn't believe it, but she felt sorry for Victoria. Of course, it wasn't hard to figure out why. This was exactly what happened when her family lost everything. At least Lacey had her mother and her children. Her friend was left with nothing, not even the big empty mansion.

Crystal spoke for the first time since they arrived. "Look, Ms. Kaiser. I know you don't know me or my family. And I don't fully understand what your situation means for them. But if there's anything you could do, I'd sure be grateful." She glanced at Lacey. "*We'd* be grateful."

Victoria stepped back into the foyer and grabbed her car keys off a table. "I'm not promising anything. But I think I know where Garrett might be." She made a beeline to the Range Rover, opened the driver's side door, and turned back. "Well, are ya'll coming or what?"

Lacey looked to Crystal, then back. "Yeah, whatever you can do, Victoria. Thank you."

"Good, let's get going." Victoria was about to hop in when she stopped and turned back. "And quit calling me that for crying out loud. It's Vicky, okay." With that correction, she slid into the driver's seat, yanked the door shut, and cranked the engine.

Lacey and Crystal darted to the Range Rover and hopped in. As they sped off from the mansion, Lacey's spirits rose. Not only did she have someone who could help her find Garrett, her old best friend was finally back.

50

Garrett moved from the crisp brightness of the beating sun to the plant's dark interior, bombarded with the stench of hydraulic fluid, grease, and the pungent smell of motor oil. With the muzzle brake of a rifle jabbed between his shoulder blades, he marched through a windowless storage room, zigging and zagging around leaky equipment until his path hit a dead end at the base of a spiral staircase.

They clanged up the metal steps, six flights to the top, stopping before a room with a closed entrance. A guard leading the way pushed the door open to a blinding flood of sunlight. Squinting to take it all in, Garrett found Holloway on the other side, with Kim lying bound and gagged at his feet.

Garrett had not even taken a full step inside when a rifle stock slammed at the base of his head. There was a moment of blurriness as his cheek hit the cement floor, and he immediately tasted the metallic tang of blood. A ringing in his ears accompanied the enveloping haze, as darkness draped over like a heavy black curtain.

TRIP FROZE OUTSIDE OF THE rusted cyclone fence, unsure of his next move. Zeroed in by the gunman on the catwalk above, he turned back for cover, finding nothing but open ground. Ahead was a railcar, much better refuge, but the barrier ahead was not fully clipped. As a supersonic round *snapped* by, he dove through anyhow, snagging his jeans on a jagged wire.

Trip lunged again, ripping a deep gash in his leg as he broke over to the other side. Low crawling, chin to dirt, he flinched as three more bullets popped beside him. He stopped short as more *tinged* off the train tracks, then found protection behind the railcar's wheelset. Unfortunately, there was still forty yards of *no-man's-land* between him and the plant.

51

Smitty strained with everything in him to keep Sanchez upright and moving forward. In his weaker moments, he was tempted to give up, but the *zip* of bullets overhead was a damn good incentive to keep trudging on. The deputy's eyelids were barely open, which left Smitty wondering if this was a lost cause. But Asadi seemed determined to live by the military's *no man left behind* philosophy and they were going to drag Sanchez to safety if it killed them all.

With the Talon guards in close pursuit, Smitty welcomed the sight of the thick wooded cover of the spring. Sanchez seemed to get a second wind spying the shade and fresh water and suddenly took on the burden of his own weight. They'd only been on the run for a few minutes, but all suffered the effects of the stifling August air. The sunbaked rocks beneath their feet intensified the heat, and the canyon walls blocked any relief from the west wind.

As they broke through into the clearing, Smitty felt the immediate cool of the natural spring and the shade of the thick cottonwood canopy. The kids had already run ahead and were down by the stream scooping water into their mouths. Sanchez broke loose, stumbled to the creek, and fell to his knees, dipping his face right in to hydrate.

As he splashed his wounded head to wash away the dried blood, Smitty kept watch. He pulled the Cabot Diablo tucked into his belt and let it dangle by his side. It was way too quiet and he got the feeling Talon's hitmen, no longer on their heels, were up to something.

ASADI HAD JUST GOTTEN HIS fill of water and looked up when he smelled the smoke. The scent didn't immediately set off any warning bells. In fact, it conjured up fond memories of campfires with the twins and Butch's famous hot chocolate. Then he remembered when a bearing went out in the hay baler, and how it had started a small fire. Fortunately, he'd been quick with the extinguisher, but the lesson wasn't lost. On a windy day, a single spark could be devastating.

Garrett had told him stories about the death and destruction an out-of-control blaze had wreaked on the Texas Panhandle. Some lost everything. Their homes. Their cattle. Their horses. All destroyed. The thought of a wildfire sent a shiver down his spine.

Ray's eyes went wide. "Ya'll smell that too?"

For the first time in a while, Tony spoke, "That's real close. We gotta get out of here."

Savanah looked to Asadi. "What are we going to do?"

Asadi wracked his brain for an answer, but none came quickly. Within the cover of the trees, they were hidden from the guards, but if a fire was moving through the canyon they were trapped. Although Tony seemed a little better after splashing his face and filling his belly with the cool water, there was no way he could climb the steep banks or hike his way out.

Asadi pointed to the ledge up above. "Need get horses."

"Horses?" Ray shook his head. "They done spooked with all the shooting and ran. Probably halfway back to the barn by now."

"No. They stay," Asadi argued. "I know it."

Savanah asked, seemingly curious at Asadi's certainty, "How can you be sure?"

"I train them stay." Asadi had worked with Butch to *ground tie* the horses. Once their reins land, they believed they were tethered to the earth. "They there. I know it."

"Asadi's right." Tony, sitting elbows to knees, looked at Ray. "Those horses will be right where we left them. Getting past those guards is the problem."

"Too big a risk to go after them," Ray argued.

Tony held his ground. "Too big of one not to. We won't beat a wildfire on foot. A blaze with some wind behind it can move fast as a car. Only way outta here alive is on horseback."

Ray looked up at the ridge above then back at Savanah. "Okay, honey, I'll go with him and get the horses." He looked back at Tony and gave Savanah a nod. "Can you take good care of Deputy Sanchez until we return?"

Savanah wasn't happy but nodded anyhow. "Daddy, you promise to come right back?"

"Of course, I promise." Ray took a knee and got eye to eye with her. "I'll be here before you know it. Quick as a flash." He looked to Tony. "You watch out for her, now. Keep her safe." Glancing up at the ridge, Ray added, "Thinking them guards aren't backing down."

Tony rested his pistol on his thigh and locked eyes. "Neither am I."

52

Kim awoke in a haze of fear and confusion. She reached up and touched her face, first her left eye, which was nearly swollen shut, then dragged her fingertips down to her lower lip, which was split open and crusted with blood. Brushing the mess of bloody blond tangles from her face, she saw Garrett lying nearby. Clambering to hands and knees, Kim crawled to her friend and put his head in her lap.

Garrett fought for consciousness as he sat up and looked around. "Where are they?"

"They're gone." Kim looked into his eyes. "Just us now."

He sat there for a few seconds without responding then grimaced as he reached to the wound on the back of his head. "Why'd they leave?"

"Don't know." Kim spoke a little louder. "But I'm guessing there's a reason. And it's probably why they untied me."

"Don't see any cameras." Garrett looked around as if searching for something. "Think they want us to talk? See if we'll say something they can use as leverage?"

Kim shook her head. "I think they just wanted us to see each other's faces before what comes next."

Grimacing in pain, Garrett struggled to his feet and glanced around. He moved to the door and worked the handle, finding out what Kim already knew. It was locked externally. He darted to the open-air platform at the far side of the room, a framework for an old fire escape.

Garrett eased to the ledge, grabbed a steel girder for stability and looked over the edge. "Not without a parachute." At the crackle of distant gunfire, he turned back to Kim and smiled. "Brought Trip along, just in case."

Kim struggled to her feet, joined Garrett at the ledge, and looked out onto the plant's expansive grounds of cooling towers, refining equipment, and network of glinting pipes. "'Just in case' kind of came and went, don't you think?

The news that her old war buddy from the Mexican border was out there didn't inspire as much confidence as it did with Garrett. Trip was good, but he was only one man against an entire team of former Russian special operations soldiers. No way he could go up against these mercenaries and come out alive.

"Not his fault." Garrett looked a little hesitant in his explanation. "Told him to hold off until I gave the signal. Just couldn't risk making a move against the guards until you were out. But don't worry, he'll get here."

Kim glanced back at the door at the muffled clanging of steps on stairs. "Well, if he's going to do something, he better do it fast. With him in the fight, they're not going to dawdle."

TRIP EYED THE BECKONING SAFETY of the building ahead, but the gunfire from the catwalk kept him pinned down flat. He rolled from his back to prone, made a sweep with his scope and saw exactly what

he feared. He'd waited too long to move and now he was being surrounded. Trip slid on his belly under the railcar to see if he could
get clear aim but as soon as he thrusted out his rifle, the *piff-piff* of
bullets chopped the earth beside him, forcing a hasty retreat.

As a group of guards moved in from the left, Trip raised his
TX10 to fire but they fanned out behind a cluster of junked equipment, likely dividing forces to flank him. He scrambled back behind
the wheelset and eased around for a shot. Careful to keep behind the
iron framework, he raised his rifle to fire. But no sooner had he got
his bearings than two more rounds sparked off the railing and sent
him scrambling for cover.

Ducking his head under the belly of the railcar, Trip scanned
the ground for more guards. He'd not even had the chance to focus
when a full-auto blast *pinged* and *tinged* off the iron. With options nil
and time nearly gone, Trip threw his barrel around the corner, found
the pipes where the above sniper was hiding, and pulled the trigger
rapid fire.

At nearly the same moment, a barrage of rounds sparked against
the steel and *thunked* into the loose soil at his feet. With every im-
pulse screaming to pull back, Trip forced himself to keep firing. He
had dumped half a magazine into the tubing when something connected that sounded like a fighter jet hitting the afterburners.

The *shriek* and *howl* of the blasting pressure from the punctured
pipe startled Trip enough to send him back for cover. But with the
shooting stopped, he swung around to find his nemesis exposed,
darting across the catwalk. Despite the odd angle Trip found his
target with ease. He had just dropped the sniper when a barrage of
bullets came in from the side.

With guards swarming the railcar, Trip rose and sprinted to open
the bay door and on through into the interior of the plant, all the

while repeating a continuous prayer: *Get me the hell outta here Lord and I'll never do this again.* As he made his way through the darkness, Trip slung the rifle over his shoulder, pulled his SIG P320 from his holster, and clicked on the tac light. He made a sweep of the room for fighters and thankfully came up empty. *At least for now.*

53

Smitty had initially taken the lead in the mission to climb out of the canyon and retrieve the horses, but Asadi quickly passed him by, maneuvering up narrow crags and taking leaps so risky it would pucker a mountain goat. Heights didn't bother Smitty, but a slip of the boot or a missed handhold would spell a nasty end.

At the top of the ridge, Asadi eased his head up and looked to the left. His eyes were wide when he turned back. "Big fire."

Smitty moved next to the boy and looked in the direction of the horses where billowing gray smoke rose to the sky. "Where them guards at?"

Asadi pointed to the opposite end of the canyon. "Back there. Where we start."

Smitty saw that the fire was about a half football field away and the Talon truck not far from it. Two men were in the back bed with their rifles at the ready.

Asadi scanned the prairie around them. "We run and hide."

Smitty understood what Asadi actually meant. There were enough clumps of mesquite brush between them and the horses to move undetected. Before he'd agreed, the kid had popped up, over the ledge and sprinted away. With no choice but to follow, Smitty clambered atop and took off after him.

Zigging and zagging through the labyrinth of thorny trees, Smitty kept his head low. Between the scorching heat and two decades' worth of cigarette smoke in his lungs, he was winded and queasy. The boy finally came to a halt about twenty yards from the horses. Despite all the commotion, the animals still had their heads down nuzzling through the brush and munching on dry grass.

Smitty took a knee by Asadi, who didn't seem tired at all. Pissed at himself for wrecking his health, Smitty took the pack of Winstons from his front pocket and tossed them in the dirt. If he happened to survive, he was going to quit. For real this time.

Asadi pointed to the horses and swirled the air. It was his odd way of pointing out what Smitty was already thinking. To get to them without being seen by the nearby guards, they'd have to come around the backside, which meant a whole lot more running. Before he could argue the kid was already back on his feet and on the move.

Smitty wiped his brow with his shirtsleeve, struggled to rise, and sprinted after him. Hugging the perimeter of the open prairie, he kept hidden behind the brush and made a wide circle around the horses, oddly content given the sprawling grassfire that was raging nearby. Asadi grabbed both sets of reins and handed one over.

Smitty swung into the saddle and felt immediately at home. It'd been over a year since he'd been riding, and though the circumstances weren't even close to ideal, a smile crept onto Smitty's face. But the good vibes didn't last long. The *pop-pop* of gunfire from the guards sent the heel of his boots backward and the big palomino in motion. Smitty was playing catchup, eating Asadi's dust at they raced back toward the spring.

ASADI RODE UP TO THE edge of the canyon, unfurled the rope as quick as he could and dallied the end around the saddle horn while

Ray pulled, his arms working back and forth like the side rods of an old locomotive. When the line was out, Ray widened the loop, and tossed it down.

Unable to see what was going on below, Asadi grew even antsier as the guards' white pickup was only about fifty yards out. "Hurry! They coming!"

Ray turned back and pushed the air with his right hand as he secured the rope with his left. "Now, Asadi! Back him up!"

With Asadi's palatal click, Skip stepped backward. The lariat squeaked and creaked as it went taut. Whatever was happening below must have been okay because Ray kept a steady and confident head nod going as he kept his eyes trained below. Asadi was wondering if the rope had no end when he saw Tony's body rise over the ledge.

As Ray gripped him under the arms and guided him gently to the top, Asadi gave Skip a nudge with his heels and sent the gelding forward to give the rope some slack. Ray hurriedly unloosed Tony from the loop, helped him to his feet and onto Ringo, who was dutifully waiting beside Moxy. The deputy sat tall in the saddle but didn't say a word.

Asadi eased Skip as close to the edge as he could while Ray tossed down the rope for Savanah. But he'd only just made the throw when the Talon pickup burst through the mesquite brush and fired two shots that zinged close by.

Ray turned to Asadi, fear in his eyes. "Ya'll take off! I'll get Savanah!"

Asadi surveyed the length of the gorge where the smoke was thicker. It was moving toward them and would be there soon. "Fire too close!"

"Go Asadi! We'll be fine!" Ray gave him a confident nod. "We'll cross on the other side where they can't get us."

Asadi held fast, uneasy with the idea of leaving them behind. But out of time, they had no choice. He eased Skip beside Moxy, then looked to Tony. "You okay ride?"

The deputy gave a weary nod. With the pickup bearing down on them, Asadi spurred Skip into a run. It would be a hard journey to the backside of the ranch—one Tony seemed unlikely to survive. But both horse and rider were following. The question was for how long.

54

Garrett had wanted to make a plan but given the obstacles facing him and Kim not a whole helluva lot came to mind. Keys jangled outside the door, the lock clicked, and Holloway marched into the room with four guards in tow. He stopped abruptly and flashed a sardonic smile.

"You should have just taken what we offered, Kohl, and moved on with your life."

"And let you destroy what took my family generations to build?" Garrett shook his head. "Not a chance in hell."

Holloway looked a little curious. "You could have just moved on. Found another place. One with better water. Better grass. You could have had it all."

"We already had it all, Holloway. That's what someone like you will never understand."

"Well, I probably understand it better than you think."

Before Garrett could counter, Kim interrupted, addressing Holloway in Russian. Holloway looked perturbed, but his reaction didn't last long. His frown morphed into a grin. "Guess you're smarter than I thought."

She mimicked his reaction. "Was going to say the exact *opposite* about you, Orlov."

It took only a moment for Garrett to remember where he'd heard the name, and then it all came flashing back. Orlov was the Russian firm Bridger had discovered that was related to Scepter Trading, the import company connected to Russia that was taking minerals off the ranch. Both Orlov and Talon used the same fire-bird emblem—the same one associated with the mercenaries Ike had seen in Africa.

Before Garrett could verbalize it, Kim filled him in. "Garrett, meet Alexi Orlov. I would say *formerly* a Russian intelligence officer, but I guess you never really retired, did you?"

Orlov looked to his guards, seemingly amused, and spoke back to Kim with a Slavic inflection. "I'm impressed. You have managed to piece together my identity. In all these years. On all my assignments around the world. No one else has done that."

Kim looked him dead on. "So are GRU pensions so bad you have to spend the rest of your life digging in the dirt?"

"It's not *always* about the money." Orlov turned and looked directly at Garrett, clearly having remembered the earlier conversation with Vicky Kaiser, who made the point that it was.

"Then it's power," Kim countered, "You said it yourself. We lap it up like thirsty dogs."

"Power and money go hand in hand. But what I have come to learn is that palaces crumble, crowns tarnish, and thrones are rigid and dull."

Garrett interjected. "So you're destroying our lives because you're bored."

"No. I'm simply here to do business."

"Then do it somewhere else," Garrett shot back.

"Battleground is in your backyard, Mr. Kohl. Bad luck, I'm afraid."

Garrett grinned. "Bad luck for you too, I guess. Found the right spot. Just messed with the wrong people."

Orlov grinned back, seeming to enjoy the banter. "We purchased your lease, as you Americans say, *fair and square*. Like we do all over the world."

"*Fair and square?*" Kim scoffed. "I've seen the photos of the dead bodies that come in the wake of your mining projects. Nothing fair about that."

"I said it was fair," Orlov countered. "Didn't say it wasn't messy." He looked to Garrett. "It's not personal. It's just war. You know a little something about serving your country, don't you?"

"You're a real patriot," Garrett shot back.

"Patriotism is for the poor," Orlov mocked. "And of course, the ones selling it for personal gain. If anyone understands why I do what I do, I suppose it would be you."

"And how do you figure that?" Garrett asked.

"Because what we do is more than a profession. It's a *calling*. It's who we are."

Garrett wanted to play it off as nonsense, but the truth of Holloway's words hit home hard. Not a day went by that he didn't question giving up undercover work. It gets in your blood and is almost impossible to let go. He'd felt it as a Green Beret, and as a DEA special agent. His profession wasn't just a job. It was his identity.

Unwilling to concede that, Garrett argued, "Maybe for you. I've got a life."

"They call it the spy game for a reason." Orlov took a couple of steps toward Garrett. "Like chess, it requires strategy, cunning, and deception. The latter of which used to be my forte." He narrowed his gaze on Kim, looking amused. "Until now apparently."

"All good points." Still hoping Trip might bust through that door at any moment, Garrett took a stab at a joke to buy some time. "Might need a day or two to think them over."

Orlov seemed to appreciate the humor. "Sorry, but we have to conclude our business." He eased closer, seeming to eye the ledge. "And a fall will do quite nicely." There was a gleam in his eyes. "Time to take care of you like I did your little Afghan boy."

He'd barely gotten the sentence out when Garrett rushed forward. But the guards grabbed hold and pushed him toward the ledge, his heels skidding on the concrete as he fought for traction. Just inches from the end, Garrett jerked his head back, smashing the guard's face behind him, then pivoted and swung a wide right hook that busted the other's jaw.

Grabbing the stunned gunman by the straps of his chest rig, Garrett slammed his forehead into the guy's nose and shoved him over the edge. With the reverberating scream as he plunged to his death, Garrett swiveled, curled his left hand into a fist and slammed it into the chin of another and followed with a front kick to the groin.

A gasp and a groan and the man fell forward, revealing Kim and the other two guards. With a rifle trained on him, Garrett anticipated the shot to come when the gunman shuddered, stumbled backward, and looked down in disbelief at the red splotch on his chest.

Garrett and Kim dove forward as the *check . . . check . . . check* of a suppressed rifle echoed in the distance. Keeping flush with the floor, Garrett counted the bodies that crumbled one by one. As Orlov fled the room, Garrett clambered over a dead body to help Kim to her feet. They both did the requisite pat down, checking themselves and each other for wounds.

Certain they were both uninjured, Garrett turned to the outside to look for Trip. But his friend was too well concealed. And it really didn't matter. The only thing that did was getting the hell out of there and making it to the ranch as quickly as possible.

Kim didn't need any instruction. She immediately grabbed the CZ rifle from a dead guard and stripped off his chest rig and Garrett did the same with the one who'd taken his Nighthawk. Seconds later, they were on the move and out the door.

55

If Lacey thought the hundred-mile-an-hour race to Borger was terrifying, it was nothing compared to pulling off the highway and veering onto a deserted county road. Crowley's massive Ford F-250 was a regular fixture around Canadian but it seemed mysteriously out of place near Borger.

Lacey turned to her so-called friend, wondering if she'd been set up. "What the hell is going on here, Vicky?"

Vicky pulled her Range Rover behind Crowley's truck and put it in park. She kept her gaze forward. "You wanted help, didn't you?"

Lacey jabbed her finger at the truck. "Yeah. Why is *he* here?"

"Because we need him."

Lacey strained her eyes but saw no one inside the cab. "Need him for what, exactly?"

Vicky exhaled and turned to Lacey. "I know you don't trust him. But he's on our side, okay."

"*Our* side?"

Vicky paused. "Well, *my* side."

Crowley leapt out of his F-250 holding an AR-15 and turned to the Range Rover. He racked a bullet in the chamber as he marched over.

Crystal leaned forward from the backseat. "Uh . . . what's going on here?"

As Lacey reached for the handle, Vicky grabbed her arm. "Lacey, you're right about Crowley. He's a crook. But he's *my* crook. Understand?"

Lacey turned and met Crowley's gaze. "No. I *don't* understand."

Vicky turned forward again, her eyes seemingly resting on nothing at all. "This is the reason I returned home. To get the business back from Talon. And Crowley's going to help me do it."

"You can't be serious," Lacey shot back.

"I am serious," Vicky affirmed with a nod. "I'm not going to let some outsiders slink into town and steal what my family built here for over a century."

"You mean what your family *stole* from everyone else."

It was a kneejerk reaction, and it wasn't exactly true. There was a difference between being cunning and a criminal, and most of the Kaisers had hovered somewhere between the two. It was only Vicky's brother who had crossed the line.

Vicky turned back again. "I know what Preston did and I'm not proud of that. But that wasn't my father. Or my grandfather. And that's why I want to restore my family's name."

Lacey knew the feeling. After losing every dime they had and her father's suicide she would've done anything to restore the Capshaws' reputation. "So, what's the game here, Vicky? You and Crowley against Talon? How's that going to work?"

"It's not just me and the sheriff. It's the families that settled this land. The families that built it. The Kaisers, the Kohls, and the Capshaws."

"And don't forget about the Smittys." Lacey turned to Crystal who'd been silent for a while. "They're in this too now."

Vicky swallowed hard, looking a little queasy. "And the Smittys, I guess."

As a convoy of one-ton work trucks and four-by-fours pulled up behind the Range Rover, Vicky rolled down the window where Crowley was standing outside. "We got everybody?"

The sheriff nodded. "Ones who ain't in the pen, at least."

Lacey took it to mean they were Kaiser devotees. By the looks of it, the ones who filed out were oil-field workers and cowboys who'd worked for Mescalero—a ragtag posse clad in boots, blue jeans, and Stetsons—armed to the teeth with pump shotguns and tactical rifles.

Lacey couldn't believe she was teaming up with Crowley and the Kaisers, but what choice did she have? The alternative was losing Garrett, and that wasn't an option. As the gang formed around the sheriff and Vickey's open window Crowley began to speak.

"Boys, I don't have to tell you what's at stake here. It's the chance we've been waiting for to take back what's ours. Once we do that, we're back in business."

Lacey suspected *business* meant criminal activity, which is what they'd done in the past. She was tempted to ask but opted to keep quiet. All that mattered was Garrett's safety. Crowley wrapped up the bizarre pep rally and his gang dashed to their trucks. He took off his cowboy hat, wiped the sweat from his brow with a handkerchief and looked right at Lacey.

"I know what you think about me. And I know why." Crowley returned the hat to his head. "I ain't claiming to be an angel, but I am *loyal*. And my loyalty lies to this empire. And I don't mean the Kaisers neither. I'm talking about *our* people. Not these damn carpetbaggers."

For the first time in her life, Lacey understood what others saw in Crowley. In a world of dirty players, he was one of their own. A native son. She didn't like him any more for it, but she saw his worth. Sometimes you need a lawman who's a little on the dirty side.

"Okay, Sheriff, what's your plan?" Lacey asked.

Crowley took a step back. "I want ya'll to hop in with me. Talon guards will be less likely to start shooting if they see an official vehicle coming in lights flashing." He winced as he added, "Don't mean they won't. But it might buy us a second or two."

A million thoughts raced through Lacey's mind and at the fore-front was her children. But neither Crowley nor Vicky was the type to put themselves in too great a risk. The duo were masters of self-preservation, which meant they were confident in their success.

Crowley flashed his campaign poster smile. "You in? You out?"

Lacey thought back to her mother's advice from earlier. *When it comes to love, never ever leave anything on the table.* That's when she made the decision that she was all in. Clearing her mind of anything else, she grabbed the handle, threw open the door, and marched to Crowley's truck with the girls behind her in lockstep.

56

Smitty hacked and coughed with nearly every breath of air he pulled into his lungs. But it wasn't the decades of puffing on Winstons that was tormenting him this time. It was the acrid fumes that were blowing through the canyon. With all the dry kindling, the flames had no buffer, moving bush to bush, tree to tree, devouring the tall tufts of brittle prairie grass as it moved toward him.

Returning to the exact spot he'd left his daughter, Smitty cupped his hand and put it beside his mouth. "Savanah! Savanah!" He turned in circles, trying like hell to keep his watering eyes open given the burn of the swirling smoke. "Just walk to my voice, darlin' girl! I'll find you!"

Smitty waited a few seconds but heard nothing but the roar of the fire. Pushing through the thick mesquite, he was scratched by the thorns. But he made no effort to avoid the barbs. The terror of losing his daughter far superseded the pain of the scrapes and gashes.

"Savanah! Savanah! Just call out to me! Please!"

Smitty had just taken the swipe of a branch across the bridge of his nose when an exposed root caught the toe of his boot and he stumbled face-first to the ground. With his hands bloody and stinging, he brushed off the shards of rock embedded in his palms. He was struggling to his feet when he heard the faint voice call out *Daddy*.

Almost too afraid to believe she was there, Smitty looked up to find Savanah curled in a ball beneath an overhang in the cliff—a little pocket of fresh air. *Asadi's cave.*

Smitty sprinted to Savanah, pulled her into his arms, hugged her tight. "You okay, darlin' girl? You okay?" Smitty let loose and looked her over. "You hurt?"

Savanah shook her head. "No, Daddy, I'm alright. But I can't hardly breathe."

"Me neither, baby." Smitty looked around. "We gotta get up above this smoke." He took her by the hand and led her to the side of the canyon, finding out it was too steep to climb. Only way they were getting out of there was to turn around and head toward the flames.

ASADI KEPT LOOKING BACK AT Tony to make sure he and Ringo were still following behind. Good news was that they'd outrun the truck that was chasing them. Bad news was there was no turning back. The flames, leaping from the canyon, had moved out onto the plains and the wind was pushing the fire in their direction. It looked as if clouds from the sky had fallen down to earth.

Feeling safe for the moment, Asadi pulled Skip's reins and eased into a walk. In a matter of seconds, Tony was beside them. Although he was pale and his eyelids heavy, the deputy held on tight to the saddle horn to keep himself righted. Suddenly, the Talon pickup roared through the mesquite and out into the open pasture.

Uncertain of their own fate, Asadi looked to Tony for answers. And as if on cue, he pulled the pistol from his holster, spurred Ringo into a run and charged the truck head-on.

57

Trip kept his eyes on his scope, panning the open-air ledge for Garrett and Kim. Given his limited view, he couldn't see beyond the walls to either side of the open bay door but assumed they'd made it out alive. Only thing left was a pile of dead bodies. As it turned out, Trip's hasty climb to the top of the cooling tower had been an exhausting but worthwhile endeavor.

He was just about to check the blind spot at his six when a gunman ran out into the courtyard below. He moved a few feet down the catwalk and repositioned above the railing to get a better angle on his target. It took only a second to realize that it was the silver-haired man in the room with Garrett and Kim—the one who'd been doing all that talking.

Trip rested the crosshairs on his head and eased his finger forward to take the shot. He was pulling the trigger when an explosion came from behind and his shot went high.

Trip dropped the TX10, jerked the SIG from his holster, and fired wildly at the door. As the rifle barrel swung around the edge and opened up full-auto, Trip sprinted for cover behind a rusted-out motor. Raising his head once taught him not to do it twice.

GARRETT THREW HIS BACK TO the wall and looked to Kim, who was on the other side of the threshold with her rifle at the ready. She eased out for a peek, but made it no further than a couple of inches when the doorframe was blasted to kindling.

In her hasty retreat for cover, Garrett hung his Bren around the corner to return fire but immediately regretted it. A flurry of rounds screamed through the door ripping everything in the storeroom to shreds. With Orlov's men regrouped and rearmed, it wouldn't be long before they rushed en masse.

Garrett was formulating a plan B when a hissing cylinder flew through the doorway and slid across the concrete until it clacked against the back wall. When glass shattered from side windows and two more canisters of tear gas rolled across the floor, Garrett knew they had only two options left—stay there and suffocate or go outside to face a maelstrom of lead.

ASADI LEANED FORWARD AND SPURRED Skip into a run behind Tony, but he could barely keep up with the fierce palomino. The wild west deputy was no longer hanging on for dear life. He was riding tall in the saddle—reins gripped in the left hand and his pistol in the right.

Only yards from a head-on collision with the Talon pickup racing toward them, Tony aimed and fired, pockmarking the windshield. He missed colliding with the truck by only inches, slowed Ringo to a trot, then lined up again. Tony spurred the gelding into another charge, aimed his pistol and fired at the gunmen in the back of the truck. He had just dropped a guard when an enemy round landed and knocked him from the saddle.

Asadi guided Skip in Tony's direction, and immediately the gunmen turned their sights on him. With rounds zipping overhead, he prodded his buckskin harder. He had just reached his friend when a shooter in the truck bed took aim and shot. Flinching in anticipation, Asadi looked up to find the source of the thundering noise that rose over the gunfire.

AS IKE MOVED HIS HELICOPTER into position ahead of the Talon pickup, he spoke to his door gunners over the intercom. "You on 'em?"

"I'm on 'em," Butch answered back.

Ike gave his bird some left pedal, opening the left side of the Hughes to the scene playing out about two hundred feet ahead. Both shooters opened fire, Butch with his Marlin and Kate with her deer rifle, hitting their targets as the chopper blasted past the truck.

One shot. One kill. The old codgers were as cool under pressure as any operators Ike had ever carried into battle. While the three in the truck bed were out of commission, the two in the cab were still alive and ready to fight. They filed out of the vehicle and fired up at them full-auto.

Ike yanked the collective to get a little lift and pushed the stick left to loop back around. He'd gone easy on his door gunners the first round but kicked it up over eighty miles an hour to make his bird a difficult target. Coming in hot over the pickup, Ike gave it some left pedal again to open up the shot and let his shooters go to work.

Kate got her target, but Butch missed. It must've been a close one though because the last gunman ran back to the truck, jumped inside, and gunned it. His wheels kicked up a dust trail as he tore away from there like a bat out of hell.

Not wanting to tangle with the bastard again, Ike looped around, brought his helo low, right over the cab. Neither Butch nor Kate were thrifty with ammo, shooting round after round until the truck rolled to a stop.

Ike pushed the stick right and circled back for Sanchez and the boy. Figuring Butch wouldn't leave his horses, he had to ask, "With that fire headed this way, I'm thinking you won't be leaving your animals."

"Not on your life, son." Butch turned and pointed to the ground. "Drop me right here and I'll get them out through the backside of the ranch. I know a shortcut."

Kate piped up from the back. "Coming with you, Butch."

"No, you ain't. Need someone here to doctor on Sanchez and look after Asadi."

"I ain't no damn nursemaid," Kate shouted back. "And that boy can look after himself. Them horses cain't. And they're in a helluva lot of trouble unless we get them out of here."

Ike hated the idea of leaving Butch and Kate behind, but he knew she was right. Circling around and landing, Butch and Kate jumped out and dragged Sanchez on board. Once the deputy was secured in back, the duo sprinted to the horses.

Asadi jumped into the passenger seat, donned the headphones like an old pro and turned to Ike. "We got get going."

It wasn't the time nor the place, but Ike had to smile. The kid was all business, just like Garrett. He gave a salute, pulled the collective and gave it some right pedal, rocketing toward the hospital in what he suspected would be a vain attempt to save Sanchez's life.

58

Smitty determined that he could go no further back up the canyon, the smoke was too thick and the heat too blistering. He lifted his daughter up and threw her over his shoulder. Finding the best path up the wall, Smitty rose one miserable step after the other. With something between the sheer will to survive and the hand of God at his back, he made it up top and over the edge, exhausted after having lost two steps in the crumbling sand for every one that had caught hold.

Once secured over the ledge, he eased Savanah to the ground then leaned over and wretched. Between the burning heat, the smoke in his lungs, and the exertion of the climb, he was all but spent.

Savanah moved to him and massaged his back. "You okay, Daddy?"

Smitty nodded, unable to speak at first, then he turned and drew her close for a hug. He looked her over and cleared his throat of the smoke. "I know you're tired, sweetheart. But we gotta keep going. We gotta run. Okay?" Then Smitty look around and realized there was nowhere to go. The wildfire had surrounded them, and it was closing in fast.

Determined not to let her see his panic, Smitty rose, said a quick prayer, and searched for a savior. And in the briefest of moments, the smoke cleared, revealing Big Yeller not forty yards away at the canyon's edge. Grabbing Savanah by the hand, he dragged her in a near sprint to the giant iron bulldozer, through the flames—across that charred ground that scorched his feet.

With Savanah screaming in pain, he swung her into his arms as he sprinted the last twenty yards, then tore up the steps to the cab, careful not to touch the burning handrail. Using his sleeve to click the button and open the door, he placed Savanah inside and threw himself into the driver's seat. Fortunately, the diesel motor was still running and the air conditioner blasting, providing a little cold air to keep the controls from burning his hands.

Smitty put the dozer in reverse and backed it from the canyon's edge at full throttle. With machinery in motion, he grabbed his sack lunch and dumped out all the contents to the floor. He snatched up the twenty-four-ounce black can of Monster Energy drink, popped the top and thrust it at Savanah, who drained half of the contents before giving it back.

After a few big swallows, Smitty poured some into his cupped hand and rubbed it on Savanah's face, wiping the smoke from her eyes. He had no plan to speak of, other than to get the hell out of there. But with smoke and flames already rising over the steel tracks, it was only a matter of time before the fire engulfed the dozer and swallowed them whole.

LACEY WATCHED IN THE REARVIEW mirror from the passenger side of Crowley's F-250 as the Mescalero posse peeled away and went in a separate direction. They were nearing the desolate grounds surrounding the Carbon Black plant when the sheriff jammed his foot on the gas as he tore off the county road and headed down the access lane to the entrance.

At first glance, the facility looked deserted. The front gate was chained and padlocked shut, a fact that didn't seem to faze Crowley. He mashed the accelerator to the floor, driving the Power Stroke turbo diesel engine into a vicious snarl.

Turning back to Vicky, who looked unusually calm given the circumstance, Lacey had to ask, "There is a plan, right?"

A very anxious-looking Crystal, who was sitting next to Vicky, looked ready to burst. "What are we doing?"

"Don't worry." Vicky had that look, the one bordering somewhere between confident and cocky. "The sheriff and his men have it all under control."

Before Lacey could even ask, Crowley shouted a warning, "Hold on tight! We're going in!"

No sooner had Lacey grabbed onto the handle and braced herself than the sheriff flicked on his lights, aimed his grille guard at the center of the chain-link entrance, and busted through the gate like it wasn't even there. They were just inside the compound when a half-dozen gunmen in the courtyard turned their weapons on them and fired.

Crowley slammed his boot on the brakes, and the Ford skidded to a halt. "Get down! Get down!"

Lacey ducked below the dashboard and looked up as the sheriff threw the vehicle in park. He grabbed his AR-15 from the console, yanked the driver's side door handle and jumped out. Taking cover behind the hood, he blasted his rifle at the Talon gunmen.

Lacey was tempted to raise for a peek over the dash when a *thunk-thunk-thunk-thunk* of bullets sinking into the truck hood and the intermittent *ping* of lead hitting the grille forced her to reconsider. The salvo raked along the passenger side, shattering the front and back windows, and ripping a string of holes through the roof.

Lacey yelled to Vicky over the rapid-fire bang of Crowley's gun,

"What do we do now?" Vicky had just started to answer when another volley drilled the passenger door by Lacey's head.

Vicky yelled back, "I don't know! But this isn't it!"

Lacey had just looked to Crowley again when she saw him crouch low, put the rifle to his shoulder and race toward the action. Assuming it was clear to rise, she poked her head above the door and surveyed the courtyard. The shooters were now gone. And it was clear by the fading echo of gunfire that the fight had moved further into the plant's interior.

As Lacey eased into the driver's seat, Vicky moved from the back, clambering over the console into the passenger's seat. Turning in every direction, Lacey searched for a way out. She had just spotted the entrance when several rounds *thunked* into the hood.

Lacey threw the truck in drive, mashed the gas, and aimed for the nearest building to take cover on the other side. It was only thirty yards but enough time for the Talon guards to shoot out her front and back tires on the right, dashing any hopes of a getaway.

Both she and Vicky followed Crystal's lead, fleeing the exposed pickup and sprinting for cover inside the front door of the main office. The plant was in complete war zone chaos, with an unceasing clatter of shooting from men darting from building to building in a tit-for-tat exchange. And for the first time ever, Lacey prayed that Sheriff Crowley was on the winning side.

59

Garrett jammed his nose and mouth into the crook of his left arm and aimed the Bren rifle with his right. Unable to stand the teargas a moment more, he burst through the doorway with Kim in tow, wincing in anticipation of the hail of lead that was no doubt sure to come. But to his shock and subsequent joy the courtyard was abandoned and his GMC waiting right where he'd left it, albeit full of bullet holes and the windows busted out.

Kim eased up beside him rifle at the ready. "What happened? Where'd they go?"

As the knock of heavy gunfire echoed through the plant, Garrett turned his Bren and aimed but found no immediate threat. "Someone saved our asses. That's what happened." He lowered his weapon and turned to Kim. "This has Mario Contreras written all over it."

"Couldn't agree more." Kim looked in the direction of the shooting. "But as far as I know he and the team are still in Virginia."

Garrett tilted his head toward his GMC. "Truck looks pretty ugly, but I think it's still running. You need to get to a hospital."

Kim gave a shake of the head. "Not leaving without you."

Garrett wasn't sure she understood how bad she was injured. "Look, Trip is still out there. And I aim to find him."

"Then I'll help."

"Kim, we got a little love from someone out there, but we're going to need more guns in the fight to finish these guys off. There's a highway patrol depot in town. Get there quick as you can and tell them we need every man they've got."

Knowing Kim would find a reason to stay, Garrett didn't wait around for her to argue. He shouldered his rifle and sprinted to the tower where he suspected Trip had been when he'd taken out the gunmen. As Garrett ran through the winding corridors of the plant he couldn't help but think back on the urban warfare he'd experienced in the streets of Iraq—the reverberating *rattle* of full-auto rifles and the ricochet of bullets on concrete and steel.

LACEY FOUND THE SHADOWY DARK corridors of the Carbon Black plant's administration building oddly serene. With the battle raging outside, there was something about the muffled gunfire and damp dewy chill within that felt like a safe haven—a place where everything might be okay.

With light coming from the window, she could see the room they had ended up in very well. The dusty office that had once belonged to Vicky's father was like the Texas version of *Mad Men*—frozen in time. Its walls were covered in trophy buck head mounts, exotics of every kind, and about a million old photographs that hung wonky on the wall.

Of all the many things on Lacey's mind the last should have been nostalgia. But as much as she hated to admit it, Lacey understood Vicky's take on Sheriff Crowley. He may be a *crook*, but he is *my crook*, she'd said. Lacey felt the same about the Kaisers. They were the devil you knew.

Lacey moved to the window and peeked outside to find gunmen darting through the compound taking cover, returning fire, and moving again. Vicky's inexplicable confidence was her only indication that the good guys would win. Lacey was beginning to wonder if she should drink the cocky Kaiser Kool-Aid when she saw a Talon gunman sprinting toward them.

SMITTY HAD EXPECTED THE SMOKE to have cleared by now, but it was only getting worse. The grayish brown plumes billowing over the cab had engulfed the dozer entirely. Keeping an eye on the temperature gauge which had tilted into the red, he wondered how long it'd be before the engine would stop running, or worse yet, what would happen if fire reached the fuel tank.

Trying not to panic, Smitty turned to Savanah and forced a smile. "Hanging in there, darlin' girl?"

Savanah returned the gesture, which looked equally strained. "Daddy, we gonna make it?"

"Of course, we are. We've just gotta get down the path a little, that's all." Smitty pointed to the windshield. "See how the wind's blowing the smoke? The direction it's moving?"

Savanah looked to every window, as if really studying it. "Going south to north, I think."

"And we're headed south. Which means we'll get on the other side of this smoke real soon. Just looks bad cause the fire line was moving toward us. We'll just be fine though. You'll see."

"But we've been going for a long time." Savanah turned to him, worry etched on her face. "Why haven't we made it yet?"

Damn good question. Smitty knew they'd never outrun the blaze, but if they could get upwind, they might have a chance. Of course, he also knew that a big fire like this one could spread. And there was a chance he was taking them from a bad spot to a worse one.

To change the subject, he pulled out his phone and checked it.

Although there was still no signal, Smitty handed it to Savanah. "Why don't you call your mom?"

It was a suggestion Smitty had put off until now. First and foremost, he was almost certain there was still no service. But the last thing he wanted to do was worry Crystal. At the same time, there was a real possibility that this was the end. And if it was, then at least they'd tried.

Savanah took the handoff and noticed what Smitty already had. There weren't any bars. "Says 'no signal.'"

Smitty nodded, still looking forward. "I know baby, but just give it a shot. Okay?"

He had no idea how cell phones worked but thought that maybe even if the call didn't make it, Crystal's phone would register that they'd tried. So she'd at least know that they cared, and in their very last moments they were thinking about her.

As Savanah fiddled with the phone trying to get it to work, Smitty looked down at the temp gauge to find it was as deep as it could go into the red. He was trying to fight his own alarm when the engine stammered, then the dozer went herky-jerky and died with a sudden jolt.

"*Daddy!*" Startled, Savanah dropped the phone. "What happened?"

Without the motor's rumble the eerie crackle and hiss of flames filled the void. Smitty worked to get the dozer started, pleading under his breath, "Come on, Big Yeller. Come on."

There was an electric hum when he turned the key, but nothing more. He tried again. And again. Then it finally sputtered to life. Clamping his eyes shut and letting out a big exhale, Smitty shifted into gear. The dozer moved several feet then locked up tight as the engine went silent.

Repeating the starting procedure, Smitty urged the dozer into action, this time loudly. "Come on! Come on! You damn piece of crap! Come! On!"

Smitty kept at it and kept at it, but no amount of verbal abuse would coax the big beast back into action. They had gone as far as they could go. The problem was that far as they could go wasn't near far enough.

Fighting back tears, Smitty turned to his daughter who was smart enough to figure that out. "Let's give your mama a call."

Stifling a sob, Savanah nodded. "Okay, Daddy."

Smitty pulled her close and gave her a hug, then reached to the floorboard to pick up the phone. After flipping it over and brushing the dust off the screen, he was shocked as hell to find the last thing in the world he'd expected. His check for a signal revealed *one single bar*. Smitty said a quick desperate prayer and swiped the screen open for possibly the last call he'd ever make.

60

Trip ducked another hail of bullets that sparked the railing above his head and tried to make himself as small as possible. He threw his back against a piece of machinery, cooked hot by the menacing sun, and felt the immediate burn of iron on skin. Unable to sit tight another second, Trip shifted his weight for a move when another *thenk-thenk* from the suppressed rifle at the doorway was supplanted by a single exploding bang.

With the Bren silenced, Trip leaned out to find Garrett in the doorway, standing over a dead body. Yanking a kerchief from his back pocket, Trip wiped his brow. "What took you so long?"

Garrett, still panting from the climb, just shook his head and smiled. "Too damn many stairs."

Trip scrambled to his feet and peered over the side in search of the answer he'd been seeking since the gun battle started. "Who are these boys on *our* side?"

Garrett moved up beside him. "No idea. But I'd say we're in a good spot to give them a hand." He exchanged his Nighthawk for the Bren. "Bad guys are in uniform. Shoot at them. See any rednecks that look like us. Leave 'em be."

Trip holstered his own SIG, picked up the TX10, and made a sweep of the ground below with his scope. The outlaw operators, in boots, jeans, and Stetsons, were unleashing hell on the Talon guards. He took three quick shots at the silver-haired gunman but missed.

"Dammit!" Off target also, Garrett lowered his rifle. "Went into the main office."

Trip put eyes on optics again to see if he could get another look. "He's the boss man?"

"Yep." Garrett gave a nod. "Russian named Orlov."

Trip couldn't believe what he'd heard. "*Russian?*"

"I'm going after him."

Trip kept the crosshairs on the office door where Orlov disappeared in case he came back out. "Want me to go with you?"

"Nah, just give me a little cover fire to get across the courtyard." Without another word, he bolted for the door, his boots clanging on the iron grating as he sprinted away.

IKE TURNED TO CHECK ON Sanchez for about the fiftieth time. As a Little Bird pilot with the Night Stalkers, he'd been more accustomed to doling out punishment than being on the receiving end. To think the deputy had made it through four overseas combat tours, only to be KIA where he hailed from was a hard pill to swallow, especially knowing that he had a family waiting for him back at home.

Planning to ignore whoever the hell was calling, Ike decided to make an exception when he saw it was Ray Smitty. Of course, he'd not told Asadi, but he'd pretty much given up hope. Snatching the phone from his console, Ike hit the Bluetooth to take the call through his headset.

"Where you at, Smitty?"

There was dead air, some crackling, then Smitty's frantic voice. "Pray to God you're close, Ike."

"Depends." Ike couldn't help but smile. "Hope like hell you're not still on the Kohl place."

"Right here in the middle of it. Me and Savanah. About a half mile west of that canyon on the south end. We're in bad trouble. You gotta come for us."

"You sure there ain't no other option?" Ike turned back to check on Sanchez. "See, I'm headed straight for the hospital and—"

"No!" Smitty cried. "There ain't no one else, man! You're it! You gotta help us!"

Ike struggled with what to do. Sanchez looked bad. Death's door kind of bad. Going back now would almost certainly spell the end for him. But if he didn't go back, Smitty and his daughter would die an agonizing death.

Ike knew exactly what Sanchez would want him to do but that didn't make his decision any easier. He gritted his teeth and pushed the stick left, swinging his bird into a tight U-turn.

"Hang tight, Smitty. Be there soon as I can."

Asadi turned to Ike. "What you doing? We have go hospital!"

"I know, buddy. I know. We're headed there soon. But Ray and Savanah need our help. We can't leave them behind."

"*Savanah?*" Asadi's face brightened. "She okay?"

Ike nodded, not knowing if she would be when they got there. "That girl your friend?"

"She my *best* friend." Asadi kept his eyes forward, head on a swivel, searching the smoke-filled horizon. "Going sit with me at lunch."

Given the desperation in Ray's voice, they were in immediate danger. But this was no swoop in and out kind of rescue. It'd have to be done among the smoke and flames. Ike hated to imagine the gruesome carnage they might find. Asadi would never recover from it.

It'd been years since the Mogadishu disaster, but to Ike it still felt like yesterday. He couldn't let this happen to Asadi this early on. Those nightmares were hard enough to bear as a grown man, much less a child. The boy had enough demons already.

SMITTY COULDN'T BELIEVE HOW FAST the heat had overtaken the dozer. Just minutes after the engine locked up and the air conditioner went off it was nearly unbearable. Even without a raging wildfire, sitting inside the cab as they were with no ventilation beneath a blazing Texas sun was assured heatstroke. He and Savanah were minutes away from suffocating.

Smitty mustered up the calmest voice he could for a man surrounded by roaring flames. "Darlin' girl, we can't sit here any longer. We gotta get some air."

Savanah looked all around in panic, knowing what Smitty knew. The only thing between them and the fire was the cab of that dozer. She broke into sobs. "But where can we go?"

Smitty pulled her into a tight embrace and kissed the top of her head. "Ike's coming for us. If we get on the roof, he'll see us better anyhow. We'll be alright, I promise."

How could he promise anything? Smitty looked around again, hoping for a break in the smoke but it was only getting worse. Ike had said that he was close, but who really knew. He was probably just placating him—the way he had just done with Savanah. He grabbed her hand and stood hunched over, his head beneath the roof.

Turning to his daughter, he kissed her on the head again, trying to think of the right words but coming up short. With nothing left to do, he took Savanah in his arms and lifted her up onto his chest. She wrapped her legs around his waist and buried her face in his neck. Smitty could feel the wetness of her tears on his collar.

Spinning around, Smitty clicked the latch, kicked the door open with his boot, and immediately took the punch of heat and smoke. Savanah screamed at the fire's intensified crackling hiss, and Smitty couldn't say that he blamed her. It terrified him to his very core. What's worse, the smoke stung his eyes so fiercely they instinctively clamped shut. Only able to force his right lid open a sliver, he stepped out onto the stairs and froze.

Could he do this? Could he climb to the top by feel, holding on to his daughter for dear life? He turned back, contemplating a retreat, but that was only delaying the inevitable. If Ike came, they had to be up top.

Smitty took a couple of steps onto the platform and felt the side of the cab. With Savanah's soft sobs his motivation, he grabbed hold of the roof, put his boots on the railing, and shimmied up and over the door to the top of the cab. To his relief, getting an extra ten feet or so gave them a little more air, but his strength was giving out and Smitty was unable to keep holding Savanah.

After easing her onto the roof, she surveyed her surroundings, which Smitty already knew were no less terrifying than what they could see from the cab. Now above the smoke, she could see the massive wall of flames heading right for them. And Ike was nowhere in sight.

61

Ike tried a fourth call to Smitty but got no answer. He hoped like hell it was lack of service and not the unthinkable, but as they flew over the area and saw the fire's destruction reality set in. The earth was charred black, and everything that once stood in the fire's way—including homes, barns, and barbed-wire fences—was all in smoldering heaps of ash and debris.

It was as close a look at Hell as Ike ever wanted.

Asadi spoke over the intercom. "When we find them?"

Poor kid had no idea this was turning from a rescue mission to a recovery operation. Ike turned back to Sanchez whose chest didn't move. If he was breathing at all it was shallow.

Ike couldn't bring himself to look Asadi in the eye. "Soon. Real soon." If he was telling whoppers, might as well tell another good one. "Almost there, kid."

Having made a pass across the length of the fire front, Ike veered right, came back in, and swooped through the smoke. He kept a close eye on his instruments—notably the altimeter and attitude indicator—making sure they were level. He wouldn't be the first pilot to get disoriented and nosedive into the ground.

Finding nothing but hazy skies, Ike pushed the stick left and circled wide for one last pass over the ranch. He was nearly out of the haze when the smoke parted between two fire lines revealing a bright yellow flash. Ike tilted the stick right and looped back around. Unfortunately, he was too late. Whatever he *thought* he saw was engulfed again by the smoke.

Afraid he'd pass it by again, Ike pulled the cyclic and slowed to a hover to get his bearings. Straining his eyes to see through the gray haze, he was startled by a sudden punch on the arm. He looked right to find Asadi hopping with excitement and back pointing in the opposite direction.

"Look! Look! Over there!" Asadi's eyes were saucers. "See! Over there!"

Ike gave his bird a little right pedal, aimed at where Asadi was pointing, and pushed the stick forward. A few seconds into the cloudy abyss and the smoke parted to reveal a big yellow dozer between the fire lines. Coming in closer for inspection, his rotor blades pushed away the smoke that had enveloped Smitty and Savanah, who were desperately trying to wave him down.

Ike dropped the thrust as much as he could and swooped in and around, hovering just high enough to keep the thumping rotors at a safe distance but low enough for father and daughter to leap from cab to cockpit. The tricky part was getting in close enough for them to jump but not so close that it would blow them off the cab.

Lowering the collective and nudging the cyclic left, Ike eased his bird to the dozer, lining up the backseat door as best as he could. The rotors had cleared out the smoke, but the damn blasting wind was bullying him off target. Hovering over, inch by inch, Ike got so close that Smitty heaved his daughter into the back where she landed with a thud.

Ike gave it a little left pedal to even up and bumped the stick to get closer. Smitty had just reached for the door when a downdraft caught the bird and slammed his landing skid into the dozer's cab, knocking Smitty off his feet and rolling to the edge of the roof. The crunch of the collision activated the *wope-wope-wope* of the Ground Proximity Alarm—warning Ike of what he already knew—they were about to crash. He was fighting the stick and pedals to regain control when Smitty scrambled to his feet, bolted to the passenger door, and made a diving leap inside.

Unable to hold his bird steady a second more, Ike yanked the collective, rocketing them off the ground, above the smoke, and high enough to figure out where the hell they were. With the Caprock Escarpment running just north, he aimed toward Canadian and pushed the stick forward.

Ike knew it was doubtful that Sanchez would make it back alive, but he'd have not died for nothing. The former Marine had spent a lifetime laying his life on the line, and this time he might've cashed it in. But if there was ever a picture worth dying for, it was the one in the backseat of a teary-eyed father embracing his little girl—the look on his face saying *I'll never let go again*.

62

As Garrett sprinted from the tower to the main office, two guards behind a Talon pickup popped out from behind and fired. The *snap-snap* of two near misses sent Garrett diving for cover. But there was none to be had. Rising to the prone position, he brought the red dot of his rifle to his right eye and swept the barrel back and forth in search of a target.

Garrett flicked the selector to full-auto and cut loose with everything he had. He'd spent nearly half a magazine before letting go of the trigger, as two bodies hit the ground. One didn't move. The other dragged himself behind the truck.

Scrambling to his feet, Garrett sprinted to the back bumper and eased past the tailgate. He'd just peered around the corner when a machine-gun roared to life. The guard was ready but his aim too hasty. Garrett emptied his gun before the shooter got off another round.

With his ammo spent, Garrett tossed the rifle, yanked the Nighthawk from his waistband and made for the front entrance of the main office where the Russian had disappeared. Knowing Orlov could be lurking inside the entryway, Garrett threw his back into the wall, gripped the pistol with both hands, and eased to the edge.

A quick glance through the open door revealed only darkness, so

Garrett bolted past it to the other side of the building. He suspected that the Russian might've reloaded, regrouped, and then snuck out the backdoor. But to his surprise, the only thing he saw was Sheriff Crowley's pickup, nestled in an alleyway close to the wall.

Given the lawman's propensity for corruption, it shouldn't have been that big of a shock. Crowley had been running interference for Talon since the company arrived. Itching at the chance to deliver up a couple of a well-deserved bullets for both parties, Garrett moved back to the entrance, checked around the doorframe and snuck inside.

Nighthawk leading the way, Garrett crept room to room, with only the scant bit of sunlight passing through bent venetian blinds to guide his pathway. With the gunfight still raging, Garrett quickened his pace. But as he rounded the corner and entered the last office, he was shocked to find Orlov was using Lacey as a shield, his Grach 9mm pistol pressed to her temple.

Garrett drew a bead on Orlov's forehead. "Don't be stupid." He was about to pull the trigger when Orlov yanked Lacey's face in front of his own. "Why don't you let her go?" With a tilt of the head at the others, he added, "Them too. And it'll just be you and me."

Orlov shifted Lacey again, their cheeks side by side. "Where's the fun in that?"

Garrett kept his sights on Orlov, but just as soon as he thought he had an opening, the Russian would move, and the shot was lost. The risk too great, he lowered the Nighthawk and held it by his side. "I know for you this is all a game. But take her from me, and you take everything. That's the woman I love."

Orlov loosened his stranglehold on Lacey but kept her near, gun barrel still pressed to the side of her head. "Not so good at keeping your cards close, are you?"

Garrett caught eyes with Lacey. "At some point, you just have to lay them on the table."

Even in the chaos of the moment, it wasn't lost on Garrett that he'd revealed the words she'd been waiting to hear. He didn't know what was to come, or if their future could even be measured beyond the next few seconds. But he wanted her to know the truth. He wanted Lacey to know that he loved her.

Orlov's mouth flattened as he gave a slight nod. "Hand over the gun."

Garrett raised the Nighthawk slowly, turned the barrel into his hand, and held it out with the grip facing outward. "You can have it. Just let her go."

Orlov inched closer, eyes trained on Garrett's pistol. Suddenly, it looked as if he suspected a trap and he halted midstride. "Why don't you come to me?"

It was clear that Orlov was getting antsy. He unfurled his arm from beneath Lacey's neck, reached out, and gave the *gimme here* motion. Garrett took a couple steps and stopped, mentally willing Orlov to keep moving forward. A few more inches would put him in front of the window where Trip would have a shot.

"You want it?" Garrett extended the pistol and waggled it at Orlov. "You can have it."

Losing patience, Orlov clutched Lacey and drew her back into the crook of his arm. "Time's up, Kohl." He mashed the barrel into her cheek.

"Please!" Lacey's voice lulled to a whisper. "Please don't."

It ripped Garrett's heart out to see Lacey so vulnerable, so scared. But he knew Orlov would leave no witnesses. The second Garrett gave up his gun they were all dead.

Garrett pushed the air. "Alright, take it easy." He took three more steps, raised his right hand, palm out, and extended the Nighthawk with his left. "Just let her go."

In the last move he would ever make, Orlov reached for the gun.

Were it not for the shattering glass of the side window, not a sound could be heard—not even from the rifle that fired a bullet into the Russian's brain.

Lacey broke loose of Orlov as he collapsed, and dashed to Garrett. He took her into his arms, squeezing with everything he had left. There was the temptation to latch on forever, but he had to get back out and end this thing once and for all. Garrett moved to the window to signal Trip that they were all okay. But to his shock, it wasn't his buddy who had saved them but an intrepid CIA operations officer, who'd forsaken her own health to stay in the fight.

Beaten, battered, and bloody, Kim Manning was standing outside, rifle still shouldered. It'd been she who'd saved Lacey—and in truth—saved them all.

Behind Kim were the flashing lights of a half dozen black-and-white SUVs with the gold state of Texas emblem on the side. Stetson-clad state troopers jumped out of their vehicles, M4 rifles at the ready and dispersed, headed into battle against what little was left of Orlov's army.

Garrett had a million questions and hardly any answers. But before he could ask any of them, he had to hunt down Sheriff Crowley.

Garrett had just made his move when the devil himself walked through the door. But even more surprising than that was that Crowley didn't look like a caged animal or a man on the run. The scumbag smiled wide, as if he owned West Texas and everyone in it. There was so much to unpack, Garrett didn't know where to begin. But none of that really mattered. Not the Kaisers. Not Crowley. And not even the damn company that started the whole mess.

Garrett's only concern now was his son. Asadi was his life. And anyone who threatened it better be prepared to lose their own.

63

Old Executive Office Building
Washington, D.C.

Less than a month later, Kim sat in silence before the desk of the deputy national security advisor, Conner Murray, waiting for the man she suspected would be delivering marching orders for her new job. Given the embarrassing revelation of Russian influence within the U.S. government, to include several members of Congress and high-ranking officials, there'd be calls for swift, but more importantly, *discreet* action to clean house.

As the CIA operations officer personally responsible for killing Alexi Orlov, it was only natural that Kim would be tapped to run the counterintelligence task force that would hunt down the other rats involved, most of whom had scattered to the four corners of the earth. Her own boss, Bill Watson, was among the traitors, and her primary target.

Kim's first job was to assemble a unit of CIA Ground Branch paramilitary operators capable of the task. After Mario Contreras gladly accepted the assignment, she made a call to Texas. Few were more capable at tracking down people who didn't want to be found than Garrett Kohl.

When Murray breezed in, Kim recognized the look of a man faking nonchalance, pretending that what had happened with Orlov and the Russian connection to congressional leadership and governmental institutions was just one of those things that happens from time to time. The truth of the matter is that foreign infiltration *does* occur but rarely is it as widespread.

Aldrich Ames, Ana Montes, and Robert Hanssen were villains of the worst kind, who had inflicted major damage on the CIA, DIA, and FBI's reputations—not to mention the harm they'd done to national security. But wide-ranging conspiracy involving Talon Corporation and Russian intelligence was unprecedented.

Murray took a seat behind his desk, gathered the loose papers on top, and compiled them into a single stack. "Sorry to keep you waiting, Kim. As you might imagine, things have been a bit crazy around here." He looked up from his tidying. "CIA director has assured us that you understand what we need from your task force. But I still wanted to speak with you in person in order to emphasize the need for discretion here."

Kim smiled to keep things courteous. "I've been doing this job for a long time. *Discretion* is the name of the game. If you have something else in mind, then I suggest you spell it out."

"Spelling it out is what I want to avoid." Murray looked back at his stack of papers in hand, clacked the bottom edge on his desktop and set it aside. "The idea is to keep this under the radar of the people manning the radar."

"You want it off the books," Kim said matter-of-factly.

Murray winced as if struggling to grab something at the far reaches of his mind. "I want you to use prudence and practicality, to handle these situations on a case-by-case basis. After all, these are very dangerous people. Who knows how they might react once you find them?"

Now Kim read him loud and clear. Her counterintelligence unit was really a hit squad. Rather than bring these traitors back for trial, it would be best if they just *went off the radar*. Because of Executive Order 12333 banning assassination, the CIA could not outright eliminate anyone. But if these individuals were to go down fighting, then that was another matter. *Assassination* was in the eye of the beholder.

"Very well, then." Kim gave a nod. "There's just one thing I'll need first."

Conner's eyes lit up. "I already told your director that money and resources are no object. This is the president's top priority. Everything in the U.S. arsenal is at your disposal."

If Kim was going to skirt the rules for Murray, she expected him to do the same. "Money and resources aren't the problem. It's a policy matter that's on my mind."

"Policy?" Murray's brow furrowed. "I thought you understood that your team will have all the latitude it needs to—"

"Not related to this, Conner. Something else." Before Murray could ask, she launched into her demand. "I want the Asadi Saleem situation resolved. Once and for all."

Conner leaned back in his chair and chuckled. "What does Asadi have to do with any of this? The kid survived, thank God. If he hadn't, we'd have a hell of a problem with his uncle. Bad enough we've delayed getting him home for as long as we have."

"Asadi didn't just survive. He *thrived*. The kid risked his own life to save others. By any standard, he's a hero in every sense of the word. And Pakistan isn't his home. Texas is."

Murray leaned forward. "I can raise the issue but—"

"Nope." Kim shook her head. "There's no raising it. This is happening."

Murray wagged his finger. "Careful there, Kim. This is starting to sound a whole hell of a lot more like a demand than a request."

"Conner, I don't know how you ever got the idea that this was a request."

"Do you realize how important this deal is with Omar Zadran? This isn't just some political favor. This is a matter of national security. We need insight into what's going on in South Asia and he is the one who can provide it."

"I'm well aware of his access, and nobody wants him on our side more than I do. But not like this. Enough lives over there have been ruined without us adding another. I can handle Zadran."

Murray let out a frustrated sigh. "And if we don't go along?"

"Then me, Kohl, and Contreras walk away."

"Fine. Then we'll get someone else."

"Okay." Kim shrugged. "Try finding *someone else* with a personal stake in the game. Someone who's shed blood over this. Had their property destroyed. Had their loved ones savagely attacked. We're the only ones with a score to settle with the Russians. Not to mention my old boss, and *your* close friend, Bill Watson." Kim let that sink in. "You really want *discretion*, then we're the ones you want. Not *someone else*."

Murray swiveled his chair, stared out the window. "The Afghan kid? You want to cash it all in for him? I shouldn't be telling you this, but you could make out like a bandit. Hell, you could probably have my job if you wanted it."

"I don't want your job, Conner. I want Asadi fast-tracked to U.S. citizenship and the adoption process streamlined to make Garrett Kohl's guardianship official. He's the boy's family now and that needs to be over and done. No more uncertainty. Got it?"

Murray swiveled back and stared her down. "Okay, we'll get it done."

Kim added with a raised index finger. "One more thing."

"Asadi *was* your one more thing."

"This still relates to him."

Murray's face was growing redder by the second. "Okay. What?"

"Asadi has an older brother. Faraz."

Murry furrowed his brow. "Thought he was killed when the Taliban raided their village."

"Nobody knows about him," Kim admitted. "But he was taken prisoner, and according to the latest intel Faraz is still alive."

Murray looked puzzled. "What does this have to do with anything?"

"I want to go in and get him. Bring him back here and reunite the brothers."

"And how do you expect to do that?"

"By getting Zadran to help broker the deal."

Murray burst into laughter. "You can't be serious?"

Kim didn't blink. "I'm dead serious."

"So, where is Faraz now?"

Kim took out the aerial photograph from her lock bag, laid it on the desk. "Right here. Tribal area." She pointed to a dot on the map and tapped it. "Compound belonging to a warlord heroin trafficker in Afghanistan."

64

Smitty couldn't believe his good fortune. Not only had he survived the wildfire and saved his daughter, but he'd also managed not to piss off Crystal in the process, which was a feat among feats that rivaled them all. Of course, she'd been on cloud nine since they moved into the hunting lodge atop the caprock on the Kohl Ranch. She'd actually called it *a dream come true*.

If she'd ever uttered those words in her life, Smitty hadn't heard them. It didn't matter that everything smelled like smoke. The place beat Misery Mobile like a drum. No nosy neighbors. No mangy dogs. Just the quiet solitude and serenity of the prairie before them. To him and the girls it was heaven on earth.

Smitty took the handoff of a two-by-four from Crystal and laid it across his sawhorse. "Hadn't seen you this happy since we first got hitched." He turned and took her all in. "Always figured you'd be partial to country life. Should've done this years ago."

Crystal gazed around at the beauty of the landscape. With the rainfall they'd had at the beginning of September, a few places that hadn't been scarred by the wildfire were green and flourishing. "It's not just the house, Ray. It's everything. New job. New sights and sounds. A whole new life."

Smitty took a quick measure with his tape and looked up at Crystal. "So, you're liking it alright over at the café?"

"Tips aren't as good as Crippled Crows, that's for sure. But I love the hours. And Lacey and her mom are good to work for. Good as Ike, I guess."

"All wonderful news." Smitty went to sawing. "Hope things work out for me too."

Crystal moved to Smitty and rested her hand on his arm to stop him. "You okay?"

"We better get moving." Smitty rested the saw on top of the two-by-four and looked up. "We were supposed to be over at Garrett's a half hour ago."

"It's just down the road." Crystal laughed. "Talk to me for a minute."

"We *are* talking." He gave her a wink to let her know he was kidding.

"Has Garrett mentioned anything about working on the ranch?"

"Nah, and I didn't want to bring it up since he gave us a place to live." Smitty took a sip of his Pearl. "Not sure if he even knows what he's doing yet. Up in the air with his equipment all burnt to hell."

"But Talon's gone for good, right? They're shutting down the mine?"

"Yep. They're done for." Smitty laughed. "Uncle Sam was extra eager to move on from that mess. But it looks like your best friend Vicky is taking control of the old business. Worked out a deal with the feds to pay back all the money her family owed. So, I guess a Kaiser will be back at the helm of Mescalero Exploration again."

Crystal chuckled. "Vicky ain't my best friend. Or a friend at all for that matter. My guess is she wouldn't even wave if she saw me at the grocery store."

"Well, I doubt Vicky Kaiser goes to the grocery store. Women like that have people for such *lowly* tasks."

"Probably." Crystal agreed. "But if she did, she wouldn't admit to knowing me. I can tell you that much."

Smitty hadn't revealed it, but Vicky had reached out to him about a job. Apparently, she was getting the old Mescalero crew back together and was looking for a few loyalists, some of whom were already on Crowley's unofficial payroll. Of course, none of them knew Smitty had been playing both sides of the law.

What exactly Vicky wanted from him he hadn't a clue, only that she promised *monetarily* it'd be well worth his while. But the thought of diving back into that world had no appeal. Of course, desperate times call for desperate measures, and with Talon gone and a Kaiser back in control of the Texas Panhandle, the offer was something he had to consider.

Smitty smiled to let her know that he wasn't worried, even though he was. "Well, let's just hope Garrett needs me out here as a ranch hand. That'd make everything perfect."

Crystal got right in front of him, stepped onto her tippytoes, and gave him a peck on the lips. "Ranch hand or not, Ray, everything already *is* perfect." She gave him a love tap on the rear. "*Now*, let's get going."

As Crystal went inside to change, Smitty took a sip of his beer and looked around, thinking how far he'd come. From crook to convict, then stoolie to solid citizen. He'd dreamed his whole life of living in a place like this with a family he loved. And to keep from blowing it all, he had to stay clean. He had to be home. And he had to be a father.

As Smitty turned to the open plains ahead and gazed out at the endless horizon, he prayed a simple prayer, hoping this time it'd stick. *Please dear Lord, don't let me screw this up.*

65

Garrett stood rigid as oak, staring at the freshly turned soil of a newly dug grave. Since the fire on the ranch, the battle with Orlov, and everything else in between, his head swam as he mentally pieced his world back together. The Kohls and Kaisers were no longer enemies, and a scumbag like Crowley was somehow a friend. Life was a lot simpler when he knew who to hate.

Garrett had enough to take care of without contemplating old feuds, particularly what was taking place back at the house, not thirty yards behind him. They call it a *celebration of life*, but he'd never really bought into that nonsense as anything other than good marketing for folks like undertakers and condolence card companies—people who were in the business of selling death.

The funeral was long over and done and supposedly so was the mourning, but Garrett still felt low, and supposed he always would. When a loved one passes, a piece of you goes with them. And the reality was he'd never be whole again.

Garrett was so engrossed in the memory of his mother that he hadn't heard Lacey walk up from behind. His sudden turn must've cued her in to his surprise. "Oh, hey there, Lace."

"Didn't mean to scare you. Just thought you might be hungry."

Lacey lowered a plate full of brisket, coleslaw, and potato salad. A big pile of bread-and-butter pickles rested atop the meat, along with Kate's famous barbeque sauce. Although it looked heaven-sent, Garrett didn't have much of an appetite given what weighed on his mind.

Garrett took the handoff anyhow. "Think this'll hit the spot." He looked back at the house to see Asadi, Savanah, and the Sanchez kids chasing each other around the yard, while the adults sat at the picnic table and on lawn chairs in the shade on the porch. Butch and Ike were still at his smoker, basting a rack of ribs he'd put on for dinner. Like it or not, this *celebration of life* would continue into evening.

Lacey took a seat on the concrete bench and patted the spot beside her. "Pull up a seat and tell me what's going on in that head of yours."

Garrett did as he was ordered and dropped down beside her. Finding a flat spot to rest his Shiner Bock and the plate of food, he turned to Lacey. For some reason, in that very moment, he'd never found her more beautiful. As the soft breeze of a mild cold front blew in from the north, it whipped her hair ever so slightly. With the wide prairie and empty horizon behind her, it felt like they were the last two people on earth.

"What's going on in my head?" Garrett only repeated the question to buy a little time to think. "Where do I even start?"

Lacey leaned in and gave him a playful shoulder bump. "Start from the beginning."

Working undercover over the past few years, Garrett had grown used to keeping his feelings to himself, hiding anything that might be used against him or his family. While Alexi Orlov had been right in saying that working undercover was more who you are than what you do, that life had grown tiresome and lonely. Garrett didn't want to keep secrets from Lacey anymore. He wanted a best friend. He wanted a partner. And he wanted to be free.

Garrett gave her a playful bump right back. "The beginning, huh?" He shook his head. "I think that's just it, Lacey. I don't know where my old life ended and my new one began."

"Well, let's start with something easy then." With that throaty voice, the one that was like music to his ears, Lacey made it easy for him. She knew where to begin, even when he didn't. "What do you think about this very spot where we're sitting? The headstone? The new trees?"

Garrett smiled. "I love it. Didn't think I would but I do."

His mother's new gravesite had potential. *More* than potential. It'd be beautiful one day.

When neighbors got wind of everything that had happened out at the ranch there'd been an outpouring of support. They'd moved her casket from the location Talon had destroyed to up by the house. They'd planted a grove of trees and trenched a water line from the barn so it would always be green. And most importantly, Butch wouldn't have far to travel for his daily visits.

It was well beyond a tribute to his mother, the hero nurse, loved by all. It was a tribute to the hearts and souls of the people who called the Texas High Plains their home. It was a tribute to all his neighbors, even the ones who lived over twenty miles away. Whether they knew him personally or not, these people were more than a community. They were a family.

Lacey gently draped her arm over his neck. "Okay, that's a step in the right direction. So, what about the rest of the ranch? Think you can start over?"

For Garrett, that was a tougher question. There wasn't much Talon hadn't destroyed in the dig, or the fire hadn't ravaged. His home and the horse barn were left untouched, by the grace of God, and the cattle and horses were saved. But his alfalfa fields, hay equipment, and tractors were all consumed in the blaze. And worse yet, his center pivot irrigation system was a twisted pile of melted junk. Without it, Garrett didn't know what would save the ranch.

"Insurance will cover most of the damage, but it's not enough to replace everything. It'll get me out of debt and that's about all. Starting over wouldn't be easy."

"No." Lacey pursed her lips. "No, it wouldn't."

Garrett scanned the horizon, beyond the destruction to the natural beauty of the sunset, with every shade of red, orange, and yellow. *God had gone and outdone himself again.* "But I love this place." He looked her in the eye. "And I'd love someone to share it with."

Given yet another cryptic revelation about their future, Garrett had half-expected Lacey to call him out for another non-plan, or to launch into him for giving up. Because giving up on the ranch was giving up on her too. But she was nothing but smiles in her response.

"Garrett, you're right about one thing. Starting over won't be easy. Or cheap. Or maybe even smart. But when it comes to love, you never want to leave anything on the table."

As if on cue, Asadi came running up to him with his new best friend Savanah trailing close behind. They were all giggles and grins.

"We gone do horseshoes. You want play?" Asadi thumbed back at his lunch buddy, who'd worn a permanent grin since she moved to the ranch. "We beat you good."

Garrett turned to the horseshoe pit to find his jarhead buddy *too stubborn to die*, banging away at an iron stake. "Dammit, Tony! Doctor said you're supposed to take it easy! I'll do that!"

As Sanchez shrugged in reply and went back to hammering, Garrett scanned the scene around his house in the backyard. Between Bridger and his family, the Sanchez brood, Lacey's kids, and a whole host of friends, neighbors, and folks he didn't even know, Garrett found that *right place* Lacey was talking about. Somehow the churned earth and charred ground seemed to matter less, and the smiles and laughter meant a whole lot more.

Garrett looked back to Asadi and playfully cocked an eyebrow. "Think you can beat me at horseshoes, huh? Them sounds like fighting words, Outlaw." He turned to Lacey and took her by the hand. "What do you say? Up for the challenge?"

Lacey stood, gazed out at the pasture, then leaned down and whispered, "I'm up for anything you can throw at me, Garrett Kohl."

As Lacey turned and walked away with Asadi and Savanah on each side, she pulled them in close as they marched to Sanchez, talking trash about horseshoes the whole way over. Garrett didn't know exactly what was said, only that it got a big reaction. The deputy flexed like the Incredible Hulk, let out a deep growl, and chased Asadi and Savanah around the yard.

It was with that scene and those parting words that Garrett knew he was there to stay. It wouldn't be easy, it wouldn't be cheap, and it probably wouldn't be smart. But it was home. And if Lacey was *up for anything* then he was too. Given his latest phone call from his good friend at the CIA, everyone in Garrett's world would certainly be put to the test. The war hadn't ended with the death of Alexi Orlov. It'd only just begun.

ACKNOWLEDGMENTS

To my beautiful wife, Diana, and wonderful children, Bennett and Maddie, who suffer with me through the long hours, seven-day workweeks, and missed vacations, I couldn't do this without your help, understanding, and encouragement. You are the reason for what I do and the inspiration behind it all. To my parents, Robert and Holly Moore, and sister, Allison Jensen, experiencing the writing journey along with you is one of the most rewarding parts of the process. I look forward to many more years of sharing this joy.

To my literary agent and friend, John Talbot, thank you for being a rock of stability and a beacon of foresight through this oftentimes daunting and grueling endeavor. The same gratitude goes out to my critique group and writing mentors, Bruce Edwards, Linda Broday, and Jodi Thomas, whose friendship and wise counsel mean more than they will ever know.

To the authors Don Bentley, Mark Greaney, Brad Taylor, Philipp Meyer, and Mike Maden, who read my debut novel and helped me to promote it, I thank you for your limited time and your very kind words about *Down Range*. The value of your support is immeasurable.

To my technical advisors Jason Abraham, owner of the Mendota Ranch, and CW4 Boyd N. Curry (Ret.), U.S. Army 160th Special

Operations Aviation Regiment, I thank you for your extensive knowledge on rotary-wing aircraft. For my subject matter experts, Joel Carpenter, Fmr. Army Ranger, 1st Battalion, 75th Ranger Regiment; Martin T. Hood, Texas Ranger (Ret.), Ranger Recon SRT 5; Dustin Pool, hunting and tracking expert; and Ian D'Costa, Director of Military/Law Enforcement, Lone Star Armory, thank you for helping me to make the combat scenes as accurate and realistic as possible.

For ensuring historical accuracy, I thank Alex Hunt, Vincent/Haley Professor of Western Studies, director of the Center for the Study of the American West (CSAW), West Texas A&M University; and William Elton Green, curator of history, emeritus, Panhandle Plains Historical Museum (PPHM) for their efforts. To my good friend Cade Browning, I thank you for both your legal and equine knowledge. To friends Mark Erickson, Justin Garza, and Ted Evans, thank you for your friendship, encouragement, and help in promoting the Garrett Kohl series.

Last but certainly not least, none of this would be possible without my publisher William Morrow/HarperCollins, specifically David Highfill, a gifted editor with a unique eye for setting cadence, calibrating tone, and fostering great character development. I would also like to thank the marketing and publicity team, who worked so vigorously to promote my debut novel. I couldn't ask for better partners.